Brush

a novel

strokes

c.s. karlquist

interlude ✦ **press**™ • new york

ISBN 13: 978-1-945053-22-1 (trade)
ISBN 13: 978-1-945053-85-6 (ebook)
Published by Interlude Press
http://interludepress.com
BOOK AND COVER DESIGN BY CB Messer
BASE PHOTOGRAPHY FOR COVER © depositphotos.com/
Max5799/Dr.PAS/rolffimages/Microstock77/
Nongkran_ch/DeepGreen/joyart/bilhagolan

10 9 8 7 6 5 4 3 2 1

interlude ⁂ press • new york

To everyone who's messed up repeatedly, but still decided to try again.

CONTENT WARNINGS:

The main character has anxiety, which affects his thoughts and actions throughout the book.

Several strained family relationships.

Brief mentions of insensitivity towards a character with hearing loss (by minor characters).

(www.interludepress.com/content-warnings)

Chapter One

GLANCING AT THE DIGITAL CLOCK on his phone, Todd winces as he drums his fingers against his thigh and watches the floors tick by in the elevator. It's an old one: forged iron made with artistic care. It's too slow for anyone with a schedule, and the inner gate gets jammed more often than not. Sometimes the worn-down button to the fifth floor, his floor, refuses to work, but today it cooperates. He's going to end up being late for work, and really it's all because he forgets time when he's at MoMA. Apparently, he never learns, either, since this isn't the first time. Whenever he researches for the kids' program, he loses track of everything else.

Mom is already waiting for him when he reaches their floor; the front door is open, and she holds up a white plastic bag the moment she spots him. She must've just come home from work, because she's still dressed in her black, knee-length skirt and the cardigan with the leather patches at the elbows. She's had that sweater as long as he can remember, and, when he was upset as a kid, he loved snuggling in her lap when she wore it. It always smelled like comfort to him. Unlike then, there are gray streaks at her temples in her otherwise ginger hair, and deep crow's feet at the corner of her eyes are evidence for how often she smiles.

"You have ten minutes to make it to work, and it's a fifteen-minute walk," she informs him, as she opens the elevator's outer gate and yanks the inner one to the side with surprising strength for such a small person, pulling him from his thoughts. He takes the bag and steps back as she closes both gates again.

"I'll run," he says, pressing the button for the first floor, and glances into the bag as the elevator starts back down. "I got stuck at MoMA. It's just, you know, cubism; I'll never understand it."

She rolls her eyes, looking exasperated, but at least she's starting to smile. "You say 'run' like I don't know you. And maybe you should stop going there before work!"

He doesn't have time to reply before she's out of sight as the elevator creeps its way down floor by floor. She's right, of course, his shift at the gallery starts in ten—probably more like nine now—minutes. Once he's outside, he picks up his pace. It's too warm to run, even if he was a running type of person, and he's sorry that he picked a black T-shirt this morning, because it's now sticking to his back after less than a block, but at least it's not see-through. August has been suffocating.

Despite being a librarian and in that sense very much interested in art, Mom tends to forget that he doesn't just go to the museum for fun. He very much enjoys art in most forms, but he also needs to be in the know when patrons ask questions. What's more cubism is the first theme for their kids' program this semester, and he needs to refresh his knowledge before Thursday. The kids ask even more complicated questions than the regular adult patron. They're also the best part of his job.

Todd clutches the bag tighter and scans the street before he crosses it. The bag is heavier than he expected, so Mom probably found more books that could be of interest for him. He hopes the evening is slow, giving him some time to read while he's at the front desk.

Todd is three minutes late when he rushes into the gallery in the old storefront. There's no one in sight—another slow day.

"Sorry I'm late! Mom gave me a bunch of books to use in the kids' art class," he calls toward the back room. If Mrs. Floral is not behind the front desk, that's where she'll be, packing and unpacking. He puts his bag next to the computer and rubs the red dents it's left in his fingers and palm.

"Barely so." Her hoarse voice is a tell-tale of how much she smokes. Last year she told him that she'd quit, but the past month she's been taking a break almost every other hour. She smells of cigarettes when she comes back—cigarettes and chewing gum. "There's coffee in the maker."

He shivers from the cooling sweat on his back. The air conditioner never quite manages to regulate properly, and it's either the Amazon rain forest or the North Pole. He grabs one of the mismatched mugs on the desk.

"Mom got me some additional information about Klimt and Lerin." He watches the steam rise from his cup as he fills it up. "I figured I should know a lot more about them, since Anderson and Fernández have similar styles."

"That's great!"

Call Todd a bad art student, but he hadn't known much about Lars Lerin before Mía Fernández, one of their showcased artists, explained her inspiration for her work. In the three books Mom got him, he sees the love for detail in the watercolors of small towns, lonely cabins, and nature. Most of the works have a lot of blues and grays. The melancholy is ever-present and sometimes overwhelming, to the point where there's a twinge in his chest. However, it's his way of incorporating light that makes Todd want to look at the paintings for days. If they're this incredible in a *book*, he can only imagine what impression they'd make in person.

While Lerin has focused on landscapes and nature, Mía captures people, except for a painting of a lighthouse that Todd fell in love with from the moment he put it up. If he had the money, he'd buy it in a heartbeat.

The bell over the door chimes, and he looks up as an older man approaches the desk. He's dressed in a shapeless tweed suit, too warm for this weather, and his back is bowed—a stark contrast to the unexpected spring in his step. Todd puts away the book and spends the next fifty minutes explaining everything he knows about the artists in the gallery and their work. Sometimes he worries that his passion for the gallery and the works displayed makes his guided tour too overwhelming, but the old man is smiling when he leaves.

Refilling his coffee, Todd notices the calendar lying next to the register and frowns. It used to have a permanent spot right there, but, for the past six months, Mrs. Floral has kept it in her office. Whenever he asked for it, she would just brush him off, saying that it's her headache and not his. Now, scanning the pages, her words make sense. There should be at least three names there, since they're ending a handful of exhibits during this quarter. But the next few weeks are empty with the exception for *Kids & Canvas*, their kids' program, every Thursday. As he flips through the pages, the following couple of months are blank too.

"Mrs. Floral?" he calls over his shoulder, still scowling at the empty pages. *This can't be right.*

"Yes, love?"

When he looks up, he finds her emerging from the back office. She has her usual checkered mug in one hand, her phone in the other. She wears a long, flowing dress and the rainbow of color is striking against her dark brown skin. She's kept her hair natural today: black graying with age. She's been like a grandma to him since he was a tot running around the gallery in awe of the art. Mrs. Floral always waved away Dad's apologies when Todd took up so much of her time with his endless stream of questions. When he struggled in high school, she and the gallery were his safe space where he could fight through his homework in peace.

"Did we put the new names somewhere else?" He points at the calendar with the pen. He is just about to put it in his mouth, when the unexpected silence stops him midway.

"No, Todd," Mrs. Floral sighs finally. Right then, she looks nothing like herself. It doesn't matter that she's wearing such a colorful dress and at least one ring on every finger. She looks *old* and tired. "It's empty because there are no booked artists from the middle of October onward."

Todd puts the pen on the counter and readjusts the back of his beanie. "Why?"

With another sigh—when has she ever sighed?—Mrs. Floral sits on the nearest chair. "I'm afraid that we're not interesting enough to attract new patrons anymore. Our regulars are aging out of the collecting market, and without them we won't make any sales. Without sales? You know where this is going, I can tell by the look on your face, but I have to say it. The artists we've always carried are aging and, frankly, dying. Without the sales we can't book new artists. Or pay the bills."

He's been working here since high school. Though it doesn't pay much, it's the best job he's ever had—the *only* one he's ever had—and considering the horror stories he's heard from classmates, he's lucky.

L'Aquarelle is an old-fashioned gallery in an old storefront and it's always interested an older crowd of patrons and showcased an older set of artists, but he's assumed there would always be a fresh crop of both.

Clearly, he was wrong.

"We're closing?" he asks, biting his lip and trying to ignore the way his stomach is suddenly empty.

She smiles. Mrs. Floral has a smile that makes him feel as if he has just had a hot chocolate in Central Park in mid-December.

"Not yet. I'm still hoping that the tide will turn. We've been in worse situations before, and things have turned around. They always do, love."

Returning her smile, Todd gives in to that tiny spark of hope that ignites behind his ribs. Evan used to call him naïve. Evan also used to say that art is of no essential use to society, and Todd long ago learned to not give a crap about Evan's opinion.

Just as he's about to ask Mrs. Floral if there's anything he can help her with, the bell over the door chimes. With the rush of sound from the street outside, Mela steps inside. For a second, the late August heat chases away the air-conditioned chill.

He hasn't seen her since she left for India to visit her grandparents at the beginning of June. His heart swells at the sight of her teal pants, too-big shirt with a peacock embroidered on it, and wide smile. The colors fit so well with her brown skin and thick black hair. She's had a bump on her nose since breaking it during a softball game in eleventh grade.

Her big, curious eyes seem brown at first glance, but Todd has known her long enough to know that they have flecks of gold and green too.

"Heya!" Her smile turns into a grin when Todd steps around the counter to hug her.

"I missed you." He lets her go before he wants to.

"Missed you too." She pushes him away and gives him a once-over. "You look good. Hi, Mrs. Floral!" She continues past him to hug Mrs. Floral. She's always been a hugger with people she knows and a firm-handshake-only with everyone else.

"So," she says as she turns around again. "There's somewhere we need to be on Friday."

Raising his eyebrows, Todd closes the calendar. "Where?"

"A party."

That is oddly unspecific. "What kind of party?"

Mela rolls her eyes. "I met a guy at the coffee shop when I was about to leave the airport. He invited me."

She has this strange superpower to connect with people at the most random of times and get invited to places, parties, and other galaxies. The most Todd has ever gotten from an interaction in a coffee shop is a thank you for holding the door.

"Who's the guy?" Todd asks.

"Why do you always get caught up in the most irrelevant parts?"

Mrs. Floral gets up. "I'll leave you kids to it. Todd has the weekend off, so there's time for a party. Don't let him tell you otherwise," she adds before she disappears into the back office.

Todd resists pulling a face. Claiming that he has to work is usually his best escape.

"So?" he demands.

Mela plops herself down on the empty chair, hums, and bobs her foot in the air to an inaudible beat, before she replies: "His name is Jesse. He has this party with his friends this weekend and asked if I wanted to drop by."

"Here in Brooklyn?"

"Not exactly."

Something in her smile makes him suspicious.

"Out with it."

"Manhattan. Frat party. Lots of jocks with muscles." Mela curls her arms in front of her in a pose. It might have been more realistic if her arms weren't so scrawny.

Heaving a sigh, Todd leans against the counter. "Since when is that your thing?"

"Since now." Mela shrugs. "If they're jocks with brains, I don't mind."

"It doesn't sound like my kind of scene," Todd tries. Frat parties? Aren't they usually all about keg stands and loud dudes in varsity jackets? "There's a new band playing on Friday. I'd rather go hear it."

Mela thumps her head back against the wall. "You'd rather go see a crappy band playing than hang out with me?"

"You'd rather go to a frat party with a horny jock than hang out with me?"

Mela snorts. "That's a good point, but I'm still not going to that gig."

Todd expects her to try to convince him, as she usually would, but instead she sits up straight, leaning forward.

"I'm really intrigued by this guy, but I don't want to go there alone. It would feel a lot better if you were there with me."

"I'd be the worst wingman," Todd mutters.

"That's okay." Mela smiles. "I'll be *your* wingman. I'm actually an *excellent* wingman."

He knows nothing about sports or keg stands and he would much rather watch that crappy band play. It's going to be a horrible Friday if he goes with her, and she has other friends.

"I can't," he says finally. "Family dinner. Dad's not going to like it if I'm not home."

"But you're *never* home for family dinner!"

"That's kind of my point."

✳   ✳   ✳

SANDWICH IS HOPPING AROUND ON the floor that Friday as though she hasn't explored the few square feet of Todd's bedroom at least a billion times. She noses his feet under the desk before she starts another lap.

Sighing to himself, Todd erases his attempt at an easy, kid's version of a cubist portrait for the kids next week and stares out the window. The sky is bright blue, almost cobalt, with no clouds in sight, and the sun is bright and sharp. He can smell Dad's cooking. Just as he's about to put his preparations for the kid's program aside for the day, be a responsible adult, and go talk to his parents, there's a knock on the door.

"Come in," he calls and spins his desk chair around as the door opens.

Dad is pale, tired-looking, and wearing the worn-out chinos he sticks to when he's sick or needs a quiet evening in front of the TV. Maybe it's been a long week for him. He wipes his hands on a kitchen towel as he watches Sandwich inspect Todd's T-shirt on the floor. Todd looks a lot like Dad, with his hair in big, dark curls—which get frizzy if he as much as looks at a shampoo bottle—the wide set of his eyes, and the same brown color to his skin. Unlike Dad, one of Todd's eyes is all brown, and the other, split almost exactly along the horizontal midline, is blue on top and brown below, as though Mom refused to let Dad have all the influence over the gene pool. Where Dad is on the short side, Todd is a little taller and less athletic in build, probably another hint of Mom but less recognizable. Looks-wise he has much more of Dad's Mexican heritage than Mom's Irish genes.

"New semester in a week," Dad says as a greeting. "Did you pick courses yet?"

Todd's stomach sinks. Dad only wants what's best for him, wants him to have a stable career and a good job so that he can support himself, but Evan's never-ending opinions on Todd's career choice have caused Dad to worry. "Yeah."

"Did you pick that accounting class that we agreed on?" Dad's eyes light up as if he just asked if Todd has picked snacks for the evening.

"No." Todd has long since given up on trying to sugarcoat anything with Dad. "*We* didn't agree on anything. *You* agreed with yourself."

Dad's face falls and Todd looks away, gaze sticking on the mess on his floor where Sandwich is inspecting one of his socks. He really needs to get better at cleaning up. At least she doesn't try to eat it.

"There are no jobs in art," Dad says, using his usual argument, one that Evan brought up when Todd first applied for college. Up until a few days ago, Todd would have disagreed, but he might be out of a job soon. Evan and Dad are right about some things, it seems.

"There are no jobs for anyone right now," Todd sighs. "The American Dream doesn't exist anymore. We're just a bunch of people leaving college in debt and with no way to pay it off."

"You *always* have use for accounting," Dad disagrees and points toward a leaflet lying on the desk on top of a bunch of fine-grain watercolor blocks. Todd hasn't noticed it until now. It has a familiar company logo on it, and Todd resists sighing. "My company has an internship program."

"For the *thousandth* time, Dad, I'm terrible with math. I barely passed it in high school."

"Accounting is different from trigonometry," Dad says, his voice kind and earnest. "I'll help you. We can sort it out together."

It hurts, because being an accountant isn't going to come easy. Anything to do with numbers is a lost cause, and he barely scraped by with passing grades in his math classes in high school. It hurts, because Dad listens to Evan more than he listens to Todd.

"I don't want to be an accountant!" Todd reaches for his phone as he speaks. "I don't want to be an accountant. I don't want to rot away in a cubicle somewhere."

"It's a *good* occupation." Dad bristles, flinging his arms out.

"Not for me." Todd types a message to Mela, as he avoids Dad's face. He has the worst way of looking like a kicked puppy, despite his age.

< **Changed my mind. I'm coming with you**

He looks away from the three dots at the bottom left corner of the screen and finds Dad still standing in the doorway. "I'm going out. I'll sleep at Mela's."

"It's family dinner!"

"I forgot and made other plans. Sorry."

They both know he's lying, but Dad doesn't call him out on it. Instead he leaves the room without shutting the door behind him. When Todd looks at his phone again, Mela has replied:

> **Awesome! Be at my place in 2 hrs!**

That brings the next issue to mind. What the hell does one wear to a frat party?

He puts Sandwich in her cage, knowing all too well that she isn't happy about it, but he needs to get ready before he can take the subway to Manhattan. He tries on black jeans and a regular T-shirt, but that makes him feel as though he's trying to become invisible. Instead, he goes for a short-sleeved button-up with a palm tree print and a beanie, because his hair looks like shit. He decides against the Doc Martens and goes for Converse. They might make his feet less sweaty.

Just as he's about to put his phone in his pocket, Evan calls. Todd swallows and mutes it. Voice mail will get it eventually unless Evan hangs up first. He usually does these days.

Todd really needs a night out to concentrate on anything but school and work. They will occupy his mind for the next few months, but not tonight. Mela wants to see this Jesse guy, and Todd is going to be there with her.

When he reaches her parents' condo in Manhattan, she's dressed in orange pants and everything else in black. *Are her lashes usually that long and thick?* Tiny, tiny rhinestones glued to the edge of her eyelids sparkle every time she blinks.

"You look amazing," he tells her.

"I like the shirt," she replies. "Thanks for coming with me."

"Anything is better than spending the evening with my dad, when all he wants to do is tell me how horrible all my life choices are."

Mela snorts. "Your dad is the best, and you know it."

"Sometimes I think he wants me to be *him*."

She gets a twinkle in her eyes when she shrugs and says, "There are worse people. And also, I'm pretty sure your dad just wants you to have the best possible future."

Rolling his eyes at her, Todd abandons the subject. "So, do you know anyone else who's going to this thing?"

"No, *I* wasn't going until you said you had changed your mind two hours ago."

"Why would you miss out on a party just because I didn't feel like going?"

She looks at him like he's crazy. "I'm not going to a frat party alone if I don't know anyone there."

"What did Jesse say?"

"He made a sad face when I had to say no and just now he sent me a smiley face because I told him the plans had changed."

"He only communicates with emojis?"

"Of course not. That was a summary."

Todd snorts, knowing that he will get details he doesn't want if he keeps pushing, and looks around the hallway. Ever since he was little, he has loved coming here, with all the little details that tell of Mela's Indian heritage. He loves the vivid colors, the *warmth*. Most of all, he loves the memories he's created here over the years. For a couple of years in high school, he more or less lived here every weekend that he wasn't working. It's a second home by now.

"Where are your parents?" It is way too quiet for them to be home.

"Some charity dinner thing." Mela shrugs. "You're staying over, right?"

Nodding, Todd holds out his tote bag. "Unless you're bringing that Jesse guy home with you."

"I told you," Mela says as she rolls her eyes. "I'm going to be your wingman."

"Good luck with that." There is no way in hell that Todd is going to hit it off with a guy in a varsity jacket.

"Don't be so judgmental."

Before he has a chance to reply, Mela grabs his tote bag from his hands and disappears toward her bedroom. When she emerges, she's got her purse in one hand and her phone in the other.

"So, I have the directions and everything. It's in some guy's parents' house. Jesse told me to call him when we get there."

Todd shifts, readjusting his beanie. "Why? Aren't we gonna be allowed inside otherwise?"

"Of course we are." Mela grins, as if she isn't worried about this at all. Knowing her, it probably hadn't crossed her mind until he brought it up, while Todd has already started preparing himself for five different scenarios where they're denied and publicly humiliated.

In the cab, she talks a lot about her trip to India, forcing Todd to focus on something other than his doubts about this party. However, as soon as they get out to face a large house with open windows and music that's a little too loud, Todd wishes he had stayed home for family dinner.

While Mela presses her phone to her ear, he sticks his hands in his pockets. A lot of people are here already. It won't be difficult for them to lose each other. They should probably set up a meeting spot and time.

"There's Jesse!" Mela tugs on his arm, and Todd spots a tall black guy exiting the house. He's not wearing a varsity jacket, but the way his white button-up stretches over his shoulders and arms makes that statement for him.

Jesse wraps her in a hug, and the way his smile warms his entire face tells Todd why she really wanted to come see him tonight.

"You must be Todd," Jesse says then and turns toward him. He's got buzzed hair, and his eyes are a few shades lighter than Todd's, closer to hazel than brown. "I'm Jesse; nice to meet you."

Todd half-expects either a one-armed hug with really brutal back-thumps or a fist bump to the shoulder. Jesse extends a hand and shakes his without trying to crush his fingers.

"Nice to meet you," Todd echoes and he's not lying.

"So the music's kind of bad," Jesse explains, as they approach the front door. "But we're thinking we'll stay for a bit and then go somewhere else."

"Sounds like a plan," Mela smiles, and Todd knows that he will be forgotten in two minutes, the way she looks at Jesse. That's okay.

The house is filled with people, and, sure, there really is a keg in the kitchen and a few dudes are wearing varsity jackets. Other than that, he's not too out of place in his palm tree shirt. He regrets wearing the beanie, because the number of drunk people in here has made the temperature go beyond that heatwave at the beginning of the summer. It's a lot darker compared to the fading light outside, and it takes a while for his eyes to adjust. The constant distraction from everyone around him causes him to lose concentration, and he apologizes five times to people he bumps into on his way to the counter where Jesse's pouring drinks.

"Beer, Todd?" Jesse offers him a plastic cup.

"Thanks." Todd accepts it, smiling, both because he knows this guy is going to be important to Mela and because beer will make him less awkward after a while. He looks around at the people talking, at the few who are dancing in the next room, and at the couple already arguing in the staircase to the next floor.

His gaze catches on a guy filling his cup at the nearest table. He's tall and blond, wearing jeans and an olive-green Henley that does great things to his shoulders and arms. He looks up, catching Todd staring at him, before Todd gets his shit together and tears his gaze away, searching for Mela and Jesse.

Crap, he's going to end up being that terrible friend following them around all night.

He finds them immersed in conversation on the second floor at the pool table. He sits on the armrest of the nearest couch and concentrates on his beer. It's pretty good.

From here, he has a decent view of the room. It's fascinating watching other people interact, especially as they're much drunker than he is.

A guy on the other side of the room is trying desperately to hit on a girl who's paying more attention to her phone than him. He doesn't seem to get the hint whatsoever. Todd rolls his eyes as he sips his beer.

For thirty minutes, Todd sits there, watching people and finishing his drink. Just as he's about to find a game on his phone that he can waste another half hour on, a girl sits on the couch next to him.

"Hello," she says, smiling and combing her dark hair over her shoulder with her fingers. She has a kind face with round cheeks and a wide smile. "Is this seat taken?"

"No, go ahead." Todd smiles back and slides his phone into his pocket. He extends his hand, because his parents did try to teach him manners. "I'm Todd."

"Sarah."

During the next hour, Todd learns that Sarah is from California and completed her first year at NYU last semester. She misses her boyfriend, who's still on the other side of the country, and Todd finds himself having a pretty good time. Not nearly as good a time as Mela, though. The personal space between her and Jesse seems to shrink every time he looks over. They are smiling and talking; their drinks stand forgotten at the nearest table. Now, however, someone else is with them. Todd immediately recognizes the blond guy he saw when he got here. He's laughing at something Mela said, and Todd loses track of his thoughts. He's got a smile that crinkles his eyes and puts dimples in his cheeks.

Naturally, the guy looks up to find him staring again—and can someone kill him right now please—because now he isn't just some random dude staring. He's just become Mela's creeper friend, instead.

He readjusts his beanie and shifts his attention back to Sarah, as the guy says something to Mela with his gaze still locked on Todd for a second too long. He knows what that usually means. *Crap.*

"Did you come here by yourself?" he asks Sarah, as she types something on her phone.

"No, but they're both talking to guys, and I don't want to be in their way, you know?"

Todd nods. "Oh, I know."

"You looked like you felt equally out of place, so I figured you'd be nice company."

Laughing, Todd ignores the buzzing of his phone in his pocket. "Did I look that miserable?"

Sarah knocks her shoulder against his arm. "You looked like you weren't exactly here for your own sake."

"I came with my friend. She wanted to meet up with this guy, and now I'm staying out of their hair." He resists the urge to look over at Mela and Jesse again, not wanting to come off more creepy than necessary.

Sarah opens her mouth to reply when another girl shows up on Todd's other side. She's slightly unsteady on her feet and, judging by the way Sarah straightens at the sight of her, she must be one of the friends she came here with.

"There you are! We've been looking for you all over the place." The girl reaches over Todd to grab at Sarah's arm, as if he isn't sitting on the armrest like a barrier between them. She's definitely drunk.

"I've been right here," Sarah says, but she still gets up.

"We're going to a club where Nathan knows the DJ."

Todd wants to roll his eyes at that, but he moves his feet out of the way when Sarah is pulled toward the stairs. She waves, looking apologetic, as she's dragged away. Waving back, Todd looks at his long-empty plastic cup and puts it on the floor next to the couch.

Alone again, he looks around the room—anywhere but in Mela and Jesse's direction—and establishes that everyone clearly is a lot drunker now than they were when he came. Talking to Sarah has made him forget about drinking, and now he's lightyears more sober than everyone else.

He brushes dust from his pants and is just about to get up to find something more to drink, when two cups come into view. Looking up, he almost falls off the armrest as he finds the guy he has been caught looking at twice standing in front of him. He's smiling. Up close like this, he's even more devastating, making Todd's stomach feel light.

"Hey," he says and offers one of the cups. "Brought you something to drink. You seemed like you were out."

He nods toward the empty one Todd has put on the floor.

"Uh, thanks." Todd tries to get control of his hands as he accepts the cup and then he's left awkwardly switching hands, as the guy extends one in a greeting.

"Daniel," he says, and his fingers are dry and a little cool against Todd's.

"Todd."

"Sorry, did you say Todd?"

"Yes, Todd," Todd says again.

"Nice to meet you, Todd." Daniel's smile turns into a little smirk, and Todd, guessing what's coming next, wants to die. "I saw you looking at me earlier."

"I didn't mean to," Todd blurts and resists the immediate urge to pull his beanie down over his face.

To his relief, Daniel only tips his head back and laughs. "Good to know."

Wincing, Todd wipes his free hand on his pants. "Sorry, I have this weird tendency to be accidentally rude when I don't know what to say."

"That's okay. Do you mind if I sit down?"

"No, not at all." Todd expects him to take Sarah's empty spot, but instead Daniel removes a few empty bottles from the coffee table and drags it closer to the couch. He sits right in front of Todd so their knees almost touch, and Todd doesn't know where to look.

Daniel, however, has all his focus on him, and Todd tries not to lose himself in the sharp lines of Daniel's cheekbones and jaw, the way his hair is so effortlessly on the right side of messy, and the intensity of his eyes. Todd can't make out what color they are in this light, but he thinks he might get lost if he allows himself to look for too long.

"Actually," he begins and clears his throat as his voice comes out raspy. "Actually, I didn't mean to be a creep like that."

"A creep?" Daniel echoes, a crease forming between his eyebrows.

"You know, with the looking."

"Come again?"

"With the looking," Todd repeats.

"I'm obviously not creeped out, since I brought you a drink."

Oh, right. Todd looks at his cup. His fingers are a little numb from clutching the cold plastic, but he takes a swig all the same to buy himself some time to think.

"That's true." It's all he comes up with, and he stares at his feet. His shoes seem dirty next to Daniel's, and his gaze locks at the inch of naked skin between the rolled-up cuffs of Daniel's pants and his shoes. It's tan. *Maybe he's been abroad during the summer. He comes off as someone who travels.* Dragging himself from his thoughts, Todd looks up. "Thanks. Unless it's poisoned."

"Poisoned?" Daniel asks.

Nodding, Todd holds up his mug. "Did you poison it?"

Daniel smirks. "I guess we'll just have to wait and see."

Biting back a smile, Todd plucks at the multicolored ties around his wrist. "Is this your party?"

"Isn't it?" Daniel says, with a nod.

Crap, the music is so loud. "No, I asked: Is this your party?"

"Sorry, I thought you said it was a great party. No, it's not my party, I'm on the same swim team as the guy whose parents live here."

"Shouldn't you be wearing your varsity jacket?"

"Should I?" Daniel counters, a sudden challenge in his eyes.

"I don't know." Todd shrugs. "I guess it would just fit with—" he gesticulates toward Daniel "—the rest of you."

He gets an exasperated sigh in return and Todd wants to escape.

"I'm sorry," he says. "As I said, I have this bad tendency to be rude when I don't know what to say."

Daniel cocks his head to the side and looks at him. "All right. How about we stick to safe subjects for a bit?"

"Like what?"

"Give me a second," Daniel says, and moves the table closer. "Sorry, the bad lighting is making it difficult for me to see you properly."

"Um, okay," Todd says. *Isn't the whole point of meeting someone like this, that they can't see you properly, so they think you're way hotter than you are?* Having Daniel so far into his own space is terrifying and exciting all at once.

"What's your major?" Daniel asks.

"I'm in art school." Todd shifts in his seat; their knees bump by accident, but Daniel doesn't move an inch. "You?"

"Poli-sci. My last year. I'm hoping to get into law school."

For some reason, Todd had expected Daniel to mention becoming a professional athlete. At the same time, law would've been his second guess. He knows it's a difficult road. Despite how predictable it might be, it's still impressive.

"Is it fun?"

"Fun?"

Todd nods.

"Would you believe me if I said yes?"

Shaking his head, Todd takes another swig from his cup. *Difficult? Yes. Prestigious? Absolutely. Fun?* "No."

"I guess I'll have to lie and say no, then."

"That's good practice for when you start working," Todd points out, and Daniel tips his head back in a laugh. Warmth blooms deep in Todd's belly.

"Probably."

"Why did you choose law?" Todd doesn't know that much about it, except what he's learned on *Law and Order* and *Suits*.

"Sorry?"

"Why law?"

"My grandfather was a judge and he told me that he thought I'd make a good one." Daniel shrugs and looks away, breaking eye contact for the first time since he sat down. There seems to be more to that story, but before Todd has a chance to ask, Daniel moves on. "Why did you choose art?"

"It was the only thing that made sense when I was applying to colleges." The fact that he's terrible at everything else isn't something he needs to tell Daniel right now.

"I see." Daniel looks at him. "Are you from around here?"

"Brooklyn. You?"

"Yes, a couple of streets over, born and raised."

The conversation dies down then, and Todd racks his brain to find something else to talk about. Daniel has been the one asking questions. It's Todd's turn now, and he's drawing a blank.

"What's being on a swim team like?" he asks, just as someone bumps Daniel's shoulder walking past. Daniel seems to know who the guy is, because he looks up and nods in a greeting. When he looks back at Todd, it's as though the previous question was never spoken.

"So Mela's your friend, right?" Daniel asks. *Is the swim team question sensitive somehow?* It doesn't make sense, but Daniel would probably not ignore it otherwise.

"Um, yeah." Todd nods and looks around for her, as he realizes that she's not where he last saw her. He finds her standing in a corner, still talking to Jesse. Clearly, it was a great idea for her to come here tonight. "She can be very persuasive if she wants," he adds to Daniel.

"Sorry, I didn't catch that?" Daniel has leaned forward slightly when Todd turns back toward him. Up close like this Todd can make out the color of his eyes better. They might be green, but it's difficult to tell with how light the color is around the pupil, and how sharp the ring around the iris is in contrast. He could spend days trying to draw them, and it still wouldn't be accurate. *Since when did reality turn into a sappy romance novel?*

"She can be very persuasive," Todd repeats and forces himself not to look away. "She made me come with her tonight."

"So I have her to thank, then?" Daniel grins, and Todd's neck grows hot.

Reaching up to scratch his neck, he tries not to stare at Daniel's mouth. And fails. *Goddammit.*

"I'm not sure you should thank her yet. It's not even past midnight."

Daniel laughs, and Todd can't help but smile. "Can I get you another drink?"

Looking in his cup, Todd finds that it's almost empty. He has no clue how this happened, but he doesn't want their conversation to end. With a nod, he hands his cup to Daniel.

"Anything in particular?"

Todd shrugs. "I prefer cold over stale but, other than that, I'm not too picky."

Nodding, looking as though he's trying not to smile, Daniel disappears toward the staircase. A moment later, Mela shows up.

"Heya!" She takes Daniel's empty spot, and Todd looks around to make sure that Daniel doesn't think he's been rejected. He's nowhere to be seen however, and Todd turns his attention back to Mela. She can't seem to stop smiling, and Todd wishes that he was the kind of person who would reach out and squeeze her hand.

"I'm taking it you're having a good time?" he asks.

"*Yeah.*" Mela nods and looks away before her smile grows even wider. "He's pretty great so far."

"Well, *you're* pretty great, so that's a must."

Mela kicks his foot gently. "So, Daniel?"

"What about him?" Todd stalls.

"He's really hot."

Snorting, Todd looks around to make sure Daniel is nowhere within earshot. He doesn't seem to need another ego boost.

"He is, and he knows it," he agrees, when he makes sure that Daniel still isn't back. "He's kind of nice too."

"*Very* nice, when I spoke to him earlier. He's friends with Jesse."

"Yeah," Todd sighs. "They're on the swim team together."

"Why do you look all down? If he's nice and hot and *smart*, what more do you want?" Mela kicks his foot again, being less gentle this time.

"I don't know." Todd hesitates. "He probably just wants to hook up."

"And you don't want that?"

Swallowing, Todd wishes he still had his cup to hide behind. "I kinda do. I just don't want to be the dude who's sad when he doesn't get a call the next day."

"You could be the one making the call."

It sounds so easy when she says it, as though she has forgotten that Todd's a total coward who has to muster up his courage to call in a pizza order.

She softens. "Just let me know when you feel like leaving. You don't have to stay because of me."

Letting out a breath, Todd nods and kicks her foot in return. "Thanks. I appreciate that."

"Allow yourself to have a bit of fun. Daniel's a decent guy according to Jesse."

"And Jesse's a decent guy according to you," Todd fills in. There's no question Daniel is both nice to look at and nice to talk to. Todd just can't come up with anything they have in common. At all.

His thoughts are put on hold when Mela gets up from the coffee table. Zoning back to reality, Todd finds Daniel slipping into her empty spot, offering him a cup.

"Sorry for taking so long," he apologizes. "I tried to find something cold."

The beer is *definitely* cold, Todd decides, as he accepts the cup. So cold that he gets momentary brain freeze when he gulps down too much, too fast.

"Wow, thanks. How did you find this?"

Daniel grins, and Todd gets the feeling that he does that a lot. He probably knows what it does to people. "Bribed a couple. Killed a few."

Snorting into his beer, Todd bites his lip to stop himself from smiling. "For some reason, I don't even think that you're joking."

"Come again?"

"I don't even think you're joking," Todd repeats.

"Seems like you've gotten the hang of me already."

"You're not that hard to figure out," Todd counters and swallows at the way Daniel's smile widens.

"I'm really not," he agrees.

Todd's spine tingles when Daniel moves the table slightly closer and their legs suddenly interlock. The music is really loud, so Todd can't blame him. He notices the difference in the width of their thighs, and his gaze gets stuck on Daniel's shoulders for a second too long. This doesn't make any sense, but it doesn't matter.

"I'm assuming that you're not in a relationship," he blurts, before he can stop himself. Expecting Daniel to laugh, Todd concentrates on taking a swig from his cup, grateful that the beer is so cold because his face is burning.

Daniel, however, waits him out. When Todd doesn't have another choice but to look up, Daniel is still looking at him. There's something in his gaze that makes it a difficult to swallow.

"If I'm in a relationship?"

Todd nods.

"I'm not. Are you?"

"No. Definitely not." Todd readjusts his beanie and gestures toward his cup. "Thanks for this. It's actually really good."

"Glad to hear it." Daniel's knee bumps against his, and Todd is about a hundred percent sure that it's not by accident. "What are your plans for the rest of the night?"

"No clue." Shrugging, Todd looks at Daniel's wristwatch. It's barely past midnight. "I'm open to whatever," he adds in a rush. He doesn't want Daniel to think that he's been blown off.

"I think we're planning on heading to a bar in a bit." Daniel nods toward a group of guys who looks like the kind of people Todd would normally refuse to hang out with. At least three of them are wearing sporty jackets with the Columbia crest. "If you and Mela want to come with us, that would be fun."

Just as he's about to nod and agree, he remembers that he has no clue what Mela wants. "I'll have to ask her."

"Sure." Daniel moves backward on the coffee table. It's not by much, but Todd really doesn't like the way it creates more space between them.

"I'd like to come, though," he adds, almost stumbling over the words, and extends his legs, keeping his feet close to Daniel's. It's an instant reward, the smile he gets for his efforts.

"Sorry?"

"I'd like to come," Todd repeats, slower this time.

"I'll go ask when and where." Daniel gets up, and Todd breathes in a hint of his cologne when he moves into Todd's space. "Maybe you can ask her in the meantime?"

Nodding, Todd gets to his feet as Daniel approaches the group of guys. He expects to feel a rush of alcohol, since he's been sitting for quite a while, but it doesn't come. Maybe he hasn't had that much after all.

Mela is in the corner with Jesse, and he's reluctant to walk over and disturb them. Luckily, she notices him hovering and waves him over.

"Todd!" Jesse exclaims. "Haven't seen you all night. Did Daniel steal you away from everyone?"

Awkward. "Uh, yeah."

"What's going on?" Mela asks, her hands not leaving Jesse's arms.

"Did we wanna go to that bar with Daniel?" It'd be easier if Jesse wasn't here. Not because he dislikes Jesse, but because his body itches from having to talk about this in front of someone he doesn't know.

"What bar?" Mela asks immediately.

Jesse looks around until his gaze locks on the group of guys where Daniel is standing.

"I don't know," Todd says. "He just asked if we wanted to come with."

"I'll ask about the plans." Jesse disappears, and Todd watches how he puts a hand on Daniel's shoulder when he reaches the group, and then gesticulates vividly about something.

"Do you want to go?" Mela asks and turns him toward her, as she scrutinizes him.

"Yeah." Todd takes a swig from his cup. "I mean, if you want to."

"Sure, as long as you don't think I'm forcing you."

Shaking his head, Todd takes another swig and—*crap*. He really needs to pee. "Can you hold this? I'll be back."

Mela takes the cup and rolls her eyes over the fact that his bladder always takes him by surprise whenever he drinks alcohol.

The bathroom isn't that hard to find, and Todd stares at his reflection. He doesn't *feel* drunk, doesn't look drunk. There's nothing but a comfortable buzz under his skin. He's a little braver, nothing extravagant. Truth be told, he can't tell if the buzz is because of the alcohol or because of Daniel.

When he reenters the living room, Mela has joined the group of guys. Todd sweats a little walking over to them; he's getting sudden flashbacks from high school when jocks blocked his locker. Daniel looks up, smiling and stepping aside to invite him into the group.

"Ready to go?" he asks when Todd is close enough to hear; he's turned toward him as if the rest of his friends stopped existing the moment Todd came back.

"Yeah, decided on where to?"

"Sports bar," Daniel says, and a smirk creeps onto his lips. "Your favorite, I assume?"

"I love sports bars. Especially how masculine I feel there."

Daniel laughs, and Todd grabs his cup with cold beer from Mela when Daniel strokes his arm.

He's grateful for the less-hot air when they get outside. He drinks it in, feeling oddly right in a company where he expected to feel out of place. Daniel is walking beside him, not saying anything, but his hand brushes against Todd's arm repeatedly.

The sports bar is crowded, but it seems as though Jesse knows someone, because no one checks their IDs. It doesn't hit Todd until he goes in with them that he's not old enough to drink legally yet. Only six months left, but he's still breaking the law.

Swallowing, he glances at Daniel, who doesn't seem to have noticed. Maybe he never has to show his ID in this place.

They get a table, though the place is crowded. It's one of those places with creaking couches in faux leather, too-large tables, and every square inch of the walls covered in something related to one of the New York sports teams. Todd recognizes the face of the hockey goalie, but that's about it. He sits at the end of the couch, and the way Daniel picks the closest chair, angling it toward him, makes him want to check everyone's reaction.

"Thirsty?" Daniel asks him.

Todd shrugs, then nods. "Kinda."

Daniel is gone before he has the chance to offer to buy the drinks this time around. To his relief, Daniel has ordered the entire round, so he's not singled out. Not that he *minds,* he just doesn't want Daniel to think that he can't buy his own beer.

"Is this your usual place? Where you go all the time?" Todd asks, as Daniel sits down.

"Sorry?" Daniel looks up, leaning a bit closer.

Todd repeats the question, surprised by the focused attention Daniel is giving him.

"It is. We're here almost weekly, even if not all at the same time."

Todd clears his throat, looks around to make sure no one is paying attention, and lowers his voice as he leans a little closer. "You do know I'm not old enough to drink legally, right?"

"You're not allowed to drink?" Daniel asks, but he sounds more as if he's making sure he's heard right, rather than appalled that he just gave beer to a minor. "By how much?"

"Six months."

"No big deal, then." Daniel shrugs, but Todd doesn't miss the relief flashing across his face.

"What, scared I was a freshman?"

"Something like that."

Todd swallows. "How old are you?"

"Old enough to drink legally."

Resisting the urge to roll his eyes, Todd says, "I'm guessing in your forties, since you're apparently really sensitive about your age."

Daniel laughs. "I'm pretty fine for a middle-aged guy, right?"

"The fact that you're still in college scares me, though."

Daniel laughs again. "Valid concern."

Looking around the table, Todd finds that no one is paying any attention to them. Mela and Jesse only have eyes for each other.

"What do you do, other than school?" Daniel asks, pulling Todd's attention back to him.

"I work at an art gallery." Todd refrains from mentioning the possibility of soon being out of a job. His chest grows heavy, as he's reminded of that particular detail.

"An art gallery? Really?" Moving his chair even closer, Daniel rests his arms on the table.

With a nod, Todd turns his glass almost a full circle. "It's not that exciting. I'm mostly at the front desk and overwhelm people when I give them a tour."

"It sounds pretty cool," Daniel offers.

"What do you do? Except for poli-sci."

"Practice." Daniel bites his lip and looks as if he is thinking. "Practice. And then of course, there's always practice."

Todd kicks his foot. "Okay, I get it. You're super fit."

There's a moment of hesitation before Daniel speaks again. "Seriously though, I do spend a lot of time doing that. I also have to study a lot."

Todd can relate to that. Most college students probably can, but since he's never had an easy time learning something new, he really has to make an effort. "Poli-sci is pretty tough, huh?"

"As is Columbia," Daniel says. "It's ridiculous."

"I don't even want to try to imagine what it's like." Pulling a face, Todd takes another swig from his glass and then another three, because Daniel has put a hand on his thigh, just above the knee. *Really, it's totally PG.*

He glances at Mela. She's at the other end of the table, discussing something with Jesse and some other dude Todd doesn't know. The bar is crowded and loud, not the same kind of loud as the frat party. Here, it's talking, shouting to be able to hold a conversation. The tables are too wide for anyone to be able to talk very well across them when it's as crowded as it is tonight.

Blinking back to Daniel, Todd puts his glass down and decides that he's old enough to not need alcohol for this.

"Does your semester start next week as well?" Daniel asks, and his hand stays unmoving on Todd's thigh. Knee. Whatever.

"Yeah, unfortunately." He grimaces.

"Why, not looking forward to midterms and finals all over again?" Daniel grins.

"Not exactly." Clearing his throat, Todd tries not to think about how he's halfway through his undergrad program. *And then what?* "Mostly because I don't exactly know what I want to do afterward."

"Work?" Daniel suggests. He makes it sound easy, and maybe it is for someone like him.

"I really hope so."

"Is this your last year too?"

Shaking his head, Todd draws a line in the condensation on his glass. "No. Two left."

"That's forever," Daniel says with an easy smile and squeezes his knee. Thigh. "You'll have it all figured out when it's time."

Todd sort of assumed that he had. He was going to work in the gallery until he found something else, maybe forever if Mrs. Floral would let him. The idea of not having that stable point in his life, which he's had since high school, scares the crap out of him. Art is all he has and the only thing he knows to any extent.

"Todd?"

Looking up, he finds Daniel frowning at him and it takes a second before he realizes that he zoned out.

"Sorry," he says, holding back a grimace. Evan has told him a billion times that he's too easy to read.

"Are you okay?" Daniel asks, still frowning.

"Yeah." Todd shrugs and nods at the same time. "I just got caught up in the terrifying idea of adulthood."

At that, Daniel laughs. "Don't worry about it now. Worry about it next year." He scrutinizes Todd. "Do you want me to get you a glass of water or anything to eat?"

"I'm not *drunk*," Todd says and immediately realizes that that's exactly what a really drunk person would say right before they tripped over their own feet. "I mean it. I've had, what, four beers including this one since I came to that house *hours* ago. I'm not that much of a lightweight. I just have a terrible tendency to zone out when I get caught up in stuff."

Daniel smiles then. It's not a grin. Not a smirk. He's *smiling*.

"All right. You have me convinced."

"So, how are you feeling about school starting next week?"

"Come again?"

Todd repeats the question, leaning closer.

"Unlike you, I'm actually starting my last year, so I have to deal with all the anxiety of applying to law school and doing the tests." Daniel shrugs as if it's no big deal, but there's a crease between his eyebrows that tells Todd something different.

"Where do you wanna go?"

"For law? I'm hoping for Harvard."

"Really?" Todd knows nothing about law schools, but he knows about *Harvard*. Everyone knows about Harvard. "Don't you need really amazing grades and to ace that test? I've watched *Suits*."

He adds the last sentence just because he might be completely wrong.

"Yeah," Daniel says. "That's why I eat, swim, study, work on a project I have with a couple of friends, and sleep. Rinse. Repeat."

"You also hang out at this place quite frequently, according to a very reliable statement made by yourself."

Daniel smiles again. "I do, when I can. I need a break from all the studying for the LSAT."

"LSAT, that's the test, right?"

"Right." Daniel nods.

"You'll get the score," Todd tells him, full of confidence suddenly.

Daniel's smile falters, then comes back in full force. "How'd you know? I might've been lying to you all this time. I might not be attending Columbia or even on the swim team."

"In that case you've gone to a whole lot of trouble to keep that charade up." Todd points toward the guys wearing the jackets with Columbia's crest.

"I don't even know them. I found them at the house and tagged along."

Todd snorts. "You're too Ivy League for me to buy this. I'm sorry."

"It was worth a shot." Daniel grins, clearly not too disappointed in not selling his lie. He pulls his hand from Todd's thigh—definitely thigh now—to grab his drink. He misses it, wants it back.

"Are you the team captain too?" Todd asks, because he *has* to.

"No," Daniel says, as he puts his beer down. "That would be Jesse."

"Wow, turns out I didn't have you all figured out."

Daniel snorts out a laugh. "Glad to hear that I'm not *that* much of a cliché."

Smiling to himself, Todd takes a swig from his beer and looks across the table in time to catch Mela winking at him. He rolls his eyes at her, because anything else would definitely make him look stupid.

His mood ebbs when he looks around the bar and notices that the crowd is thinning out. A quick check of the watch on Daniel's wrist tells him that it's been a couple of hours already. *When does this place close?* He's not ready to say goodbye yet.

"Don't worry," Daniel says, his voice easy and warm. "We still have a couple of hours."

Mind reader.

"That obvious, huh?" Todd asks.

"Took a guess based on my own thoughts."

Meaning Daniel doesn't want this to end either, right?

Todd half-expects to have a mini freak out. Instead, it's as though someone has poured hot liquid into his belly.

"Just admit it," he says, trying to divert his own attention. "You're a mind reader."

"All right." Daniel holds his hands up. "I admit it."

"See, I told you I have you all figured out."

Daniel's hand returns to his thigh then, and Todd doesn't need to reach for his beer this time. He puts his hand over Daniel's.

The tiny twinge of nervousness is instantly chased away when Daniel smiles at him again. Todd can't stop himself from smiling back.

The following few hours pass so fast that, before Todd knows it, they're asked to leave because the place is closing. He can't believe he's had a better night in a *sports bar* than watching his favorite band. Worried that Daniel will just simply disappear, he trails after the group, even though Mela is still putting something in her purse.

To his relief, Daniel is waiting for him by the curb, slightly separated from his friends.

Unsure if he has full control over his feet, Todd walks over to him and forces himself not to shove his hands into his pockets.

"Do you need to leave?" Daniel looks a lot less self-assured than he did five minutes ago. Todd's stomach swoops the way it does when he's standing on a ladder, and he doesn't even consult with Mela before he shakes his head. He'll take a cab by himself if he has to.

"No, do you?"

"They're going to go back to the house. We could tag along." Daniel's eyes are bright, and Todd thinks he looks hopeful.

"That sounds great. I'll just talk to Mela."

He gets a very familiar elbow in the ribs for that. "We're going there too," Mela says and she sidles up next to him. "I'm not even close to tired."

Normally, Todd would be exhausted and way ready for bed at this time, but it's as if he's got a spare battery charging him.

"Hungry?" Daniel asks, and Todd thinks that maybe he can get used to the way Daniel's intense focus is on him and no one else, as if they're the only ones around.

"Maybe a little?" Todd doesn't want to check, because he hasn't had dinner and he's usually starving if he doesn't eat every four hours. He really doesn't want this night to be ruined because he can't focus on anything other than his growing black hole of a stomach.

"I'll get something on the way back," Daniel says, smiling. "I'll meet you there."

Todd watches him get into a car with a few of the guys in Columbia jackets and climbs into the one Jesse pushes him toward. He barely pays attention during the ride; his head is somehow so loudly empty now that Daniel isn't around. His brain is getting ready to take off, crouching in its mental starting-blocks, when a familiar hand squeezes his. Mela doesn't say anything, but Todd knows what it means. *Don't overthink this.*

Taking a breath, he watches the city pass, and dares to revel in the fact that he's going to spend more time around Daniel, that it's ridiculously late, borderline *early*, and his night still isn't over. Unable to stop the smile from spreading, he squeezes Mela's hand back. He's okay.

The house is a lot less crowded, and the music isn't as loud, but there are still people around, when Todd climbs the stairs behind Jesse and Mela.

"I'm going to have to help Jordan clean up tomorrow," Jesse sighs, just barely audible over the music.

Glancing around, Todd can see why, because there are plastic cups and empty bottles *everywhere*. He doesn't want to know what the rest of the house looks like.

"Todd, how do you feel about me beating you at pool?" Jesse asks suddenly, as they walk back into the same room where they spent most of the night. It's close to empty now.

"It sounds like something my ego doesn't need right now," Todd answers truthfully, but he also doesn't have anything else to do until Daniel comes back. "But apparently I have no self-respect so I'm going to say yes anyway."

"You don't even know the rules!" Mela protests, but she's laughing, and Todd suspects that she's secretly pleased that he's making an effort for the guy she's into.

"How difficult can it *be*?" he asks, rolling his eyes as he reaches for the stick Jesse offers him. "So how do I hold the stick?"

Jesse is painfully patient for someone who's had a lot to drink, and teaches Todd the basics of the game, like how to break and how to hold the stick. Apparently, it's called a *cue*, and Todd is definitely not an undiscovered pool talent, that's for sure.

He's less horrible by the time Jesse stops and nods toward the door. Glancing over his shoulder, Todd doesn't know what he expected to see, but it wasn't Daniel with two paper bags in his hands. He jerks his head and that probably means that he wants Todd to leave the room with him.

"I guess this means I lost?" Todd offers Jesse, as he gives the cue to Mela.

Laughing, Jesse shakes his head. "*This* means you lost?"

"I'll come grab you before I leave," Mela tells him. "Do something reckless. You need it."

Todd really hopes that Daniel didn't catch that, because to someone else that probably didn't sound like the *dare to have fun* Mela meant.

That swooping sensation in his stomach is back as he approaches Daniel, who doesn't look as patient as he did a moment ago.

"Come on; we'll get some air and eat." He nods toward an open door farther down the hallway. Todd is pretty sure that it was locked before, because he tried it when he was on the hunt for a bathroom, but now it leads to a bright bedroom with two large glass doors. The balcony on the other side has a beautiful cast iron rail that's probably been there since the house was built. It's something, all right.

"Are we allowed to be here?" he asks, just to make sure. When there's no answer, he looks away from the rail and finds Daniel looking at his phone. Todd nudges him with his elbow and smiles a little when Daniel looks up at him. "Are we allowed to be here?" he asks again.

"As long as you're not thinking about destroying anything on purpose," Daniel says with a smirk. It fades into a smile, almost shy-looking, as he holds up the paper bags. "It's easier to talk when there aren't as many people around. It makes it difficult for me to focus, and I'm already really tired."

If the intense attention Daniel has been giving him all night is him having difficulty to focus, Todd isn't sure if he's ready for this.

As soon as he follows Daniel through the balcony doors, he decides that he *definitely* isn't ready for this. There's a dark gray blanket on the balcony floor, along with a few throw pillows in different shades of dull green, and the soft glow of the outdoor string lights makes the pale, early morning light seem almost magical.

"I just wanted to get some time alone, if that's okay?" Daniel asks, as if he's taken in all of Todd's big-eyed reaction.

Blinking, Todd stares at him before he remembers his words. "Yeah, yes, that's okay."

He's known Daniel for less than twelve hours but sitting on a blanket on a balcony with him and carefully placing the food containers between them, is somehow exactly where he wants to be right now, where they should be.

Todd eats sweet potato fries and looks out at the morning fog over the lawn. It's small but a luxury in the middle of Manhattan. Right now, it's almost as if they're in a different world. Out here, everything is so quiet.

"Tell me more about art."

Looking away from the lone apple tree, Todd finds Daniel's eyes on him. He looks content, relaxed against the bars of the rail, with his legs folded, and he's holding a half-eaten burger.

It's such an open request. Not: *tell me why you like art,* or *why did you decide on art school?*

"Um." Todd wipes his fingers on his jeans and chews his lip as he tries to sort out his thoughts. "It's such a powerful thing, you know? For messages and statements and exploring the world somehow. *Telling* the world. Whenever I think I've seen it all, there's something new that blows my mind. A combination of colors, or techniques, or just something that really hit home that day."

"Sorry, I didn't catch the last part?" Daniel frowns, leaning closer across the array of containers. He's got salt on his lips.

"Um," Todd says, trying to remember the last thing he said. "There's always something new? With colors or techniques."

"Techniques?" Daniel asks and, when Todd nods, he gestures for him to go on.

"Right now I'm very into art from around the Mexican Revolution, and especially José Clemente Orozco—"

Daniel interrupts, "Is that the name of an artist?"

"Yes, he's very political. It's all so political? And also a way of making sure history is kept alive. I think art has in many ways been the only way to take a stand sometimes. When something is forbidden, it's like there's even more attention drawn to it, and it's just so amazing how you can create something that makes other people *feel*. It doesn't always work the way you intended it to, but it's kind of incredible, isn't it?"

His cheeks heats as he clamps his mouth shut, realizing that he's probably said a bit more than Daniel intended.

"I guess I've never seen it that way," Daniel says but he sounds thoughtful. "Anything that can evoke something in people is powerful."

"Tell me about swimming," Todd says, because he doesn't understand it at all. But right now, with Daniel in front of him, he wants to.

"Well, I guess that's the one place where I don't have to constantly compensate. Where it's effortless. Something that comes natural to me, unlike most things."

It's not at all the answer Todd expected and it doesn't make all that much sense to him, but Daniel is so open in front of him, stripped down, somehow, and Todd doesn't want to ruin that with questions.

"I'm hard of hearing," Daniel says, as though he's heard Todd's thoughts. He pauses, eyeing Todd's face with care as if he's searching for something. "So I have to compensate a lot on a daily basis."

For a second, Todd can't find his words. It usually happens when he's angry or hurt, but right now, he's more worried about causing the hurt.

"Um," he ventures. "Is there anything I can do to make it easier?"

The corner of Daniel's mouth tugs up, just barely, but definitely. "Repeat anything you just said without question if I ask you to. Don't turn your face away from me when you're speaking."

"I can do that." Todd nods to himself, jotting down mental notes of Daniel's requests. His head is spinning, but the lack of sleep and spending a night drinking has made it difficult for him to sort his thoughts. "Do you sign?"

Daniel nods and looks away. Now, when Todd knows to look for them, he can notice Daniel's hearing aids only partially hidden by his hair. He can't believe he didn't notice them before, but maybe that's thanks to the alcohol. "In English, meaning I sign the way I'd speak. English is my first language, so the grammar and syntax of ASL doesn't come natural to me, but I'm working on it. It takes a lot for me to read lips and it drains my energy, and, sometimes, like with you, I don't have a choice, but I'm willing to make the effort anyway."

Todd's face heats up, and he has to bite his lip to hold back a smile. He can't be that successful, because Daniel smirks.

"I appreciate that," Todd says. "Since I can't sign yet."

He watches as Daniel closes his eyes briefly, and, when he opens them again, something raw in his gaze makes Todd's chest clench. They just look at each other, and Todd's brain isn't working, but that's okay.

"Tell me about palm tree shirts," Daniel says, sliding a foot over to nudge Todd's with his own, and, though the moment has passed, Todd doesn't think it's gone.

The sun is rising when Mela knocks on the glass door, and Todd isn't sure if it's been five minutes or maybe another two hours. He does know that all the food is gone and that he'd do anything to stay in this moment.

"Ready to go?" She looks tired in that good, happily exhausted way a person does after a great night out with people you really enjoy.

He isn't, but he nods anyway, because he should. Daniel follows him in silence down the stairs and stops at the curb while they wait for a cab.

"Can I see you again?" Daniel asks.

"Yeah, I'd like that a lot." Todd immediately steps closer when Daniel reaches for his hand. "I've had a really great time, despite my doubts."

Daniel smiles. "I'm glad. I've had a really great time as well."

They look up when a cab slows in front of them. Time is running out.

"That's your ride." Daniel squeezes his fingers. "Can I kiss you goodnight?"

Nodding, Todd licks his lips; his pulse picks up as Daniel closes the remaining distance between them. Todd closes his eyes when Daniel cups his cheek and has enough brain capacity left to put his hands on Daniel's waist.

Daniel's lips are warm against his and taste faintly of beer and salt from the fries. At first, it's just a brief brushing of lips, but when he feels Daniel start to pull away, Todd can't help but chase after him. If this is the only chance he gets, he's going to make it worth remembering.

He sinks into the kiss when Daniel's hand slides to his neck and is fingertips dig into his skin slightly. Todd can't do anything but hold onto the fabric of Daniel's shirt and kiss him back, until a car honks.

"Are you sure you don't want to come with me?" Daniel asks as he pulls away, and Todd can't remember how to swallow.

"I want to," he blurts. "But I can't." He nods toward Mela, who is waiting patiently by the cab, looking smug as hell. It's going to be a horrible ride back to her place.

"Fair enough." Daniel gives him another, much more brief, kiss. "You should go. I'll text you tomorrow."

"Okay." Biting back a stupid smile, Todd watches him walk back to the house, before turning around and getting into the cab with Mela.

"You're paying the five bucks he wants for waiting while you made out," Mela tells him when they pull away from the curb.

"You're paying the rest, because I only came with you so you could suck face with Jesse." Todd is still lightheaded.

"I can't believe you said *suck face*." Mela groans as they slow at a traffic light. "But all right, you have a point."

They end up splitting the fare fifty-fifty. They always do.

It's quiet coming home to Mela's place. It smells almost as much like home as his own does. He remembers the first time he was here, five years old, and terrified that Mela would force him to play with dolls; they've always creeped him out. They ended up pretending to be bats by hanging off the back of her couch by their knees and have been best friends since.

He's always been comfortable in her room with its warm colors. She's not one for white and minimalism, that's for sure, despite the color of her walls. Instead her furniture ranges from a cherry wood bookcase, to a teal, plush arm chair by the window. She has an addiction to throw pillows and blankets in every color she can find. There is clear evidence of her interest in science in the books and notes scattered everywhere on her desk, the one she managed to convince Todd to paint petrol blue one summer when he was weak and bored. She's collected odd thrift shop finds over the years. Todd has tried to talk her out of at least ninety percent of them and, when people ask why he hasn't improved his bargaining skills over the years, he wants to tell them about every object she's put back on the store shelf. His least favorite is the collection of animal horns in her bookcase that she uses to display jewelry. But being here always warms the pit of his stomach.

"So," Mela prompts from the en suite bathroom as she washes off her makeup. "I'm assuming you had a good time since you *sucked face* with Daniel?"

"Yeah," Todd says, hoping that he only sounds breathy to his own ears. "I don't know what happened."

"I know what happened. You saw a hot dude, found him nice, and really wished you weren't such a great friend so that you could've ditched me and gone home with him."

Todd can't stop the grin from spreading over his face. Luckily, she's not here to see it. "That's only about half true."

"I asked Jesse about Daniel, obviously, since I'm the best wingman ever and wouldn't set you up with a douche."

"And?" Todd straightens in the teal armchair, where he's been trying to unlace his shoes.

"He's really nice. A huge flirt, but really nice."

Swallowing, Todd yanks at the laces, finally getting them to untangle. "What does that even mean?"

"That he didn't stick around you all night just in hopes of getting laid."

She knows him so well. It's ridiculous.

"We talked before he came over to you."

Right, Daniel had been talking to Mela and Jesse before he sat on the coffee table.

"What did you talk about?"

"You know, the general polite-y stuff, and then I told him that I came with a friend; he asked me about you and was obviously curious. So, I told him that you're single and that he's definitely your type—"

Todd groans. "He is *not* my type."

Emerging from the bathroom, Mela quirks an eyebrow at him.

"I mean he *wasn't* my type, until he was."

"See." She braids her hair over her shoulder with scary swiftness, as she eyes him. "I told you I'm the best wingman."

"I know I should be annoyed, but I'm just going to say thank you and blame it all on being drunk." Undressing, Todd creates a pile of his clothes on top of his tote bag and sits on the futon that she has already prepared for him. "How was Jesse?"

"Awesome. Unsurprisingly. We just click really well."

Smiling to himself, he looks up to find her gaze lost somewhere outside the window. "So you're seeing him again?"

She blinks, returning to the room and him. "Definitely."

He checks his phone, remembering that he hasn't done so all night. That is unusual for him, since it is most often glued to his palm.

Two texts wait for him. One is from Mela.

> Daniel is awesome. Mela-approved. Go for it.

Rolling his eyes, Todd notices that she sent it about when Daniel brought him his first drink.

The second text is from his mom.

> Evan called. Please get back to him when you have the chance.

Locking his phone, Todd pushes it away, display down, on the cushion. Nothing gets past Mela, however.

"What was it?" she asks.

"Mom. Evan called."

Mela sits on her bed, facing him. The crease between her eyebrows tells him there's so much that she wants to say but decided not to. "When's the last time you talked?"

Shrugging, Todd pulls the covers around him. "When he moved to Vancouver. Give or take."

"That's a year and a half ago." Her voice is quiet; the words are spoken reluctantly.

"I'm exaggerating." He isn't. "I don't want to talk about it."

"Okay." Mela tosses him a pillow that he catches with his face. "Are you seeing Daniel again?"

"I think so. He said he was going to text me tomorrow." *If time would only go faster.* If he would've already slept for a few hours and would wake up to a text waiting for him. It would save him a lot of anxiety.

"That's great!"

Todd is just about to agree, when his stomach drops. "Shit."

"What?"

"I didn't give him my number. And he didn't give me his."

With a dramatic sigh, Mela flops backward on the bed, barely avoiding smacking her head against the headboard. "You guys are *terrible*."

"Damn," Todd whispers. "What do I do?" Maybe he can find Daniel on Facebook, or—

"You calm down and remember that your best friend is dating *his* friend and that we'll fix this for you." She picks up her phone. "I'm sending Jesse your number right away."

Collapsing on the futon, Todd tries to calm his heartbeat. It's fixable. Nothing he needs to get worked up for. It'll be fine. Mela will make sure that Daniel gets his number in no time, and it will be fine. *Unless*, his brain provides unhelpfully, Daniel didn't get his number on purpose, because in that case—

"No! Stop that!" Mela flicks a pen at him. "I said that he's a flirt. Not a dickbag."

Todd pulls a face to hide his instant relief. Maybe they've been friends for too long. He can't even have his thoughts to himself these days. "I guess we'll see tomorrow."

"Trust me on this."

Todd tosses the pen back at her, missing by a good two feet.

When they say goodnight, it's long-since light outside. He smiles to himself, face pressed into his pillow where no one can see. If he closes his eyes, he can still replay the kiss.

It *was* a really good night.

Chapter Two

TODD WAKES EARLY THE NEXT morning. Blinking against the sharp sunlight flooding the room, he reaches out for his phone. Ten-thirty. *What the hell.* He hasn't been asleep for more than a couple of hours, but he isn't tired.

There's no text from Daniel, not that he thought there would be. Jesse hadn't gotten his number until early in the morning, and maybe he was already asleep by then. If he hadn't been, it's possible that Daniel was asleep when Jesse forwarded the number to him.

After checking that Mela is still asleep, he goes on Facebook mostly to keep from going crazy. Much to his disappointment, she isn't friends with Jesse on Facebook yet. There can be many valid reasons for that, such as exchanging numbers and not thinking of Facebook, or maybe Jesse doesn't have an account. It's an inconvenience, since he won't be able to snoop out Daniel's profile through Jesse's. *It's probably for the best anyway*, he decides and puts his phone away. Daniel promised to text him. He'll wait for that.

Last night was so much of everything, but now, in the stillness of Mela's room, with the morning light flooding through the window—they must've forgotten to close the blinds before crashing—he goes back to Daniel and their moment on the balcony. So maybe Todd didn't have him all figured out. Thinking back on the night, it all makes more sense now, how Daniel's attention was solely on him when they spoke and how he didn't reply to questions Todd asked when he was looking the other way.

Learning a new language will be a challenge, especially on top of his regular school work, but it'd take some of the pressure off Daniel. The sooner Todd starts learning, the faster they'll be able to communicate on Daniel's terms.

He picks up his phone and types a note to find a way to learn ASL. There's got to be a way that doesn't require him to take another class.

Sighing to himself, he turns over and manages to sleep for another few hours, until Mela's phone wakes them both with that horrific whistling tune she has picked for her incoming texts.

Groaning, Todd pulls the cover over his face. He's already wide awake, though, and it's too late to go back to sleep now. He should head back home soon and make sure that Sandwich is fed.

"Daniel now has your number," Mela announces, sounding as if she's in need of three gallons of water.

"Great." Todd folds the cover down from his face. He means to sound casual, but he doesn't think he quite pulls it off.

"Are you having breakfast here or going home?"

"Here," Todd decides, despite his earlier thoughts. The less time he has to wait alone for Daniel to text, the better.

He lingers, eating breakfast and then dozing on the couch in front of a TV show, until he no longer has any excuse but to head back home. Sandwich really needs to get fed, and a proper nap is starting to sound really good.

He almost falls asleep on the train back to Williamsburg but manages to stay awake by sitting stiffly upright in his seat. It's New York City, no one seems to notice that he's acting strangely.

Only Dad is home when Todd unlocks the front door. He's sitting at the dining room table reading with a mug in front of him when Todd walks through on the way to his bedroom. Dad looks up, and the tense lines around his eyes smooth out.

"Had a good time?" he asks.

"I did, thanks. You?"

"Dinner was lovely," Dad says pointedly and then adds, "Evan called."

"I know; Mom told me." Todd sighs and clutches the straps of his tote bag.

"Call him when you can."

"Yeah." He won't.

Entering his room, he finds Sandwich hopping around on the floor, and her food bowl has been refilled. It even looks as though her cage has been cleaned. If that isn't an olive branch.

Swallowing, Todd walks back into the living room. "Thanks," he says to Dad. "For feeding Sandwich."

Dad smiles then. "She was hungry."

"She's always hungry," Todd mutters to hide the tightness in his throat. "I think I'm going to take a nap."

"Did you have lunch?"

"Late breakfast."

"All right. I'll wake you for dinner if you're not already up."

Curling up under the covers is one of the best things he knows. The sheets are cool, despite the suffocating heat outside, and Todd presses his cheek to his pillow.

Instead of allowing himself to worry about the lack of texts from Daniel—*it's not even four, dammit*—he concentrates on last night. He's already having trouble picturing exactly what Daniel looks like. He knows the hair, the smile, and the eyes, but the full picture is getting blurry.

There are things he *does* remember without difficulty, though: their conversations, Daniel's laugh, the way his hand felt against Todd's thigh, and how his lips tasted. Todd's belly swoops, and he allows himself to focus on this, to not worry for once.

He's woken up by a text. Again. For a second, he's annoyed with himself for not muting his phone. A moment later, he is wide awake, reaching for it.

It's Mrs. Floral wanting to know if he can work tomorrow. She has a meeting. Ignoring his disappointment, he texts her back, letting her know that he'll cover for her. It's almost seven, and he's really hungry.

Sandwich is eating in her cage, having lost interest in the rest of his room for now. She'll take another round later, the way she always does.

Grabbing his phone, he types: *how to learn ASL* in his browser and hits SEARCH. The first result is a page listing apps and other resources. Todd spends a good forty-five minutes clicking around, and he's downloaded two apps before he puts his phone down. He can do this.

Mom is prepping dinner next to Dad in the kitchen, when Todd gets there. She looks small next to him, with her meager five-foot-three and slender limbs. Compared to Dad's darker skin, she looks strikingly pale, matching her ginger hair. Todd smiles to himself when Dad kisses her cheek, and she nudges him until he gives her a proper one on the lips.

"You're awake," Mom says when she notices him in the doorway. "Did you have a good night?"

"Yeah." Todd gratefully accepts the banana Dad gives him. "It was great."

"Where did you go?"

"Some frat party in Manhattan and then a bar."

"They let you into a bar?" Mom looks up from her chopping, eyes narrowing.

"They gave me a wristband, so I couldn't drink."

Dad gives him a look that clearly says he doesn't believe that for a second, but he doesn't comment. Mom nods her approval and turns her attention back to the vegetables. She has this idea that at least half the plate needs to consist of vegetables, and Todd isn't sure he agrees.

His phone buzzes in his pocket. Even though he doesn't want it to, his heartbeat picks up. *It's probably just Mela*, he tells himself, as he slides the phone from his pocket.

It's not. It's Daniel.

> **Hey! Jesse gave me your number, thank god. I hope you've had a great day. Thanks for last night. /Daniel**

Todd's not a hundred percent successful in biting back his smile. He reads the text twice before putting the phone on the kitchen table, screen down. When he looks up, he finds Dad watching him.

"It was just Mela," he says.

"Uh-huh," Dad replies, not sounding the least bit convinced.

Todd's face heats, but Dad doesn't push it. In fact, he looks as if he's perfectly enjoying himself. *Unbelievable.*

During dinner, Mom talks about work, but Todd doesn't have it in him to listen. He's too caught up in eating and thinking of how he's going to reply to Daniel's text. There's no energy left to pay attention to people asking for weird books, or even weirder research subjects. Working in a library seems nothing like the quiet peace it should be. Mom really loves her job, though, and he figures that that's what's most important.

His thoughts return to Daniel's text. He has no clue how to reply, except for the obvious *my day has been good, thanks.* Maybe it doesn't have to be more complicated than that.

"What are your plans for tomorrow?"

Dad's question pulls him back to reality. Todd shrugs.

"Mrs. Floral asked me to cover for her a bit during the afternoon. Other than that, nothing. Why?"

"Just checking if you'll be home for dinner. I'm making chilaquiles."

"Definitely home for dinner, then," Todd decides. No matter how frustrating Dad can be, he means well, and his cooking is beyond amazing. He hates missing out on it just because Dad keeps bugging him about school, especially as he knows that Dad only wants what's best for him.

Dad nods. "Good."

An hour later, Todd's on his bed with Sandwich on his stomach, and he still hasn't figured how to reply.

"Why is this so hard?" he asks Sandwich and pets the soft fur between her ears. She stills before she continues her carrot chewing as if nothing happened.

"Maybe you're right." He sighs and picks up his phone for the seventh time in the last twenty minutes. "I'm making this unnecessarily complicated."

< Hi! My day has been good, but I've slept for most of it. How was yours? I had a good time last night as well :)

He removes and then adds the smiley—*it looks sarcastic without it, doesn't it?* He sends the text before he has a chance to change his mind, and then obsessively pets Sandwich to keep his mind off of it. At least she knows him well enough not to pee on him anymore. He probably smells enough like her property by now.

To his surprise, Daniel doesn't take three hours to reply, unlike Todd.

> **I've been studying for most of the day, and then practice. When can I see you again?**

Todd frowns over the studying part, but then he remembers that Daniel must be sweating over the LSAT already.

Giving up on waiting with replying—Daniel hadn't, after all—he types back.

< **Maybe next week? I hope studying went well.**

He gets a reply almost immediately.

> **Sounds like a plan! How's your evening?**

Biting his lip, Todd contemplates letting Mela know, but decides against it.

< **Pretty good. I'm doing nothing right now except for trying to digest dinner**

> **Same. Basically just waiting for it to get late enough so I can sleep. How's your work and school schedule next week?**

< **Only working the closing shift on thurs.**

> **How's Friday?**

< **Free**

> **How does coffee sound?**

< **Sounds great :)**

Todd smiles stupidly. *Friday. That's less than a week away.*

*   *   *

WORK IS SLOW THE FOLLOWING day. Mrs. Floral is fidgety but doesn't want to tell him why. Todd concentrates on trying to come up with any way he can help with getting new artists to exhibit. *If they need a younger crowd, maybe a younger artist is the way to go?*

There are people in his school who are scarily good. He knows this. The problem is that he doesn't know *them*. Studying usually takes up so much of his time that he doesn't have much left to be social, what with working and all. He's got a small group of people he hangs out with between classes, but he mostly befriended them by accident the first weeks of college and then stuck with it.

It's possible that some of them can introduce him, however, and he starts trying to figure out which one of his friends would be the best to start with.

His phone buzzes in his pocket as he welcomes a stray patron. It's one of the few regulars, who sometimes likes to sit on the second floor and look at the pieces for hours. He checks his phone as soon as she has disappeared out of sight.

It's Daniel.

> **I'm in your hood!**

Just as Todd is about to reply asking what the hell has possessed Daniel to make him leave Manhattan, the bell over the door chimes, and Todd's brain short-circuits.

There, stepping inside, is *Daniel* with three other people.

Daniel notices him almost immediately, looking confused to see Todd. He opens his mouth, but is interrupted when Mrs. Floral appears, ushering them toward the office.

Still too shocked to be able to grasp that *Daniel is here*, Todd doesn't reflect over the other people until he notices the man in the dark suit trailing behind them.

That's Stanley, the gallery's landlord.

Todd can't piece it together, but then suspicion dawns on him: They're here for the gallery, the *space*. They must be. There's no other logical explanation for why Stanley would be here, and it would explain how out of character Mrs. Floral has been behaving today.

Todd has no clue how Daniel plays a part in all of this, but he's in there with the rest of them. With his stomach in knots, Todd does his best to concentrate on something else, despite the fact that he would rather press his ear against the door. Truth be told, he probably would do just that if the door wasn't mostly glass. He's going to have to wait until Mrs. Floral is done and then ask her about it.

He sends a semi-desperate text to Mela, belatedly realizing that she's on Coney Island with her cousin and most definitely isn't checking her phone. She's impressive like that.

The meeting takes almost two hours. Todd doesn't understand what could possibly take this long. Even selling the place should go quicker.

After Todd's dusted the front desk twice and gone through the stack of papers next to the register, as well as giving another stray patron a tour, the group finally emerges, and Todd instantly wishes that the meeting would have taken longer.

His gaze keeps switching between Stanley, Daniel, and Mrs. Floral, not really noticing the other two. Daniel looks almost bored, while both Mrs. Floral and Stanley seem annoyed. Daniel's face brightens when their eyes lock, and Todd is too confused by this entire situation to not get a tumble behind his ribs as Daniel approaches him.

"I was *really* in your hood it seems," he says, leaning against the counter.

Todd tries not to stare at the way his arms look, stretching the shirt fabric over his biceps and shoulders. Swimming has its perks, apparently.

"Yeah, I'm still really confused," Todd admits. "I wasn't prepared to see you until Friday."

Daniel grins. "I'm considering this an extra treat."

Snorting, Todd glances at the rest of the group. They seem too caught in wrapping up their meeting to pay attention to them.

"So, it's a good thing that our friends are dating," he blurts. It's his turn to keep the conversation going. "With the phone number mishap, I mean."

"Jesse giving me your number?" Daniel checks, and when Todd nods, he continues, "tell me about it. I almost had a heart attack when I came home and realized that I didn't have your number, or even your last name. It was a painful fifteen minutes, before I remembered Jesse having Mela's contact info."

"Yeah, same. She sent him my number right away."

Daniel rolls his eyes. "That guy sleeps like the dead after a few drinks. He sent it to me the next day, and I didn't notice until late because I was studying."

"I'm impressed that you can keep away from your phone for that long."

"I can't," Daniel admits. "I have my sister hide it for me."

"Ambitious." Todd doubts that he has the self-control to ask someone to do the same for him. He checks his phone every time he isn't busy doing something else. Mom tells him it's a problem. He isn't sure he agrees.

"Well, I don't have much of a choice."

At that, the man who arrived with Daniel clasps his shoulder. Something about him is familiar. He can't pinpoint what it is, but then he notices that Daniel looks a lot like him: the same hair color and similar sharp features. It must be his dad.

"I'll see you Friday," Todd offers as a goodbye when Daniel straightens and pushes away from the desk.

Daniel grins and waves before he disappears out the door.

"What was that about?" Todd asks, turning toward Mrs. Floral as soon as the door closes.

She sighs and sinks into the nearest chair. She's aged five years in the past week and tripled her daily quota of cigarettes. He should talk to her about that, but there never seems to be a good time. "They're interested in the space. Apparently, the son wants to use it for some kind of club."

Todd's stomach drops to the soles of his feet. "That guy?"

"The one you were speaking to, yes. Daniel," Mrs. Floral says. "Do you know him?"

"No," Todd decides, his chest empty. He doesn't.

✳ ✳ ✳

TODD'S HEAD IS STILL SPINNING when he gets off an hour later. Daniel wants to use the gallery space for a freaking *club*? It hurts between his ribs at the idea of Mrs. Floral's life work being torn down, packed away in boxes, and replaced with strobe lights and pounding basses. Todd knows every crack in the sidewalk from his own front door to the gallery. He knows where he has to be extra careful during winter, because the ground always gets slippery there and where he can pick up a good coffee on his way to work. Above all, he's been there, watching Mrs. Floral pour her heart and soul into this place. He's kept her company late at night, when she's wanted to finish putting up new works before the weekend, even though he should've been studying. Every corner of that place is something she's created, and now she's so close to losing it. It aches to breathe.

Things aren't exactly better, considering that his classes start tomorrow. Before today, he had one thing to worry about: the gallery closing. Now, he has that, plus the fact that the guy he has been all starry-eyed over is the one who's trying to take it from him. Mrs. Floral's life work. His safe space.

Todd decides to take a longer way home. It's hot, despite the sun starting to set, and the humidity ruins his hair in a few blocks. However, the strain in his legs as he walks is clearing his head. It makes him focus on something other than what just happened.

Everything smells heavenly when he gets home. *Right, Dad is making chilaquiles.* That is a positive thing at least.

"Hey," he says, sinking down at the kitchen table.

"Hungry?" Dad asks, with a quick glance at him before returning his attention to the cooking.

Not really, but he can't say that. "Starving."

Dad's entire face lights up.

Todd ends up eating so much that he's nauseous, but it's worth it because Dad doesn't stop smiling and he doesn't ask about school even once. All things considered, it's a pretty terrific dinner.

He checks his phone once he's in bed. Mela has replied with a row of question marks. There's no text from Daniel.

Heaving a sigh, Todd presses CALL on Mela's name.

"You send me the most cryptic text and then don't call me until *now*?" she greets.

"Dinner. Sorry." Picking at a loose thread in his shirt, Todd chooses his words carefully. "I don't know what it's all about yet, but it's already bad enough."

Mela hums on the other end.

"So, the gallery has been doing badly financially for a while. I only found out last week. Today I get this text from Daniel saying that he's in my hood, and, the next thing I know, he's walking into the gallery for a meeting with Mrs. Floral and the landlord and people I think are his parents."

"Seriously?"

"Yeah, it's too weird. Then I find out that he's the one wanting the space for a *club*."

"Uncultured swine," Mela mutters.

"I don't know what to do," Todd confesses and sighs. "Before I knew that he was involved in this, I said yes to coffee on Friday."

"You go, of course."

"He's trying to close the gallery."

"He probably had no idea that you work there until today."

Thinking back on Daniel's surprised expression when he saw Todd, Mela is probably right, but he's so freaking *stupid*.

"I don't know. That place means a lot to me and everything to Mrs. Floral."

"Well, if you give Daniel a shot, maybe he can mean a lot to you, too."

She says it as if it's easy, as though Todd is supposed to overlook the fact that he might be out of his safe space and Mrs. Floral might lose everything she has because there's a possibility for him to be with Daniel.

"He wants to make it into a *club*."

"Would you have cared if it was Cruella's gallery?"

Todd resists the urge to hang up. "Of course I would."

"Liar."

"I'm not lying. Art is important."

"I'm not disagreeing with you on that. I'm just saying that you would have gladly sacrificed *art* just to finally see Cruella go."

"It's not entirely true," Todd mutters. *Not entirely false, either.*

"Coffee with Daniel is a good thing. You should go. It also gives you a chance to talk to him about this."

"Maybe."

He looks at Sandwich, who's already sleeping in her cage, stretched out to look twice as long and half as fat compared to what she usually does. Maybe he should try to get some sleep, too.

⚹　⚹　⚹

FOR ONCE, THE FIRST-WEEK-OF-CLASSES-CONFUSION IS something Todd is grateful for. He's forced to keep his mind busy while trying to get a grasp of the curriculum and figuring out what classes will take more effort.

On top of that, he's making a list of people he would like to showcase at the gallery. Several seniors are already starting to make a name for themselves, despite not being finished with school.

There isn't much room to think about Daniel and everything surrounding him until Thursday, when Todd can no longer avoid answering his texts.

He's sitting at the table on a pink stool way too low for his height and watching as the kids have a go at a cubist portrait. There are six of them, of varying age but similar background. The program is free, and anyone can apply online when the spots are released before every semester.

Some travel quite far with their parents to get here, just because they can't afford to go somewhere else. Some live closer by, and their parents took an opportunity for them to learn more about art. They're not from well-off families, and some parents have a strain in their voices and around their eyes when they ask Todd if the program is free next semester as well.

Farthest down the table, Najwa is doing pretty well on her own, but she's also the oldest in the bunch, turning ten next week, and she's been around since the program started. Clara, she's six and the youngest, has long since decided that she'd rather draw scary spiders than *weird faces, Todd, because spiders are the coolest*, and that's fine. She explains three times over the course of an hour that since spiders have eight legs, they're not actual insects. Jamal went to the bathroom twenty minutes ago, and Todd should go look for him. He's probably stuck in front of one of the pieces in the gallery. It's more rule than exception that he gets distracted on his way back from the bathroom. He's already finished with his piece, and it's a beautiful creation of primary colors on one half, and their complementary colors on the other. They talked about that last semester, and Jamal has a thing for making colors pop.

He slides his phone out of his pocket and chews on his bottom lip. If he replies to Daniel's text now canceling their coffee date tomorrow, he'll still have about thirty minutes with the kids and thirty minutes of cleaning up after them to distract himself.

"No phones, Todd!" Raina shouts across the table.

"Sorry, sorry," he says, holding his free hand up. "I have a really important text to reply to and then I'll put it away, I promise."

"Only if you bring cookies next time," Clara says without looking up from where she's drawing tiny, tiny hairs on her spider's legs.

He's such a pushover. "I might."

"Okay, I don't see any phones," Raina sing-songs.

"No phones at all," Logan agrees, giggling under his breath. He's paying a lot of attention to one side of the portrait, but he always works slowly and meticulously.

Todd's chest grows heavy from wondering where the kids will spend their Thursday nights if the gallery closes. He won't be able to see them again, and they're the highlight of his week. Their open, unashamed fascination with art and whatever he shares with them is so refreshing compared to the critical eyes of himself and his classmates. They're not afraid to share their opinions and never worried that they might have one that's considered *less*.

He opens his phone and the text conversation with Daniel. There's a new one waiting for him.

> **Hey, where did you want to grab that coffee tomorrow?**

Raina is now showing her work to Logan, asking for his suggestions. Sourness spreads in his stomach. Some of them claim that this is their best part of the week too.

< **I think I'm getting sick, sorry. Rain check?**

Then, he types a second text to Mela. It's easier if he isn't the only one who knows that he lied.

< **Said no to grabbing coffee tomorrow. Can't do it**

She replies in an instant.

> **Are you serious?**

< **The gallery is too important**

> **Oh for fuck's sake Todd!**

He doesn't reply. There's no use when she's already decided that he did the wrong thing. She might be right, but his heart screams *betrayal* every time he thinks about going on a date with Daniel, when he wants to take over the space after the gallery closes. This place is everything to him and even more to Mrs. Floral. It means a lot to these kids.

"I think I'm starting to see phones at the table," Raina sing-songs after a while, and Todd hurries to put his phone back in his pocket.

Daniel replies twenty minutes after Todd has come home.

> **Sure, let me know when you are back on track. Feel better!**

He doesn't feel guilty. He doesn't. Sinking down on the floor in his room, Todd ignores the sudden hit of nausea and pets Sandwich's smooth ears. Her nose twitches, but she stays still.

"I think you need some exercise."

After building an obstacle with an empty DVD case and erasers to keep it steady, Todd pushes Sandwich toward it.

"You need to jump it." He ignores the skeptical look she gives him. "Bunnies like that."

She refuses to go near the case, and when Todd lifts her over it to show how she's supposed to go about it, she hops back into her cage as soon as she's back on the floor. At least she's faster on her way there than she usually is.

"Well, I guess that's better than nothing," he mutters.

On Saturday, he agrees to go to a bar with a few people from one of his classes. Sitting at home makes him want to message Daniel and apologize. Maybe he should.

The small place is in a basement, where the air is already running out of oxygen, and the owner might've spent more time and money on unknown beer brands than on interior décor and comfort. Pushing away his thoughts, he focuses on Giselle, who's friends with the guy who invited him. Todd has seen her work. She's on his list.

"So this is your last year?" he asks her while nursing his coffee. The band playing isn't that great, but he's comfortable in this crowd. As long as he can focus on what's important—the gallery—he'll be fine.

"Yep! It's so scary." She pushes a stray, strawberry blond corkscrew from her face. It has escaped the messy braid hanging over her shoulder. She's very short, only reaching Todd's shoulder, and chubby. He's never seen her wear anything but skirts and dresses. She smiles, creating dimples in her rosy cheeks. Nothing in her innocent look correlates with the dark anguish in her art. He once spent over an hour staring at a portrait of a man whose face is decaying until it seemed to come alive. "What about you?"

"Two left, including this one. Thank god."

"Do you have plans already?" she asks him.

"Nah, can't say I do. I'm still hoping that I will have figured it out when it's time." Shrugging, Todd looks at the other people around them.

He hasn't talked to them much until this week. Does this mean that he's exploiting them, even though he likes their company? But they're getting something out of this too. At least Giselle will, if she says yes.

"What about you?" he adds, remembering to be polite.

"Well, I'm hoping that I can maybe concentrate on my art for a bit. I've had some luck so far, but you know the business. It's all about knowing the right people and getting exposure."

Todd is all too aware. While it requires a lot of talent, it's also about being *right*. He's seen people who would've been incredible if they had been doing five years ago what they do now. It doesn't mean that they lack talent. They're just not... *current*.

"I know it's not much, but I work for a smaller indie gallery in Williamsburg. If you'd like to honor us with your work, I'm sure we'd be happy to showcase it for you."

Suddenly sure she's going to laugh at him, he doesn't quite dare to look her in the eye.

"Really? That would be really cool, Todd. I think my stuff would work best in a place like that."

"Think about it and let me know what you decide. I'll talk to the owner." He straightens in his chair. It's a silver lining, if nothing else.

"Do you guys do this a lot? Student's works?"

"We didn't previously," Todd tells her and hopes that Mrs. Floral won't hate what he says next. "But we're thinking that maybe we should. I think that everyone would gain."

"I think so too," Giselle says, nodding. There's a glow to her now; color high on her cheeks almost matches her hair. "I'll get back to you for sure."

Back in his bedroom, Todd manages to make Sandwich jump the DVD obstacle once. He also manages to eat the entire Tupperware container of chili that he found in the fridge, pretend not to see the missed call from Evan, and avoid replying to Daniel's text sent at two-thirty.

> **I hope you'll feel better soon. I'm really looking forward to that coffee :)**

The only reason Todd smiles is because he's so relieved over Giselle's *I'll think about it.*

There's a knock on his already-open door, and he looks up to see Dad standing there in his pajamas.

"Are you still up?" he asks, despite the obvious answer to that question.

"Yeah, came home a little over an hour ago." Todd checks the time on his phone. "Well, make that two."

Dad smiles, all sleepy. "Had a good time?"

"It was fun. Hung out with some new people I haven't really gotten to know before." He really did have a good time, despite the crappy music.

"What did you get up to?"

"There was a new band playing, and we hung out. Might've recruited someone to exhibit at work."

"Sounds like a good night." Dad nods toward the empty Tupperware container on the floor next to Todd's thigh. "I take it you didn't eat out."

"Uh, no, sorry. I was starving."

"It was in the fridge for a reason." Dad shakes his head, smiling.

"Thanks. Did I wake you?"

"No, bathroom. While I was up, I figured I might as well check to see you made it home."

Swallowing the sudden lump in his throat, Todd rubs his chest. "I did. I'll go to bed in a minute."

"You wash that up first." Dad points at the container before he disappears toward his and Mom's bedroom.

Sighing, Todd grabs it and rinses it carefully before he disposes it in the dishwasher, knowing all too well that Mom will kill him if he has managed to stain one of her containers permanently—again.

*　*　*

TODD'S CLASSES ARE GOING SURPRISINGLY well for someone who procrastinates like a professional. Two weeks into the semester, and he's not behind in a single class. That's an improvement by a week and a half compared to last year.

In the middle of Friday afternoon painting techniques class, Giselle texts him. He wipes the paint off his fingers the best that he can, hoping he won't ruin his phone as he unlocks it to read the full text.

> **Hi Todd! If the offer still stands, I would love if you could talk to your manager about the possibility of displaying my art.**

His pulse picks up; his fingers tremble as he types a quick yes. Her text is a welcome break from staring at the gallery's books, unable to comprehend what the numbers stand for, or the constant textbook-reading and quiz-taking that he does when he isn't working. It also lightens the heaviness of his bad conscience, even if just by a fraction. He's told Daniel that he has a severe case of pneumonia, instead of confessing what the real problem is. Not only is Mela disappointed in him, but he has also managed to paint himself into a corner. He'll have to face the music at some point. It's just easier to leave that for the future.

He isn't sure if it's because of Mela's busy for the first two weeks of school or if she's so disappointed in him that they have barely talked since classes started. When she texts him during his walk from the subway stop to his building, it comes as a surprise, a welcome one.

> **Wanna go out tonight?**
< **I'm working tomorrow :(**
> **Just for a couple of drinks? No late night out!**
< **All right, just because I miss you**

It's a bar close to where she lives with a very obvious sports theme. She's already there when he arrives, sitting at a corner table with Jesse. Todd slows and swallows. He's supposed to be home and very sick. That's what Daniel thinks, at least, but Mela knows the truth. He has no idea if Daniel has told Jesse or if Mela has. Maybe they both have told him, and he might have put two and two together. *Shit.*

Sticking his sweaty hands into his pockets and squaring his shoulders, Todd walks over to them.

"Hi."

To his surprise, Jesse smiles and reaches over the table to shake his hand. He doesn't seem to notice how sweaty Todd's palm is. Mela makes a kissy face.

"Heya."

Todd sits down as the waitress walks over and he orders a coke, because she asked for his ID before when he tried to order a beer. She probably doesn't remember, but Todd is not taking any chances tonight.

"Did you talk to Daniel yet?" Mela, always so blunt, asks when he gets his drink.

Todd glances at Jesse, but he doesn't bat an eye. Maybe Daniel didn't tell him about Todd being sick. Jesse clasps his shoulder as he heads toward the bathroom.

"No, I'm still sick." Sighing, Todd scratches his cheek. "I'm starting to feel bad."

"You're *starting* to feel bad? Mind you, you're ruining your chances with a possibly great guy."

Todd concentrates on the condensation on the outside of his glass. It's not exactly true that he's only now starting to feel bad, but it's becoming too heavy to ignore. He doesn't want to talk about this and doesn't feel like pointing out that Daniel clearly isn't such a great guy if he thinks it's cool to take away people's life work just like that.

"Speaking of a possibly great guy." He draws a pattern in the condensation with his fingertips. "How's everything with Jesse?"

Mela's smile tells him everything. "It's great so far. We've only met a few times since the party, not including today, because of school. It's been worth it making time for him, though."

"So he's really great, then?"

"So far, so good." The way she lights up when Jesse comes back to their table makes Todd's chest ache for her. She deserves every second of this.

"I'm gonna go get a new drink," Jesse says and nods toward the bar. "You want one?"

"I'll come with you." Mela slips around the table, heading toward the bar before Todd can blink.

He looks after them and doesn't understand the sudden rush until he looks at the door. Right inside, probably having just arrived, is Daniel. He looks around, clearly searching for someone.

"Seriously?" he hisses at Mela while she's still within earshot and fights the urge to rush out in sheer panic.

"What?" she turns around, eyes narrowing. "Imagine how much less awkward this would've been if you had just talked to him like a grown-ass human being instead of making up excuses?"

With that, she strides to the bar, where Jesse is already standing. He wants to hate her, but he can't, because she's right.

His gaze finds Daniel again, and he watches, with a growing sense of dread, how Daniel first spots Jesse and Mela at the bar, smiling wide and waving. Jesse signs something and points toward the table, toward *Todd*, and Daniel looks his way. It takes one, two, three seconds—Todd counts them in his head—until their gazes lock. Daniel's face falls.

Then everything just stops. Todd can't tell if his heart is still beating. The look on Daniel's face makes it obvious—he had no clue that Todd would be here.

Daniel looks away and bites his lip before he rolls his shoulders back and walks up to Todd.

"Feeling better?" Daniel asks, hands in his pockets, as he stops in front of Todd. He's not sitting down.

Todd is grateful Mela and Jesse are still at the bar. They must have planned this. He's also scared half to death being left alone with Daniel.

"Yeah, about that," he starts, voice a little higher than he intends. "Uh, I—"

"—lied?" Daniel supplies helpfully. "Because it sure as hell doesn't seem like you're *eating ice cream and watching a movie in bed* to me."

Todd winces, swallowing desperately as he tries to find words. "I'm sorry."

"That you got caught."

Ouch. "For being a dick."

Daniel heaves a sigh and sinks down on the opposite side of the table.

"You could've just told me that you didn't want to see me again, instead of stringing me along."

Todd reaches up to readjust his beanie, but his hand falls back into his lap. He wants to say that it isn't as easy as not wanting to see Daniel, but the situation is too complicated to explain. "Yeah, I should have."

"Better late than never, I guess."

Daniel seems less confident than the guy Todd met at that frat party. Maybe that comes with rejection, even for someone like him.

"If it's any consolation, I did want to see you again until I found out that you were trying to take the gallery away."

Todd bites his lip. He doesn't have alcohol to blame for letting that slip out.

"Come again?" Daniel says, and Todd repeats himself. It's even more stupid the second time around.

"Seriously?" Daniel stares at him. "*That's* what this is about?"

"Don't make it sound like it's nothing," Todd blurts. "It's culture, you know, *art*. It's culture. It's valuable for society." *And I have kids there*, he wants to say, *who don't have much else in their free time. Whose parents can't afford any other activities. Who have talent and interest, and this is their only option.* He doesn't. Todd juts his chin out, knowing full well that he looks exactly like a five-year-old when he does it. Evan has told him often. It just comes automatically when he gets defensive.

"What? I lost you."

He doesn't *want* to, because it makes him sound like a child, but he can't refuse to repeat anything that Daniel hasn't been able to catch. So he repeats himself, wincing as the words come out whinier than the first time.

"Sure," Daniel agrees, easy, as if he doesn't have a conflicting interest. "There are hundreds of galleries in New York."

"You want to make it into a *club*," Todd points out. "There are *thousands* of clubs too."

"There really aren't," Daniel snorts.

Todd sees red. *Seriously? He's going to deny that there's a club or bar on almost every corner around here?*

"I don't think we're talking about the same city."

"Clearly not." Daniel gets to his feet. "Or maybe you can consider the possibility that you've misunderstood something? Like the fact that I want to make it into a meeting place for deaf and hard of hearing kids to meet others like them. Not a goddamn night club."

He leaves before Todd has a chance to say anything. A second later, Mela and Jesse come over. They're not even trying to pretend they haven't watched the entire interaction from the bar.

"He wants to make a club for kids who are deaf or hard of hearing?" Todd asks, still staring at the door where Daniel disappeared.

"It's a project he's been working on with a few of his friends for a while now. It's very important to him." Jesse shrugs.

Todd's brain screeches to an abrupt halt. This must be the project Daniel spoke about the night they met. "Oh, god."

Todd doesn't know what to say . His brain echoes empty, and he spends the rest of the evening staring into his glass. Mela and Jesse give up on trying to talk to him pretty quickly.

He's not stupid. People with hearing loss are a minority, and a safe place to hang out must be incredibly important. For kids it's probably even more so.

Todd glances over at Jesse and Mela. They're in their own bubble, discussing something, touching, sitting so close together. He knows that he should be angry with them, goddamn *furious* even. For some reason he can't quite muster the energy. Daniel finding out the truth was bound to happen. Much like ripping off a band aid, it'll hurt like hell for a while, but maybe things will be better afterward. He hopes it hurts more for him than it does for Daniel. It wouldn't be fair for Daniel to take the biggest hit for something that's seventy-five percent Todd's fault. *Okay, maybe closer to ninety.*

Either way, he can't really see how things could get any worse.

After an hour, he leaves without saying goodbye. When he's at the station waiting for the train, he texts Mela to let her know where he is and then stuffs his phone in his pocket.

He messed up. There's no other way to put it. Daniel won't want to talk to him again. Truth be told, Todd doesn't want to talk to himself either.

Mom and Dad aren't home. They would've known that something is up just by looking at him. He's always been easy to read.

Making a nest on his bed out of blankets and pillows, Todd curls up in front of a movie. Right now, he wishes that he really was sick. *Dying, even. Okay, maybe not dying, but somewhere close.* It would've been less horrific coughing his lungs out than having this concrete weight on his chest that's making it difficult to breathe.

He barely registers what's happening on screen, because all his focus is on that angry text he expects from Daniel, but his phone stays quiet all evening.

"I suck," he mutters to himself.

Sandwich twitches her nose, going still in her cage. Todd suspects that means she agrees. He can't blame her.

Chapter Three

ON THE PLUS SIDE, IT'S a lot easier to focus on school when he doesn't have to worry about coming up with excuses to not see Daniel.

On the down side, the concrete weight is still there two weeks later, chafing whenever he has a moment to himself. Todd has typed out an apology text at least once every night. He hasn't sent any of them. An apology doesn't make up for any of this. During the days he tells himself that it's for the best. They met once—that time in the gallery and the last time don't really count—and they don't know each other at all. But as soon as he's in bed, his mind starts spinning without permission.

Where would they be be now, if that coffee date had happened? Every time he goes down that road, he gets a sinking feeling. Daniel *still* wants the gallery to close, he has to remember that, even though it doesn't make it okay for Todd to act like a grade-A dick. He can't overlook the fact that Daniel's club means, no matter how great a cause it is, that Todd's safe space and Mrs. Floral's life work is gone.

It usually takes a couple of hours of feeling bad, reminding himself why, and then going back to feeling bad again before he's so exhausted that he passes out.

He buries himself in schoolwork to occupy his head with *anything*, and, even a month in, he's not behind in any of his classes. That feels pretty great. Mrs. Floral said yes to exhibiting Giselle's art. Logan finished his cubist piece. At least some things seem to be working out.

"I really want company," Mela tells him on the phone two days later. "I can't go by myself."

"Why not?"

"Because I don't know *anyone*."

"Neither do I." Todd has tried really hard to forget Daniel and everything about him. The last thing he needs is to show up to a swim meet. Sure, it's for Mela's sake, and she's going for Jesse, but it's not as though Daniel will become invisible just because Todd is there.

Still, ten minutes later, he hears himself say, "Fine. You're buying me coffee afterward." *And extensive therapy sessions.*

Mrs. Floral is happier since she's seen Giselle's work. She's stopped sighing and doesn't smell of cigarettes as often, and Daniel hasn't been around again as far as Todd knows.

"How many more new artists do we need?" Todd asks, after handing a new patron a sheet with short information about the artists.

"It's hard to say. We've got limited space, but it's better to have a queue lined up than always signing at the last second."

"I'll see what I can do." There are more people in school who are incredibly talented, and Giselle knows a whole bunch of them. If he can work up enough courage, maybe he can ask her to help him out. He still finds himself a bit awkward around her.

"You're such a good boy, Todd." Mrs. Floral pats his cheek gently. "I don't know what I would do without you. I remember when you were skinny and short and so nervous that you were shaking when you asked if you could spend time here. You're all grown up now."

Todd straightens where he stands, trying not to smile before she disappears into the office.

He grew up here, more or less, learning how to hang new works and slowly getting comfortable talking to the patrons about them. Mrs. Floral coached him with such patience that she should get a prize. He found his love for art and experienced the electricity under his skin whenever he discovers a new piece that moves him. He found himself here too. Mrs. Floral was the second person he told, after Mela, that he likes boys. She taught him how to drink coffee without cream and stayed with him after closing hours all through high school to help him finish his homework when it seemed too difficult. Losing the gallery is terrifying, not only because it's so important for Mrs. Floral—it's her life work—but also because of what it means to him. If the gallery closes, what's left of him?

Maybe, *maybe* they can pull this off.

The next second, the front door bangs open and Cruella—*Gloria*—sweeps in. She's wearing fur, even though the weather is still quite warm.

"Todd!" she exclaims and flings her arms out, as if she's expecting applause for showing up. She's in a glittering dress under the fur and wears shoes with little fluffy balls at her toes. Per usual, she's wearing bright red lipstick and has styled her hair in stiff, unmoving waves over one shoulder. It's as if she's walked straight off the pages of a comic book.

"Gloria." He greets her. Despite owning the gallery next door, her visits are surprisingly rare. They have never come with anything but bad news, either.

"How's business?"

"Pretty good." He leans against the counter. "How are the minks?"

Eyebrows drawn together, she looks at him, then shakes her head, clearly deciding that he's not worth a follow-up question.

"It just looks a tad *empty*, doesn't it?" She gestures around the room.

"It's Thursday evening. We're closing in ten minutes. People are having dinner with their families."

"It's such a pity in such a picturesque… atmosphere."

Rolling his eyes, Todd bites his tongue. "Did you have anything to say?"

She looks at the list in front of him where he has been writing down names of potential exhibitors. He turns it over as she steps closer.

"No. I just wanted to check in and see how you are doing."

"It's Mrs. Floral's gallery," Todd reminds her.

"That's impossible to forget." Then she breezes out, letting the door bang shut, without saying goodbye.

"Was it something I said?" Todd says under his breath. Shaking his head, he logs out of the register, before locking the front door and going to the office and Mrs. Floral.

"Cruella was here."

"*Todd.*"

"What? She looks the part, with the fur and all."

She shakes her head, unable to hide her smile completely. "I can't be angry with you for being rude behind her back when I know how hard you're working to keep us afloat."

"I really like this place." Sitting on the edge of the desk, Todd looks at her. "This is, by far, the best job I could've asked for and you're the best boss anyone could ever have. I'll do everything I can to keep all of this, if it's possible. I just feel like we need to try."

"You are absolutely right. We should do all we can." She squeezes his hand and then hesitates before she says: "What happened with that boy who was here with his parents? Daniel?"

Todd swallows. "I don't know."

"You very pointedly didn't know him, but you sure seemed like you did."

"I know." He sighs, not wanting to talk about this, but Mrs. Floral is too nice for him to refuse her anything. "We met a few days before that and I was a bit interested until I learned that he wants this place."

"*Todd.*" This time, when she says his name, it isn't reprimanding but so very soft.

"I mean, I *know*, I know it's not really true, but I can't help but feel like, if I'm dating him, I'm betraying something that's so important, that's your life work, and a second home to the kids in our program, to *me.*" Getting to his feet, Todd grabs his jacket. "I'll see you Sunday, Mrs. Floral."

"Have a nice weekend, honey."

They both know that he's fleeing, and Todd expects her to bring this up again soon.

＊　＊　＊

TODD HAS NEVER BEEN TO a swim meet. Until the other day, he didn't even know that they were called *meets*. Whatever he had imagined them to be like, this is different.

It's extremely humid and surprisingly crowded. For some reason, Todd had expected the place to be empty except for him and Mela, but this is clearly a big deal.

"So, when's Jesse up?"

"I don't know." Mela looks excited. She's always liked sports and used to play softball in high school. Todd never understood the big deal with competing and all the *exercise*.

"I hope it's soon. My hair is going to look like shit in two seconds." Humidity is the arch enemy for his curls.

"Oh, please, it'll totally be worth it when you can drool over Daniel."

Todd glares at her, ignoring the sting in his chest. She knows everything and still she keeps teasing him like this, as if things are the way they were a month ago.

"You know that we're not talking."

"Have you tried?" she asks, voice light as though it's the easiest thing in the world.

"No."

"Maybe you should."

"No," Todd says again. "I was a dick to him."

Mela looks at him for a long moment. Sometimes Todd thinks that they have been friends too long, because she doesn't sugarcoat anything.

"So maybe start with an apology."

Todd resists the urge to pull his knees to his chest. "I can't. I need to focus on the gallery. It's too important."

The way Mela takes his hand is such a contrast to her deep sigh. "Sometimes you're your own worst enemy."

"I'm not."

She elbows him in the ribs. "You need to talk to him about this."

"I really don't," Todd mutters and tunes her out as the loudspeaker calls for contestants to line up.

Despite the humid air, the swimmers look bare in their suits. They are so focused on the task at hand, they don't seem to realize that there's a crowd looking at them.

"No Jesse or Daniel," Mela says, just as Todd comes to the same conclusion.

"What if we have to be here all day?"

"You'll live."

They're not the most eventful few heats in Todd's opinion. Swimmers line up and off they go, until they've completed however many laps they're doing this time around, and climb out of the pool. Rinse, repeat. Two schools are competing, and they seem to be fiercely competitive.

He straightens in his seat when a new set of swimmers takes their places on the white platforms. In the middle of them, lane five, is Daniel. Todd has no clue how he recognized him in that black, skintight suit, the cap, and goggles, but it's definitely him.

"Is that Daniel?" Mela asks.

"Yes." There's no hesitation.

"I hope he wins."

Todd doesn't reply. When the loudspeaker calls for the swimmers to take their mark, he zeroes in on how Daniel curls over on the platform, gripping the edge, his body tense as a coil. Todd can't read his face from here, but the way he holds himself shows how focused he is. Every muscle in his body looks as though it's vibrating in anticipation.

The start buzzer sounds and there's a flash of light, and they're off. Daniel is fast. Todd knows nothing about swimming, but he's just seen several heats, and, if he remembers the numbers on the scoreboard correctly, the other swimmers weren't this fast.

He holds his breath when Daniel turns, and the guy next to him is not much behind. Digging his fingers into his thighs, Todd leans forward and watches as Daniel somehow manages to pull ahead in the last few yards.

"Not so boring now, is it?" Mela asks, sounding smug, as Daniel climbs out of the water.

Todd can't remember words, but manages at last, "Uh, sure."

As it turns out, it's more fun to watch someone you know compete. He has no clue why he's surprised that both Jesse and Daniel win all their heats, but he is. Daniel did tell him that Jesse is the team captain and maybe that should have given him an idea of what to expect. Despite Todd's lack of knowledge in the sport, he thinks that Jesse must be the best swimmer on their team.

"We're gonna grab coffee afterward," Mela tells him as the crowd thins.

"You didn't tell me that." He probably shouldn't count on Daniel not coming.

"It's not like I'm going to come watch him compete and then *leave*. Plus, you required me buying you coffee to even show up."

That makes sense. Todd had assumed that he could sneak away unnoticed. That was really stupid of him.

The thought of seeing Jesse again is almost as stressful as the possibility of Daniel joining them. Todd *lied* to Jesse's best friend. He wouldn't be very keen on hanging out with someone who did that to Mela.

"Stop angsting." Mela bumps into his side as they walk down the stairs together. "It'll be fine."

That's easy for her to say.

Todd's stomach is in knots while they wait outside. Sure enough, when Jesse exits the building, Daniel is about two steps behind him. Todd doesn't miss the way Daniel's steps falter when their eyes meet.

His stomach grows heavy, as if he's swallowed a dozen stones.

"Hi," he greets, pleasantly surprised when Jesse gives him a shoulder squeeze and a friendly *how's it going?* Todd doesn't have an answer to that.

Daniel steps away from hugging Mela, and Todd wants to leave. Daniel's hair is damp and there's a shine in his eyes, making them look greener than Todd remembers.

"Hi," Todd says again, not remembering where to put his hands or how to stand properly.

"Hi."

"So, coffee?" Jesse asks, locking gazes with Daniel, who shrugs. For the first time, Todd notices that he signs as he talks. He's only seen them interact once, the first evening Todd met Daniel, and then he must've been too drunk to realize that it was more than just hand gestures.

"Sounds good to me."

Todd doesn't like the coffee at the commercialized chains very much, but he's not going to voice his opinion in this company.

Jesse picks a square table for them, giving them a side each. It takes a second for Todd to realize that it must be easier for Daniel to lip read if he's able to see everyone around the table.

"I'll get your usual," Mela tells Todd as he puts his phone on the table.

Then he's alone with Daniel, who's looking a little to the left of Todd's face. It's such a contrast to the night they met, when Daniel's intense focus had only been on him.

Sucking in a breath, Todd presses the HOME button on his phone. There's missed call from Evan. *Great.*

"Who's Evan?" Daniel asks suddenly, taking Todd by surprise.

Looking up, Todd finds Daniel's gaze immediately. Swallowing, he goes for a shrug and breaks eye contact to delete the notification on his phone, careful to keep his face in Daniel's line of sight. "Uh, my brother."

"Your brother?"

Todd nods.

"Aren't you going to call him back?"

"No."

When he looks up again, he finds that Daniel is watching him with guarded curiosity in his eyes. It's just there for a second before he looks away and the conversation is over.

The two minutes they sit in silence before Mela and Jesse return are tenser than Todd's ever experienced. Daniel doesn't even bother to pretend texting on his phone. He's just looking the other way.

Todd concentrates on his coffee when Mela hands it to him. Daniel, on the other hand, politely partakes in the conversation. The way he talks to Mela makes Todd suspect that they have met several times. They even have *inside jokes*. Todd doesn't miss the fact that Mela has learned to sign a few things as well, but Jesse seems to sign most of the things she's saying, apologizing the few times he forgets.

What would things have been like now, if he hadn't lied to Daniel? Would he be a part of the conversation too? Or would they had gone on that coffee date and then decided that there wasn't anything between them to build on?

Swallowing, he puts his empty mug down. "I have to head home. Thanks for the company and congrats on the victories. Well done."

He doesn't quite look at anyone.

"You can't stay longer?" Jesse asks, face falling.

"Nah, school stuff and all that." Todd clears his throat. "Sorry."

Daniel doesn't say anything, not even goodbye. *That's okay.* Todd doesn't care.

*   *   *

DAD IS IN THE KITCHEN when Todd gets home. The way he looks up and zeroes in on Todd makes it clear that his self-pity is showing.

"What happened?" Dad prompts and points to one of the kitchen chairs.

"What hasn't happened?" Todd mutters but sinks down on the chair all the same.

"Take it from the start."

Todd considers saying no and going to his room. But the truth is, he's *lonely*. Everything with the gallery and with Daniel is wearing on him. It has been for a while now, and he's *tired*.

"Well," he starts, fiddling with the newspaper on the table. "A month ago, give or take, I met this guy when I was at a party with Mela."

Glancing up, Todd finds Dad stirring the pot with his back turned, but he nods, humming.

"He was great. You know, nothing what I thought I would be interested in, but ticking all the boxes I didn't know I had, kinda."

Dad hums again.

"And we hung out all night and decided to see each other again. It was all good, until I find out that he's trying to take the gallery and turn it into... something else."

Dad looks up then, frowning. "He spent time with you just to get more information about the business?"

Todd shakes his head. "No, I think he was just as surprised to find me there as I was to see him walk through the door."

"So it's nothing personal from his side?"

"No." Todd pauses. "It's a coincidence. The gallery isn't doing that great financially and he needs a space for his thing."

"I take that this is upsetting you?"

"It's so important to me, and I'm so scared of losing it. I can't help that I feel like he's trying to take it from me."

"Todd," Dad says, voice soft. He puts the ladle on the counter and removes the stew pan from the stove. "Why would you look at it that way?"

Because it's easier than being helpless and sad.

"I don't know." Todd would be more upset if it wasn't for Dad using the same voice he had when Todd was fourteen and not doing that great in school. Todd remembers so well how he had expected a lecture, fully aware that Evan excelled, but instead had been told that the only person he had to do justice to was himself. It was easier to make an effort after that, to see every passed test as a victory. To him, passing has never been a small feat.

"These are two separate issues." Dad pulls out another chair. "The gallery is not doing well, and the landlord is looking for other potential renters. That's the first issue." Dad holds up a hand when Todd opens his mouth to explain. "And then there's another, with this boy that you've met, who's trying to start some kind of business, and he's looking for somewhere to have it. If he doesn't rent the space should the gallery close, then someone else will. The survival of your gallery doesn't depend on him wanting the space or not."

"But it's… the gallery is so important to me and to Mrs. Floral. It's all she has. She's put all her money into this. He's trying to take that away." Todd knows that he's sounding like a petulant child, and, somewhere in the back of his mind, there's a little voice saying that Dad might be right. It's just not what he needs to hear right now.

"Think about it and try to talk to him if you want some answers." Dad reaches over the table to ruffle his hair before he goes back to the stove.

Todd gets up from the chair, suddenly drained and with his temples tight, as if he has a headache coming.

"Go get some rest," Dad says. "I'll call for you when it's time for dinner."

"Thanks."

Todd buries himself under a pile of blankets and keeps his mind busy with completing this week's quizzes. Dad's put his head in a spin with a bunch of unwelcome thoughts. The last thing he wants right now is to consider that maybe he was wrong.

AS IT TURNS OUT, ASKING Giselle's friends is less easy than he thought. Giselle is reluctant, possibly worried that they will be competition. Todd can understand that, but he also knows that one college student isn't going to be enough to save his safe space and Mrs. Floral's retirement. It doesn't matter how talented she is or how great a career she will have in a few years. Her name just isn't that well known yet. She's not enough to save them.

"I was contacted by a California-based artist yesterday," Mrs. Floral tells him during his shift the following day. It's exactly what he needs to hear. Unpacking pieces, fighting the sticky tape, isn't such a hardship suddenly.

Todd pauses, freeing his index finger from an especially stubborn piece of tape. "Really?"

"Yes. He's seen our webpage and wants to showcase."

He can't keep himself from smiling at her use of webpage. "I assume you said yes?"

"Of course." She smiles, and Todd wipes his hands on his jeans before he hugs her.

While things are going better with work and school is going steadily according to plan thanks to late nights and not enough sleep, everything Daniel is going really bad.

"I'm having a bunch of people over for dinner on my birthday," Mela tells him, mid-October, when she's lying on his bed, reading something for school. She has a pink marker pen balanced on her nose.

"That's nice."

"You're coming, right?"

"Like you even have to ask. The only time I've missed your birthday was when I visited abuela. In *Mexico*."

Mela removes the marker pen and looks over at him. There's a moment of silence before she says, "I'm going to invite Daniel."

Todd freezes, betrayal flooding his gut. "*Why?*"

"Because I've hung out with him a bit, and he is a really great guy. We're friends."

"Okay." Todd saw the indications of that during the coffee disaster, but he didn't know that they were friendly enough to invite each other to birthday dinners. It shouldn't be such a surprise. Mela is the best person he knows and she's dating Daniel's friend. It's only natural that they see each other every so often.

"Are you okay with that?"

Is he? He doesn't have much of a choice. It's her birthday dinner. She can invite anyone. "Sure."

"It's also so that Jesse has someone he knows, except for me and you."

Jesse hasn't exactly come off as the kind of guy who can't talk to people he doesn't know, but Todd isn't the one dating him, so he's not going to question. Above all, she doesn't need to defend the people she wants there when she celebrates her birthday.

When Mela's birthday comes around, he stands in his room with the contents of his closet all over the floor. He's tried on at least a dozen shirts and every pair of pants that he owns and attempted to tame his hair into some kind of submission. In the end, he goes for jeans and a turquoise, paisley-patterned button-up, with a purple bow tie. That's about as formal as he gets, unless someone gets married or dies. He found her a piece of a moose horn in a shady thrift shop last week. Someone doused it in glitter, and his hands sparkle whenever he touches it, which is *awful*, but Mela is going to love it. He found a necklace with her birthstone, too, most likely fake, but it looked pretty. The horn is probably going to overshadow it anyway.

He's early. Mela asked him to help her prepare, and he doesn't tell her that he's relieved she still needs him, but she must understand that anyway. It's not as if he *actually* worries that she would ever switch him out, considering how long they have been friends, but sometimes he gets those weird brain ghosts that tell him differently.

"You look great," she greets, but *she* looks smashing in a bright teal dress. "We match!"

"Happy birthday." He hugs her tight. A tiny space in his chest fills each second she holds on to him. "You look amazing."

She twirls on the spot; her skirt poofs out. "I'm glad you could be here early."

"What do you need me to do?" He hands over the gift box, neatly wrapped in pink gift wrap and an origami butterfly as decoration, and her entire face lights up. One of his secret talents is gift wrapping.

"Nothing." She shrugs, eyeing the box as if she's two seconds away from shaking it, but then she puts it on the dresser right beside the front door. "I just wanted to hang out for a bit before everyone gets here. How are you?"

"I'm doing okay." Taking off his jacket, Todd avoids her gaze. "I mean, I should be doing great because we have two more artists for the gallery and I'm *ahead* on school work."

"But?"

He leaves her question hanging while he mulls it over. They make tea and curl up on the couch together, backs against an armrest each, feet touching. Todd remembers when they could do this with their legs stretched out and they'd have to point their toes to touch over the seemingly endless couch cushions. Sometimes he isn't sure if it's just that they grew, or if maybe the couch got smaller too.

"I don't know," he sighs, clutching the mug until his palms burn. "It's all the *what ifs.*"

She smiles, nudging him with her foot. She has surprisingly big feet for such a tiny person. When they were kids, she told him that it was so she could walk on water. He believed her for several months. "It'll be fine. Maybe you just need some time. There's nothing wrong with that."

"It is if I was the one turning *him* down."

"No, because you didn't do it because the interest wasn't there. Don't be so hard on yourself."

Todd takes a breath and looks at her. It's her birthday dinner. He's not going to ruin it for anything in the world.

"Okay," is all he says, and they talk about everything else until their mugs are dry.

Jesse arrives next. Todd is nervous for all of two seconds until Jesse squeezes his shoulder and asks him how he's doing.

Todd has met all of Mela's guests. Most of them are mutual friends Todd has gotten to know through her. It's comforting, considering that Daniel is coming. This way, Todd will probably not feel that left out; he'll have a whole bunch of people to talk to that he hasn't lied to.

Todd is talking to Michaela, a girl from Mela's high school softball team, when Daniel shows up. He has a huge bouquet of pink flowers and a bottle of champagne; the label has the shape of a shield, but Todd can't see the brand. Todd's brain partially quits on him when he takes in Daniel's olive-green slacks and crisp button-up. His hair looks just as Todd remembers it: carefully styled to look effortless. While Todd has a hard time deciding what he feels for Daniel, he can't help but warm at the way Daniel smiles at Mela and how he hugs her.

He isn't the only one who has trouble focusing as Daniel politely shakes hands with everyone. He smiles, looks them in the eyes whenever he's not looking at their mouths, repeats their names, asks several of them to say it again or to spell their names on their phones. Todd waits, conveniently last in line, and his pulse picks up as Daniel comes closer.

"Todd," Daniel says, when he's the only one left.

"Hi." For some reason he expects Daniel to say something more, but he doesn't. Instead he seeks out Jesse.

Todd resolutely turns his attention back to Michaela, who's clearly dying to know what that was about. Todd really doesn't feel like telling her right now—or ever.

During dinner, Daniel sits across from him, between Jesse and Hannah. Todd has known Hannah for almost as long as he's known Mela, but they've never gotten along well. He distinctly remembers her trying to boss him around when they were playing and promptly refusing to do anything she suggested, however fun it sounded. They get on better now, but he looks away when Daniel gives her all his attention. He knows so well what it's like to be in her shoes, and if things were different, maybe he still would be.

Todd concentrates on Mela, whenever she can tear her gaze away from Jesse, and Michaela, who has just come back from a semester abroad.

"Denmark is great," she tells him. "I wish I could've been there longer, but the exchange program at my school won't allow it."

"That's a shame." He glances at Daniel and Hannah and sees how their food seems to be forgotten. He can't help but overhear their conversation. Hannah sighs in frustration and shrugs.

"Sorry, can you repeat that? I can't tell what you're saying when you're facing away from me," Daniel says.

"It wasn't important, so never mind." She waves her hand and smiles before she empties her glass.

Daniel frowns and looks away. Todd opens his mouth to tell her to stop being an asshole, but Daniel squares his shoulders and smiles again, albeit stiffly.

"We can use my phone?" he suggests and holds it out to Hannah, who lights up and nods.

"That's a great idea!"

It takes him a moment before he realizes that he's zoned out and Michaela is looking expectantly at him. "Uh, how's the weather there?"

Oh, god, of all the things he could have asked, he goes for the *weather*? Michaela takes it in stride, but her gaze flicks to Daniel before turning back to Todd.

"Kind of cold and rainy during fall, winter and spring, but the summer was fine. It's very green, and, even though it was super expensive to live there, it's easy and cheap to go to other countries. Europe is great like that."

"That must've been really cool," Todd says, ignoring his own jealousy at only having been to Mexico.

"It really was!"

She excuses herself for the bathroom. Todd's gaze catches on Daniel again. He's typing on his phone, and Hannah is nowhere to be seen.

He should say something. He isn't sure if his sudden urge to talk is because of the wine or the chafing lump in his stomach that hasn't gone away. Blinking, Todd comes back to reality and finds Daniel looking back at him.

"Did you say something?" Daniel asks.

Todd swallows. "No."

"Did you just sit there and look at me for five minutes?"

"Uh. Yeah." It's out before Todd can filter himself, and his face heats as he hastily adds, "There's no way that was five minutes!"

Daniel presses his lips together and looks away without saying anything. Todd doesn't think he looks annoyed, though—quite the opposite. His eyes are crinkling at the corners.

Todd wants to say something—anything—especially now, when he's reminded of how they met.

At times like these, when he gets emotional and nostalgic, he needs to remind himself that it was just one night, that things went south after that, and then *even more* south. Todd doesn't know exactly why he's uneasy with Daniel and Hannah picking up conversation when she returns to the table. Maybe his nostalgia is to blame for that too.

He flees to the balcony, sucks in a big gulp of New York air, and revels in the silence. The sound of traffic several stories below him is just a distant hum.

It takes twenty minutes for Mela to find him.

"Heya." Her voice is soft, and, when Todd looks over his shoulder, he finds her smiling. It's her pity-smile.

"Hi."

"What are you doing out here?" She closes the door behind her and sits on the chair next to his.

"Getting some air and rest for my head. All the talking is exhausting my brain."

"That's okay." She hesitates. "Does this have anything to do with Daniel and Hannah?"

Taking a breath, Todd looks at the skyscrapers, at people walking in a hurry and cars waiting at traffic lights. Maybe because he's had a bit to drink, maybe because he really is tired of this, he's heavy and his body feels worn all of a sudden.

"No. I don't have the right to have any opinions about that."

"How about feelings, though?"

Todd worries his bottom lip between his teeth and considers just shrugging it off. But this is *Mela*. Since when won't he talk to her about these things?

"I'm kinda torn. On one hand, I'm semi-jealous, because I know *I* had a great time with him at a party. On the other hand, I still feel like an idiot."

"Why?"

"Because I was so ready to see him again, and then I find out that he's trying to take the gallery."

"Todd," Mela sighs.

"I know, not *technically*, but it still feels that way."

"Have you even considered talking to him about it?"

Todd squares his shoulders. "I did mention it when we met at the bar."

"The same day he found out that you had been lying about being sick?"

Todd winces. That wasn't his finest moment. "Yeah."

"He was probably hurt. Rejection hurts."

"He probably doesn't get rejected that much, so I think he'll live."

"Seriously," Mela says, her voice stern now. "Daniel is one of the nicest people I've met, and I really think you should give him a chance. But if you don't want to, then maybe you should ask yourself why you react like this when he flirts with other people."

"I guess I wanna eat the cake and have it too."

"That's a possibility. Or maybe you're regretting rejecting him so quickly."

Todd shrugs. He can't be annoyed with her when he's been thinking the same thing himself.

"It's too late now anyway."

"You don't know that until you've tried."

"Why are you being reasonable?" he mutters and gets a grin in return.

"It's my job. That's why you keep me around. Then she leans across the armrests of their chairs and hugs him tight. "I just really want you to allow yourself to be happy."

Todd agrees with that wholeheartedly. It's a lot harder to do it in reality than just thinking about it, though.

"Get back to your party. I'll be there in a sec."

"If you don't, I'll come back for you."

"Don't threaten me." Todd snorts.

He stands at the railing, looking at the traffic below, for another ten minutes until the door opens again. Assuming that it's Mela who's coming to drag his sorry ass inside, Todd turns around.

It's not Mela. It's Daniel.

"Mind if I join you?" he asks, hesitating in the doorway.

"No, go ahead." It's not as if Todd can refuse him. "Needing some air?" he asks, because he's going to say something stupid if it gets awkward and quiet between them.

"Things got a little loud."

Todd hums and he's just about to agree when he remembers. Meeting Daniel's gaze, he finds a peculiar glint in his eyes.

"Funny," he says instead.

Daniel smirks, and Todd's heart flips over. *Stop it.* "I just needed some air."

"Same."

Todd considers doing what Mela told him to—talking to Daniel about everything—but Hannah almost trips through the open balcony door.

"I guess that's my cue," he tells Daniel, who opens his mouth as if to say something, but then closes it again when Hannah grabs his arm.

"See you inside," Todd adds and leaves them alone.

Jesse drags him into a conversation immediately, and the next thing Todd knows it's past midnight and half the crowd, including Daniel, has left for a club.

"Since you're staying over, I'm not," Jesse tells him, and Todd's stomach sinks despite Jesse's smile. His button-up is wrinkled now, and there's a wine stain on his sleeve.

"I can try to find a cab."

"*No.* Mela wants to have you over. She's missed you. I'll see her again on Monday."

"Are you sure? I don't want to intrude."

"Todd," Jesse says, suddenly serious. Todd's discovered during the past couple of hours that Jesse is one of those people who turn into a professional life coach when he gets drunk. "You're her best friend. You've known her for a really long time. She would never stop spending time with you because of me. I don't want her to, but even if I did, you and I both know that she would never allow it. I like you. I'm sure you're a nice guy. Stop beating yourself up about what happened with Daniel. It already happened. You can't change that now. He doesn't hate you, and neither do I."

Todd's had some to drink as well, and, while he's normally not a fan of being Dr. Phil-ed, that's exactly the reassurance he needs now.

"I was a grade-A dick to him."

Jesse actually smiles at that. "Yeah, but to be fair, I don't think I know a single person who has never been a dick to anyone in their life. Sometimes we make mistakes and do things we regret. That's okay, as long as we own up to them."

Todd squints him. *Who is he? Jesus?* "I should probably apologize to Daniel."

"I'm sure that he'd appreciate that."

"Thanks for being nice even though I was a dick to your friend."

"Right now, I don't think my friend benefits from me being angry with you. I think you guys need to talk."

"That's what everyone says." Todd heaves a sigh.

"There might be something to it."

"Yeah." Todd agrees, because he *knows*. He would give the same advice if this was anyone else. "I'll think about it."

"Good." Jesse squeezes his shoulder. "All right, I'm out. Have a nice evening with the birthday girl."

"You know it."

Mela is clearing the table when Todd finds her.

"Didn't you wanna go out with them?"

"Nah, I had more fun here. Plus, you're still a baby."

She's missing out on fun because he's not twenty-one. "I could've stayed here or gone home."

"I haven't seen you in forever. Properly, I mean. That's the best birthday gift for me right now."

Todd hugs her and doesn't let go for a long while.

✳   ✳   ✳

IT'S ONLY A COUPLE OF days later when Todd sees Daniel next. He's grabbing coffee at his favorite café and he's got his laptop with him. There are a bunch of articles and assignments he needs to deal with before class tomorrow and trying to focus at home makes him nauseous lately. This place only serves organic and fair trade, and, unless it's super busy, they don't mind people studying at their tables for hours. The lighting isn't the best—yellowish and dull from the industrial lamps— but the place is warm and smells of freshly brewed coffee and croissants.

Todd has already zeroed in on a corner table with a power outlet— someone must've just left because those are sacred here—and fewer people nearby talking when he notices a familiar head of hair at another table across the room.

Stopping dead in his tracks, Todd stares. Because, one: this is Brooklyn, what the hell is Daniel doing *here*? And two: this café is the least Daniel-like café Todd has ever seen. However, the person sitting opposite of Daniel fits in better. She's dressed as if she shops for clothes in the same places as Todd and a lot of people in his school.

If it wasn't for the fact that she's taking notes, Todd would have assumed that they were on a date. They're signing, and Daniel looks relaxed in a way Todd's never seen him, not even the night they met, when things were going well. He's laughing, signing in a flurry, and the girl signs as well, only pausing to take notes.

Wow.

Though Daniel told him the first night they met that he does a lot of compensating, Todd hasn't fully grasped what that means until now. This, this is what being around Daniel would be like if Todd knew how to sign, if Daniel didn't have to ask him to repeat things or focus so hard on his lips to puzzle out the conversation.

Realizing that, caught up in his own realization, he's staring openly, Todd's about to head over to the corner table again, when Daniel looks up. Should he go over there and say something? He looks at the girl again—she's still taking notes—and decides that it's not appropriate to disturb them. He nods his greeting. Daniel nods back and then he smiles, making Todd bite his lip as he finally escapes to the table.

It's surprisingly easy to concentrate on schoolwork, despite Daniel sitting across the room. He makes it through three articles and jots down a few notes for the questions in the assignments. While it's still a huge effort for him to learn all the theoretical stuff, it's a lot easier when he doesn't have a deadline hanging over his head. Stress makes his brain quit. Knowing his professor, they'll discuss the articles before the lecture starts, and Todd would very much like to have something intelligent to say. Being prepared for class is pretty big, even for this new Todd, who's way ahead on schoolwork.

"Can I sit down?"

Startled, Todd blinks away the blurriness that come with switching focus point too quickly. There's Daniel holding a takeaway mug.

"Yeah, sure." Todd bunches his notes into a haphazard pile next to his laptop.

Clearly hesitating, Daniel puts a hand on the back of the chair. "Are you busy?"

"Nah, I was just preparing for my class tomorrow, and I'm basically done." He can skim the articles again in bed.

"Ambitious," Daniel comments as he sits down.

"It keeps me from thinking too much."

Daniel looks at him for a long moment before nodding.

"What were you doing here anyway? It's a bit far from Manhattan just for a coffee."

"No, thank you." Daniel holds up his travel mug. "I already got one for my ride."

"Oh, no." Todd hurries to clarify. "I can see that you have coffee. I was saying that it's a bit far from Manhattan for grabbing a coffee."

"It's what?" Daniel leans forward, and Todd mentally curses the bad lighting in this place. "Sometimes when I'm in a coffee shop, with so many distractions, and I only manage to get the last word like now, I assume they're asking if I want coffee."

"It's okay. I'm the one talking too fast and not thinking about how dim it is in here." Todd clears his throat. "Before, I said: It's a bit far from Manhattan for grabbing a coffee."

Leaning back in the chair, Daniel slides a fingertip around the dents in the plastic lid of his mug. "It was an interview for a school project. She was interested in my swimming. I think I gained a new friend, though." He clears his throat. "Now I'm waiting for my car."

Of course he is.

"That's cool. You're a good swimmer," Todd says and then hastily adds, "based on the very scientific research I made from going to one of your meets."

Daniel grins. "You're right. I am good."

"Cocky," Todd mutters, but Daniel's grin only grows wider.

"Did you have a good time on Saturday?" Daniel asks then and removes the plastic lid to take a sip from his coffee. Todd wants to ask if he's completely missed that there's a hole in the lid for that exact purpose, or if there's another reason to why he removes it. He doesn't.

"I did," he says. "Did you?"

"Sure. We continued to a club."

We.

Todd closes the lid to his laptop and immediately regrets it. There's so little between them now. "So I heard. Was it fun?"

"It was a good night out. I like dancing."

Todd doesn't think that's another one of Daniel's jokes about his own hearing loss, but he isn't comfortable enough to ask. He's saved from replying at all when Daniel's phone lights, vibrating on the table.

"My ride's here. Thanks for the chat." He stands, puts the lid back on his mug, and gives Todd a smile. "See you around."

Watching him go, Todd resists the urge to pinch his arm. Did he just have a somewhat normal conversation with Daniel?

He repeats Dad's words to himself as he packs up his things. Someone would be interested in the gallery's space no matter what. The finances aren't adding up, and they can't keep the place. They're two different things. Daniel just happened to be the guy who wants the space.

While it sure does suck that he might lose a safe place and Mrs. Floral might lose her dream soon if things don't get better, it's not Daniel's fault.

Sighing to himself, earning a concerned look from the girl reading at the next table, Todd puts his laptop in his bag and heads home. Before bed, after he's tried—and failed—to concentrate on his articles, he writes a couple of messages to people in school whom he knows are very talented artists. He's twitchy with anxiety afterward, but he'll take it over the bad conscience from not doing enough.

When he crawls under the covers, his body is as heavy as though he's run five miles and he's unable to stop the *what ifs*. They stick longer tonight, possibly because he talked to Daniel today and it wasn't awful.

In an attempt to silence his brain, Todd grabs his phone from the nightstand and hovers over Evan's name—and chickens out.

Tomorrow, he'll call tomorrow, after dinner.

Chapter Four

WHEN TODD SEES DANIEL AGAIN, he's trying to survive midterms, and the people around him seem to be competing about who's stressing the most. Mela has been isolated. Todd might've done the same thing if it wasn't for the gallery. Some days he hates going to work, and others he's grateful for an excuse to busy himself with something non-academic and see *people* for a change. Thursdays are his opportunity to breathe and get out of his own head for a bit. For a change, the kids are quiet, focusing on their projects and raising their hands whenever they need his help. Maybe they can sense that something is bothering him. Jamal is still there after everyone else has been picked up by their parents, one by one.

"Wanna help me clean up?" Todd asks, when Jamal has finished putting everyone's pieces on the wall. It's an uneven row and a little low for a grownup to look at them properly, but he's been so careful with every single one.

"Mom's working," Jamal says, not quite meeting Todd's eyes the way he usually does when she's late.

"I know. She'll come pick you up as soon as she can. Sometimes hospitals get busy, you know?"

She works in the E.R. where sometimes she can't get away on time.

They clean the room and put away the supplies in the storage room. They're running low on a lot of things lately, but it's not the right time to ask Mrs. Floral to buy more.

"I really like art," Jamal says, when they're sitting at the front desk having hot chocolate. It's been almost an hour, but Jamal's mom called a few minutes ago, apologizing profusely and promising that she's on her way.

"Me too. What is it that you like?"

Jamal sighs, fiddling with the hem of his shirt. "I don't know. The colors. And that you can make anything you want."

For a second, Todd thinks he's looking at himself at the same age. "That's true. What's your favorite thing to make?"

"Haven't found it yet. Every time you teach us something new, I think I've found it, and then there's a new thing again."

He knocks his elbow against Jamal's shoulder. "You don't have to pick a favorite if you can't."

"Can I like all art?" Jamal glances up at him, chewing his lip.

"For sure, and sometimes you like some art depending on how you're feeling that day. That's the cool thing about it, you know."

"I made something in school too; you wanna see?"

They look through Jamal's notebook until his mom arrives, out of breath and with guilty conscience written all over her face.

"It's fine," he says, when she starts apologizing again as they're leaving. "I'm happy to stay here a little while longer. We had a good time, right, Jamal?"

"We had hot chocolate," Jamal agrees and then puffs out his chest. "And Todd likes my art."

"Exactly." He ruffles Jamal's hair and holds the door open for them. When Jamal's mom meets his gaze, he adds: "Seriously, don't worry about it. I don't mind."

During his next shift, Mrs. Floral catches him before she leaves for the day.

"I saw the security alarm wasn't set until well after Kids & Canvas ended. Did something happen?"

Shaking his head, Todd concentrates on the box he's packing. "I stayed to study. I can't stand being at home and stare at the books there. No need to add extra hours."

When she remains quiet, he looks up and finds her frowning.

"Seriously, it's midterms. It was just a nice, quiet place to get some studying done."

"Okay, if you say so."

On the upside, midterms have people grasping for opportunities, as they face a precarious future after graduation. Some of his long shots agree to think about his offer, though he's pretty sure that they could do better. Others reach out to him on their own, having heard about the opportunity to exhibit from friends. Apparently being talented doesn't save you from worrying about the future.

It shouldn't be that much of a surprise to see Daniel walk through the doors, looking just as exhausted as every other college kid.

"Hi." Todd closes the *History of Modern Art* he's been reading behind the front desk.

"Hey." Daniel smiles, looking a lot less sleep deprived in an instant. "I'm here to see Mrs. Floral."

"I'll go get her." Todd also wants to ask her why she didn't warn him about this. When he glances over his shoulder on his way to the back office, Daniel is picking up his book, flipping through the pages.

Mrs. Floral is unpacking a new piece when he finds her. She's got tape stuck to her hands and she looks a little sweaty. Glancing into the box, Todd finds a heavy-looking sculpture.

"Your guest is here."

"Mr. Berger?" She straightens, and Todd winces at the sound of her back popping.

Todd pauses, realizing that he doesn't actually know Daniel's last name.

"Um. The guy who was here with his parents and Stanley."

"That's Mr. Berger." Mrs. Floral smiles at him. "I promised him a tour. All the back rooms and the smaller spaces."

"That's nice." Todd shifts, trying to shake the uneasy feeling under his skin. *It's not Daniel's fault.*

"Would you be able to do it?" She holds up her tape-covered hands. "I'm rather occupied."

"Jesus." Todd wonders if he should offer to help her. "Sure."

"Thank you, honey."

Daniel has put the book back when Todd comes back to the front desk.

"You wanted a tour?" Todd asks to make sure, gesturing around the space. It would be just like him to start showing Daniel around only to find out halfway through it that he just wanted to leave a message.

"Mrs. Floral said it would be okay."

Nodding, Todd wipes his palms on his pants. "Yeah, of course. She's busy unpacking a bunch of stuff. Would you mind getting the tour from me?"

Daniel frowns, a slight crease forming between his eyebrows. "Are *you* okay with that?"

"It's no problem. Unless you very much want her to do it instead?"

The crease disappears. "I'd be happy to get the tour from you."

Readjusting the back of his beanie, Todd nods and gestures toward the main room on the first floor. "We could start with the open areas and then take a look at the back rooms?"

"Come again?"

When Todd repeats the question, Daniel nods and follows him when Todd steps around the front desk and heads toward the next room. There are only a few patrons left at this hour, but a few weeks ago, there were even fewer.

"So, I'd say that this is the largest open space we have. We've divided it with those fake walls to fit more works." He stops when Daniel clears his throat and puts a hand on his shoulder. Mouth dry as if he's just swallowed a pound of sand, Todd turns around.

"I'm sure you said a whole lot of interesting things just now." Daniel gives him a small smile that doesn't reach his eyes. "But I'm still hard of hearing, so I need to see your mouth."

Smacking a hand over his face, Todd wishes that he could go back in time to have Mrs. Floral do this.

"I'm really sorry. Talk about being a dick."

"It happens." Daniel shrugs.

That makes it even worse. "Well, it shouldn't. I know better."

Daniel shrugs again, and Todd gets the impression that he doesn't feel like talking more about this.

"All right, so this is the biggest open space we have," Todd repeats, staying turned toward Daniel and doing his best not to flush. "These—" Todd gestures at the fake walls "—you can remove these easily. We move them around all the time."

"Good to know."

"Do you wanna look around?" he offers.

"Sure."

He watches Daniel move around the room. To his surprise, Daniel stops to look at some of the pieces and not just the layout of the room.

Todd is showing him the second floor when he stops mid-step and turns around to point out the fire exit. Daniel is just behind him, and unable to stop, he smacks right into Todd. Stumbling backward, Todd has enough time to think that he's going to bash his head open against the brick wall and that's a really shitty way to die, when Daniel grabs his arm and steadies him.

His face burns and Todd pretends to smooth his shirt. "Thanks. Sorry."

"Are you okay?"

"Sure." Todd straightens, feeling a bit disoriented. "You're very solid."

Daniel laughs. *Laughs.* Todd doesn't think he's heard Daniel's laugh since the night they met.

"I'm going to take that as a compliment."

"You should," Todd blurts before he regains control over his mouth. "I was gonna say that the fire exit is right there."

Daniel is still smiling, eyes twinkling. "Good to know."

Todd doesn't realize that Daniel's hand is still on his arm until he's about to turn around again. His need to apologize to Daniel for how he behaved in the past grows stronger.

He shows Daniel the areas upstairs and is again left waiting when Daniel gets caught up in one of Fernández's pieces. This one is of a lighthouse in the middle of a foggy lake. It's in watercolor, and Todd spent a long time looking at it when they put it up.

"That's my current favorite," Todd says, when Daniel turns toward him. "It's a bit sad."

"I think it's kinda hopeful too, with the light through the fog."

"Could you repeat that?" Daniel asks, and Todd does. Daniel looks at it again and hums. "You could be right."

Discussing art with Daniel isn't something he thought he would do in a million years. Actually, discussing *anything* with Daniel was off the table for a while. "So, we only have the back rooms left."

"Do I need to see those?"

"I just assumed—" Todd shrugs. "We have a lot of them?"

"Okay, show me."

It's not until he gestures around the first back room that Daniel blurts out a laugh. He's somewhere between embarrassed and amused when Todd turns around, with color on his cheeks but still a smile in his eyes. "Oh, I thought you said bathrooms. I've been walking around thinking that you're going to show me all the bathrooms the entire tour. I didn't realize until now. You said back rooms, right?"

"Oh, my god," Todd says and then can't help but laugh too. "No, we have two bathrooms, and a million back rooms."

"It does make more sense to show me the back rooms," Daniel says with a grin.

Todd takes him around each of them, opening every closed and locked door. There are *many* for a pretty tiny space.

Downstairs, he pauses in the back room containing the boxes with new pieces. Mrs. Floral is putting them on display now, meaning that Daniel and Todd are alone in a confined space with a lot of cardboard. The new art supplies he got on sale are on the shelves. Since he used his paycheck to buy them, it's almost if Mrs. Floral bought them herself, and that's what he'll tell her if she asks.

"We use this for storage," Todd says. "And unpacking pieces. You could probably use it for something else, if you'd like."

"You're always in need of storage."

Taking a breath, Todd tries to muster up some courage.

"This is the last room." Biting his lip, he looks at Daniel who meets his gaze with patience that tells Todd he knows there's something he wants to say. It makes it easier and harder at the same time.

"So," Todd says slowly. "I've been wanting to apologize for being a dick. With the lying, and the general... dickishness."

"I appreciate that," Daniel says after a beat of silence. "I've gathered that this place means a lot to you and Mrs. Floral. It's nothing personal."

Nodding, Todd looks away. It still stings. "I know that. It's just difficult. It's my job and I've spent so much time here, plus this place was supposed to pay for her retirement, you know? It's scary knowing that we might lose that."

Daniel's gaze is so intense that Todd has to meet it. "I'm not trying to take the place away from you. I'm interested in the space, if it becomes available."

"I know. I'm sorry it took me so long time to come to terms with that." Todd tries smiling, but he isn't sure how convincing it is. His cheeks are stiff.

"Sometimes we need a while." Daniel hesitates. "When are you off?"

Checking his phone, Todd realizes that it's been over an hour. "Fifteen minutes ago?"

"Would you like to grab a coffee?"

"Sure, yeah, I'd like that." Clearing his throat, Todd adds, "I really want us to be friends. I don't want it to be this awkward when we're with Mela and Jesse."

Daniel looks down, and Todd takes three breaths, convinced that he's said something stupid, when Daniel looks up again. His smile is a bit tired, but, then again, it's midterms for him as well.

"Friends, yes, I'd like that too."

The relief must have been clear on Todd's face, because Daniel's tired look disappears. "Come on. Get your stuff."

Mrs. Floral's smile is pleased when Todd tells her goodbye.

They go to the coffee place where they bumped into each other last time, and they sit at the corner table again after getting their coffee orders.

"Do you have any midterms left?"

"What?"

"Midterms, do you have any left?"

"Only one, thankfully." Daniel grimaces and hugs the mug in his hands. "It's been a rough few weeks. It's not like we've had less practice, either."

"Do you have a lot of that? Practice, I mean."

With a shrug, Daniel sips his coffee before answering. "Five to six days a week, depending. It's usually two hours in the morning and two hours after classes."

Todd's eyes grow big. Jesus. "That's *rough*. And you have a lot of things in school, right?"

"I suffer from fatigue a lot, related to school," Daniel explains. "I have interpreters for most of my classes these days, but it's exhausting trying to keep up with socializing with classmates and concentrating on the professor."

"There's no way to make it easier?"

"To make it easier? Sure, the best way for me is an interpreter. I always prefer visual presentations, because I can look at the slides before and after class. A study partner makes it easier too. Whatever I can't catch, they might." Daniel bites his lip, and Todd gets the impression that he doesn't like talking about this too much. "What about you? Are you done with your midterms?"

"I have three left." Todd resists the urge to face-plant on the table. "Two of them are the same day, and the last one is the day after that."

"Ouch. How are you holding up?"

"Even though I've been surprisingly caught up with schoolwork this semester, I still kinda want to die a bit."

"You're usually not caught up?" Daniel says it as if it's a foreign concept to him.

Laughing, Todd shakes his head. "No, I'm the guy who has to be up all night before an eight a.m. deadline and hate myself and then I do it all over again next time."

"Except for now?"

"Yeah, well, I've been feeling pretty bad about lying and I have this bad habit of overthinking everything, so concentrating on school has been the only thing that's kept me from never leaving bed."

Daniel gets that crease between his eyebrows again. "Why didn't you say anything sooner?"

Yeah, why?

"As I said," Todd begins, and bites his lip. "It took me a while to come to terms with the fact that it wasn't really your fault that the gallery hasn't been doing that well."

"Better late than never."

"You must've been so pissed," Todd says, in an attempt to lighten the mood. To his surprise, the crease between Daniel's eyebrows grows deeper.

"Why would I be pleased?"

After a second of frozen confusion, Todd's brain manages to connect the dots. "No, *pissed*, angry."

The expression clears on Daniel's face and he looks away. "Sorry, pleased and pissed look very similar to me."

"No need to apologize," Todd assures him.

"Anyway." Daniel clears his throat. "To be completely honest with you, I think I was mostly hurt."

Wincing, Todd digs his fingers into his thighs under the table, where Daniel won't see. "Sorry."

"It's all good now. I felt, I don't know, like a fool for a while there, but as I said, we've moved on. I appreciate the apology, and it's definitely going to be easier hanging out all of us."

"Mela is going to be really relieved." Todd doesn't say that *he* will be too, now when he won't have a nervous breakdown every time there's a possibility of bumping into Daniel.

"We have a meet next weekend and we get the day after off from practice. We're going out. Do you want to come with? Mela is coming."

"I'm still not twenty-one." But he wants to. His coffee cup is standing forgotten on the table in front of him. It's probably cold by now, but he still takes a sip and manages not to make a face over the lukewarm coffee taste.

"Don't worry about that. It worked last time, didn't it?"

Saying no is tempting. He strongly suspects that *we* refers to more people than just Jesse, Daniel, and Mela. However, Daniel is offering him an olive branch, and who's he to refuse that?

"Okay, sure."

He texts Mela as he walks home, and she calls him immediately.

"You had coffee with Daniel?" she says as a way of greeting.

Todd sighs. "Calm down. I showed him the gallery, and then we had coffee afterward."

The silence on the other end tells him that she's waiting for something. Sometimes she has this creepy sixth sense.

"And I apologized."

"You did?"

Why she says it as if it's a huge thing, he doesn't know. *Well, okay,* he does. Apologizing is something he's rarely done to anyone except her or Evan, even when they were kids.

"I did. And then we agreed on being friends, and he asked me to come out with you guys next weekend."

Mela lets out an awed sound. "Wow, I don't know how all of this happened, but I approve."

"So, can I crash at your place?"

She's quiet too long, and Todd's good mood plummets.

"Sorry," he winces. "Of course you're staying with Jesse."

"I can change that."

"God, no, never." He's not going to be that friend—ever. He sidesteps a person staring at their phone while stumbling over his own feet.

"I'm sure my parents won't mind if you crash in my room by yourself."

Todd's sure about that, too, but it would make the entire evening awkward. He was hesitant to agreeing to begin with, and now he has an excellent excuse that won't make Daniel upset.

"No, don't worry about it. I'll join in when you guys are in Brooklyn."

"But I want you to come along," Mela protests.

"I have no way of getting home and I'm never again deciding to stay up late enough to catch the first morning train." It's not that the subway is unsafe at night. Actually, Todd knows that crime levels decrease after eight or nine in the evening—he knows, because he's googled this, and Dad's told him a billion times. However, since that time he almost got mugged, he refuses to take the subway after midnight.

"Just because last time—"

"We don't talk about last time!" Todd interrupts.

Mela laughs, but then she quickly grows serious again. "I don't want you to feel excluded."

"I'm not. It was a last-minute thing. I should've understood that you have plans with Jesse. Obviously. Don't feel bad about it. There's always the next time."

"Okay," she says, voice soft. "I'm really proud of you for apologizing."

"It took me two months to get there."

"But you *did* get there," she points out.

"Yeah," he admits, and his steps grow a little lighter.

"See you this week?"

"Sure, I work Monday and Thursday."

"I'll get back to you."

Todd tries some of the signs in the apps that have been untouched since he downloaded them and makes Sandwich jump over the DVD obstacle twice before he goes to bed.

✳   ✳   ✳

THREE DAYS LATER, HE RECEIVES a text from Daniel.

> **Heard from Mela that you're not coming with us on Saturday. If you need a place to crash you're free to stay here.**

Why is he suddenly out of breath, as if he's run five miles? *Sleeping at Daniel's? Did he offer, or did Mela ask him to?*

"Daniel offered to let me crash at his place," he says when Mela finally picks up on the fourth ring.

"What?"

"Did you ask him to offer?" Todd prompts.

"Offer what?" She sounds genuinely confused.

"Offer me a place to stay, because you're staying with Jesse."

"I didn't. I've told Jesse that you can't come, so I'm guessing he must've talked to Daniel." She adds, before Todd can ask, "I didn't ask him to do it, either."

"What do I say?"

"You say *yes*, of course, dumbass!"

Todd stares at Daniel's text. He reads it four times just to make sure that he isn't making wrong assumptions and making a fool of himself. But the text is pretty straightforward.

< **Would that be okay? Don't feel pressured**

> **Sure. My parents are away and my sister doesn't care.**

< **That's really nice of you. Thanks!**

> **No problem. It's more fun when everyone can come along.**

Does this mean that he needs to bring nice underwear for sleeping? This is a new kind of nerve-racking. It's not as though he hasn't slept over at a guy's place. It's just that he still isn't quite sure where he stands with Daniel. He's practiced some basic signs a lot over the past couple of days, but they just don't seem to stick.

< **Do I need to bring anything?**

> **Just yourself.**

Todd rolls his eyes. He can't picture Daniel writing that with a straight face. Daniel obviously wants them to be friends, and that's way more than Todd dared to hope for.

✳ ✳ ✳

COME SATURDAY, TODD IS IN the crowd by the pool in the seat next to Mela's. Despite the humidity and the smell of chlorine, it's decidedly less strange this time around.

When it's Daniel's turn to swim, it dawns on him just how hot Daniel actually is. He forgot about that somehow while he was upset. Daniel looks nothing like the kind of guy Todd would usually find attractive, but he's not *blind*. Daniel obviously lucked out with his gene pool.

This time, Todd cheers with the rest of the crowd when Daniel wins.

Afterward, his skin is crawling in a mix of anticipation and anxiety as he waits with Mela outside.

"Jesse and I will come by as soon as we're ready, so we can have dinner before we head out."

"Okay." He's going to be alone with Daniel for several hours, probably. *Jesus.*

When Daniel exits the building, Todd forgets how to breathe. He has his bag slung over his shoulder and a dark-green, nice-looking jacket. His hair is still damp and darker than usual, and his eyes have that shine like the last time Todd saw Daniel after a meet.

"Hey," he says, stopping in front of them. "Jesse will be out any second."

"Hi," Todd says.

"Did you bring your stuff?" Daniel asks, and Todd pats his own bag.

"Yeah, but I'm sure I forgot something."

"Let's hope it's nothing vital," Daniel smirks.

"I'm not too sure." To be honest, right now someone could have told him that he needs meds every five minutes to stay alive, and he would've believed them, because right now his brain is too busy registering the smell of Daniel's cologne.

"It's really sweet of you to offer to have Todd sleep at your place," Mela says, after tapping Daniel's arm to get his attention, as if she knows Todd's mind is useless right now.

"It's no problem. We have guestrooms, so it's not much of a hassle."

Todd is simultaneously relieved and disappointed about sleeping in a guestroom. He tries not to think too much about either of his reactions.

"Still, thanks," he says, once Daniel has turned back toward him, remembering his manners.

Daniel smiles at him. "We'll have a good night. It's always more fun when everyone can be there."

"I've been looking forward to this a lot," he confesses. "Last time was a lot of fun."

"It really was," Daniel agrees.

When Jesse emerges, Daniel bumps Todd's shoulder. "Ready to go?"

Nodding, Todd hoists his own bag farther up on his shoulder. "Is it far?"

"We'll take a car. My legs are dead."

Todd grins. "Okay."

"See you in a few hours!" Mela calls after them, and Todd waves at her over his shoulder as they turn around.

Once they're in the sleek, black car that's taking them to Daniel's place, Todd taps his arm to get his attention. "So, what are the plans exactly?"

"What the plans are?" Daniel asks, and Todd nods. "Getting ready and having dinner. And then we're going to a pre-party at a friend's house."

"Sounds good." Todd clears his throat. "Are you sure I'll get in?"

"Almost positive," Daniel shrugs, "but if you don't, we'll leave. It's no big deal."

"You can still stay."

"And leave you waiting outside? That's not going to happen when you're sleeping at my place."

As it turns out, Daniel is basically next-door neighbors with Central Park. He lives in one of those white, fancy townhouses just a couple of streets from where they first met.

"This is nice," Todd says, except that *nice* isn't the right word. Then he remembers Daniel mentioning his sister. "I don't know how to ask this without being impolite or rude, but is your sister hard of hearing too?"

"That's not rude," Daniel says, as he digs out a set of keys from his jacket pocket. "And no, she isn't. It's just me."

"Oh, okay."

Daniel gives him a long look before he unlocks the door. The entrance hall looks like something from an interior design magazine. It's all sleek and white, gray, and brass with fresh flowers in vases and hardwood floors.

When Daniel takes his shoes off, Todd does the same. "Wow."

"Sorry?" Daniel turns toward him.

"I just said wow." Todd flexes his fingers, to resist shoving his hands into his pockets.

"It's all my mom."

"Is she an interior designer?"

Daniel looks at him as though he isn't sure if Todd is serious or not. Todd has no idea why, because this place looks like a magazine spread.

"No, but she thinks it's important to have a beautiful home," Daniel says finally, as if he's decided that Todd's question was sincere.

"You fit in," Todd blurts, and if there was a hole in the floor he could fall into, that'd be great.

"Thanks." Daniel isn't entirely able to conceal his smirk, but at least he's trying.

"I guess I've migrated from rude things to embarrassing things." Todd doesn't know if Daniel will get the reference to their first conversation. Daniel laughs, and Todd is momentarily light, as if gravity just checked out.

"Let me show you where you're going to sleep."

Daniel takes off up the stairs, and Todd suspects that his whole *my legs are dead* was a lie to save Todd's dignity, because he's forced to climb four flights of stairs and, while he's panting as he reaches the final floor, Daniel isn't even a little out of breath.

"That's my room." Daniel motions toward a closed door to the right. Most of the floor is a lounge area, with couches and a TV. It's the perfect place to hang out with friends.

"The guestroom on this floor is over there. We have another guestroom on the second floor that most people use, so I usually have this floor to myself. I figured you'd rather be up here, though."

Being alone on a different floor in a house where he's never been? *No thanks.* "That's... yeah, I think that would cause more anxiety than necessary. Thanks."

Daniel pushes the door open, and Todd takes in the queen bed and the white sheets. There's a gray armchair in the far corner with a sheepskin thrown over the back and an ottoman at the foot of the bed, which is mostly covered by a soft-looking, beige blanket. It's very light and sleek. It must be horrible to dust this place, with all the white. It's also a bit sterile. He doesn't say that out loud, though.

"Where, exactly, are we going tonight?" Todd asks before he puts his bag on the ottoman. It seems wrong to put something so worn and covered in paint stains on furniture so *pristine.*

"First to Mick's place and then to a club."

Todd's pretty sure that he's a lot less likely to get into a club than a bar but he's not going to be whiny. He also has no clue who this Mick is.

"That sounds fun." It doesn't, but on the other hand, Todd had a great night the last time he went somewhere unexpected with Daniel.

"Do you like dancing?" Daniel doesn't look entirely convinced.

"I don't *dislike* it," Todd amends. "What about you?"

"It's okay. It can be fun in big groups." Daniel shrugs.

During one of his google sprees, Todd's learned that there's a decently famous DJ who's deaf, so his surprise that Daniel kind of likes dancing is because he's *Daniel.* Todd can't imagine him pulling off any smooth moves whatsoever.

"Thanks for letting me stay." He clears his throat. "Stay over. Here. That's really nice."

"You've already thanked me."

"Well, yeah, but still."

Daniel clasps his shoulder, and it's so different from when Jesse does it. Todd's never felt as though Jesse's hand is burning through his clothes, but right now the skin on his shoulder is a little tender. "It's no problem. I invited you to go out with us and I'm glad you could make it."

They get ready while they wait for Mela and Jesse. It's strangely quiet. Todd's alone in the guestroom and Daniel is in *his*.

He lingers in the room after putting on his clothes and dealing with his hair—it looks good for once. Actually, *he* looks good too, in black jeans and a navy shirt. The color brings out the stark contrasts in his left eye, making the brown darker and the blue clearer. But this also means that he doesn't have any excuses left to not seek out Daniel.

Daniel's standing by his bed pulling a shirt over his head when Todd knocks on the open door, and there's an awkward moment when there's no reaction. His next urge is to bang his head against the wall. *Of course there isn't.* Todd wonders when he'll finally learn.

When he takes a couple of steps into the room, Daniel looks up.

"Is it okay if I come in?" Todd asks.

"Sure, I'm just getting ready."

Todd looks around the room. It's less sterile and smaller than he expected. There are photos on the matte, gray walls. Most of them show places and people. If he could spend an hour inspecting every single one of them, he'd learn so much about Daniel, he's sure of that. On the far wall, below the impressive, arched window a white desk is buried under a chaos of papers, pencils, notes, and textbooks. The mess is like Todd's desk without the drawings and doodles. Against the opposite wall is a wide dresser, and on top of it are piles of neatly folded clothes. Todd has to clasp his hands behind his back to keep himself from reaching out to touch them, just to see how soft the fabrics are. The bed is wide enough for two, covered in soft, blue linen and a folded knit blanket. Next to it is a cluttered bedside table on one side and a butterfly armchair in worn-looking leather on the other. Sinking down in it, he meets Daniel's gaze.

"This is nice," he comments, gesturing around.

"Thanks. It's all right, since I have the floor to myself."

Nodding, Todd looks at the book on the nightstand. It seems to be a textbook from one of Daniel's classes, unless Daniel reads books about strategies for national security for fun, which wouldn't be too surprising. "That makes sense."

"Do you want anything to drink?" Daniel asks him as he digs through a drawer.

Todd is about to say yes when he hears someone stomping up the stairs. He points toward the door when Daniel looks up at him expectantly.

The next moment a girl enters the room. She must be Daniel's sister, because she has the same hair color and eyes. However, where Daniel is mostly sharp angles, she's softer: rounder cheeks and an upturned nose—definitely younger.

She opens her mouth to say something, clearly annoyed, when she spots Todd.

"Hi," she says.

"Hi," he replies, getting to his feet and offering his hand. She eyes him silently before she shakes it.

"I'm Todd," he says.

"Ava."

"This is my sister," Daniel explains, completely unnecessarily. "And this is Todd."

"Uh-huh," Ava says in a tone that makes Todd suspect that she might know something about his behavior in the past.

"Nice to meet you," he tries.

Great. Todd is sure that Daniel's entire family hates him.

"Todd is staying over," Daniel explains quickly, as though he doesn't want Ava to reply.

Her expression slowly changes into one that makes Todd uncomfortable for a completely different reason.

"In here?"

Daniel rolls his eyes. "In the guestroom across the hall."

She turns to Todd, signing as she speaks. "That's what he always says."

"Did you want something?" Daniel asks, voice sharp suddenly.

"Yes. Your new Netflix password."

Judging by the look on Daniel's face, this isn't the first time she's asked for it.

"There's a reason I changed it."

"Well, there's either the new password or I'm going to stay here and talk to Todd."

"Oh, for god's sake," Daniel mutters and then turns toward Todd. "Sorry. I'll be right back."

"That's fine."

The moment they're out of the door, they start signing in a flurry. Todd watches, mesmerized, for the ten seconds it takes them to disappear.

He seizes the opportunity to look at the photos on the wall and immediately spots one of Ava and Daniel. They're a lot younger in the picture. Daniel might've just started high school and he has *braces*. Todd smiles and continues to the team photo and the one of Daniel and Jesse.

When he hears Daniel's steps on the stairs, he quickly moves away from the photos.

"Sorry about that" is the first thing Daniel says when he walks through the door.

"No need to apologize."

"There definitely is," Daniel objects. "Sometimes I don't know if our parents ever taught her manners or if they gave up when she was five."

"Well, she did shake my hand."

"While being super rude," Daniel sighs.

"In her defense, she probably acted that way because I was rude to you." *Rude* is not exactly the right word for his behavior, but Daniel seems to get the picture, because he waves in dismissal.

"We already sorted that out."

Todd knows that he needs to drop this, but his guilt has etched itself into his ribs. Daniel acts as if it's no big deal, and Todd doesn't ask how Ava found out about it.

"You look nice," Daniel says then. Maybe he's just trying to change the subject, but it's working.

"So do you."

"Did you want something to drink?" Daniel asks, as though he just now remembers what they talked about before Ava interrupted.

They end up sitting at the kitchen counter, and Todd has a glass of wine. It's cold and dry, and *grown up* in a way that he isn't used to. Watching Daniel holding a glass of his own, his stomach clenches so hard that he has to look away. The wine is so cold that a drop of condensation is running down the foot. He catches it with his fingertip. *What if things were different?* Maybe they wouldn't have so much space between them. Maybe he'd have Daniel's hand on his thigh like that first night.

"So, did you find more artists for your gallery?"

The question takes Todd by surprise, and suspicion swirls in his belly until he tears his gaze from his glass and sees the earnest look on Daniel's face.

"Not really," he confesses and mentally repeats to himself that the gallery's financial trouble is not Daniel's fault.

"No? How come?"

"Well, we used to have a big group of patrons, but they're all getting old and there aren't that many left and the ones that are don't buy a lot of art these days. I think we exhibit the wrong artists to attract a younger crowd too."

"You think what?"

"I think we have the wrong kind of artists right now. They don't attract a younger crowd."

Daniel nods, diverting his gaze as he takes a swig from his glass. When he looks back at Todd, he adds, "It's difficult to make the place work like that. I think having students exhibit could be a way, but no one really knows that we exist anymore, so it's not enough."

"Of course. Basically, you'd need someone who can bring a big crowd and with that, revenue, so that it would benefit the newcomers."

Todd has never thought about it like that, like a *strategy*. It does make a lot of sense.

"I guess, yeah." He hesitates. "I've never really... considered that."

"You could possibly promote it as some kind of responsibility thing," Daniel suggests. "Giving back to the community, so to speak. If you managed to get someone more famous, they could bring a new, younger crowd and by that help get the newcomers recognized. Plus, your gallery would be back on the map as something a little different, maybe?"

"Huh." Todd blinks. "Even better if they were alumni from my school."

"Oh, *yes*." Daniel's eyes light up, and Todd's belly flips over. He's excited now. "*That* would definitely give you a reason to reach out to media as well. I'm sure lots of local sites would find that interesting."

A familiar spark ignites behind Todd's ribs, and he can't help but smile. A moment later, he can't stop the small voice at the back of his mind asking why Daniel is so eager to help.

"Why are you helping me? You don't want us to make it." He winces at how harsh the last part sounds. "I mean, for your club. That you want the space for." Heaving a sigh, he resists the urge to face-plant into the marble countertop. "Sorry, I guess I'm back at being accidentally rude."

Daniel's lips quirk upward. "You know, if you lose the gallery, I'll be happy to take over the space. But if you can save it, I'd be just as happy to find some other place to be. It's not my only option." He pauses. "And it's obviously important to you."

Todd shifts in his seat, trying to get rid of the weird swelling in his chest. "Yeah, it is." He decides to steer the subject away from himself. "But it's really far from where you live. Wouldn't it take away a lot of time from practice and school? Especially if you're planning on going to Harvard."

"Remember that I told you that this is a project I'm working on with a few friends?" Daniel scoots his barstool closer to the counter. When Todd nods, he continues, "They all live in Brooklyn and they've been part of Deaf culture for a long time, and I'm still just learning."

Daniel falls silent, gaze averted and a crease between his eyebrows, as if he's debating something with himself.

"I want to try and make a difference where I can," Daniel says. "I wanted to be a part of this project, which is entirely my friends' idea and not mine, because I feel like I haven't … *contributed*."

"Contributed to what?" Todd puts his glass on the counter. When Daniel looks at him, he smiles slightly, hoping that it comes off as encouraging.

Daniel gives him a tiny smile back. "To anything. This is the first thing I'm doing that I feel is important to someone other than me."

Todd wants to squeeze his hand, offer some kind of comfort now that Daniel is so vulnerable, but there's an entire counter between them.

"It's a balancing act, I guess. When you grow up like this—" Daniel gestures around and smiles again, but this time it's bitter, self-deprecating "—it's kind of hard to keep a concept of what's normal and where you should take the backseat. We tend to think that we need to save people with money. So I'm letting my friends make all the decisions, because they're the ones with the knowledge, you know? I'm backstage, helping out where I can and where I'm wanted."

"Thank you for sharing that," Todd says, tentatively, because this is new territory for them.

Daniel opens his mouth, and the doorbell rings and a light flashes.

Todd startles, but Daniel gets to his feet and heads toward the front door. Todd realizes that *of course* this is a visual sign for the doorbell.

He recognizes Jesse's voice, and a moment later Mela is in the kitchen with a bag of Korean takeout.

"You okay?" she asks.

Frowning, Todd gets up from the chair to help with the food. "Yeah, why?"

"Just making sure that it wasn't too awkward."

Shrugging, Todd takes out the containers and places them on the counter. "No, it was fine. We talked about stuff."

"And had wine," Mela points out, with a nod to Todd's glass.

"And had wine," Todd confirms.

She squeezes his hand but lets him go when Daniel and Jesse come back.

Dinner is pretty great, and Jesse interprets for Daniel. Sometimes they have to pause and make sure that Jesse can keep up or clear confusion where he's missed something and to give Daniel room for questions. If Todd didn't know better, he'd think of it as a double date. But he does know better.

He's buzzed and filled with energy when they leave for Mick's house. It's not as crowded as Todd assumed that it would be, nowhere near the number of people who were at the frat party. He gets introduced to some. Jesse's the one doing it, though, which makes it simple and just *This is Todd, my newest friend*. It sounds nice, put like that, as if it's an honor to be Jesse's newest friend. If there was a badge, Todd would wear it.

Once again, Todd's taken by surprise by how nice everyone is. *But why wouldn't they be?* He knows he has to stop expecting the worst of people.

Somewhere between a game of beer pong and a surprise delivery of pizza, Daniel slides his arm across Todd's shoulders. It's heavy and warm and it fits, as if it belongs there.

"Hey," he says.

"Hi." Todd turns toward him and sticks his hands in his pockets to stop himself from touching back. "Are you having a good time?"

"I was just going to ask you the same thing." Daniel smirks, and Todd gets flashbacks from when they met. "But yes, I'm having a good time."

"Me too." He is. If anyone asks he's going to deny it, but beer pong *is* kind of fun.

"Glad to hear that." Daniel's arm squeezes him slightly. "Are you ready to go dancing?"

Todd snorts. "Question is, are *you* ready for my dancing?"

Did that just come out, like, out loud? Todd puts his glass down and looks around for water.

The laugh Daniel lets out is such a great reward, though.

"I guess we'll just have to find out."

Todd has no clue how he got in. One second they were in line, and the next he was handing his coat to the coat checker. Maybe they hid him in their group of people, but no one has asked for his ID. The place is packed, and the music is too terrible and too loud for him to be able to think clearly. The melody is lost to him, but the bass vibrates through his body with every beat.

It's perfect.

He looks around, finding familiar faces at a couple of couches and heads over. It'd be just like him to get lost. Sitting next to a guy he thinks that he shook hands with at Mick's place—Todd still doesn't know who Mick is—he looks around.

Mela is already dancing close to Jesse, and they're smiling at each other as if there aren't a hundred, sweaty people nearby. Todd would bet anything that it won't take long before they decide to leave. He keeps searching, finding Daniel a little farther away, and he's dancing as well, with a girl Todd doesn't recognize. While Daniel said that he enjoys dancing, he's not the most graceful person Todd's ever seen, and he's seen *himself*. Daniel is seriously terrible. He's stiff and awkward, and despite keeping the beat unlike some of the other guys around him, and Todd too probably, he isn't in tune with his limbs *at all*. For someone who's so in control of his own body when he's swimming, they seem to have different lives with no connection whatsoever right now. Todd smiles to himself, the inside of his chest suddenly tender like a bruise. Watching Daniel now though, how he laughs and smiles and leans in closer when the girl he's dancing with shows him something on his phone—Todd *burns*.

The guy he sat next to—*Joey or Jim*—is talking to him. He evidently has been talking for a couple of minutes. Todd hasn't registered a word.

"You live in Brooklyn, right?" he asks, and Todd's pretty sure that he's said this before.

"Yep."

"How are you getting home?"

"I'm not. I'm staying with Daniel." He easily finds Daniel's hair in the crowd. He's still dancing with the girl, and Todd thinks that maybe she didn't come with them, because she isn't familiar.

"Wow, that's gonna be awkward," Joey-Jim says.

For a second, Todd wonders if even this guy knows about his asshole tendencies. *No, that's not likely.* He has to ask. "Why?"

"Are you gonna be three sharing that bed, or what?"

Todd hasn't considered that at all, that Daniel would take someone home with him.

"I sleep in the guestroom," Todd says, intending to add *we're just friends*, but the words get stuck in his throat, and he hopes that it's enough to end this particular topic.

Joey-Jim starts talking about football. Todd doesn't know jack about football, so he just hums and hopes that it's enough.

When a girl, sitting opposite of him, catches his gaze and rolls her eyes he sees an out.

"Wanna dance?" he mouths, and she nods eagerly. Todd grabs her hand without hesitation, and they make it through the sea of people to the group they came with.

"Thank you," she shouts over the music.

"No, thank *you.*"

"You're Todd, right? I'm Gemma."

He doesn't remember her, but he doesn't say so. Instead, he gets into his dancing. Soon, he's warm and sweaty at the neck, and his hair probably looks *nothing* like it did when he left Daniel's place. But he's having fun and he's *laughing.* Gemma's got some ugly dancing skills that Todd's never seen, and he has to pull out all his aces to keep up with her.

Todd doesn't know how long they dance—maybe hours. His legs and arms protest his every move, and he's out of breath. But it's as if the bass has migrated into his body, vibrating through his limbs, and he's having the best time he can remember having in a while. When Daniel comes up beside him, he's pulled back to reality. The girl Daniel danced with is nowhere in sight.

"You getting ready to go?" Daniel asks, leaning close to Todd's ear, before he pulls back enough to see Todd's reply.

He grabs Daniel's arm and checks the time on his wristwatch. It's past three. *Holy shit.* Todd swallows his ragged breathing long enough to speak.

"If you are?"

Daniel nods and takes his hand. Todd freezes, but, of course, Daniel only wants to make sure that they don't lose each other in the crowd.

He turns to say goodbye to Gemma, but she's making enthusiastic thumbs up at him and she's already dancing with another guy. Todd isn't sure if the gesture is because she thinks Todd is leaving with Daniel for *that* reason or because the new dude is pretty hot. Possibly both.

Outside, he sucks in fresh, cold air in big gulps, and walks backward to be able to talk to Daniel. He has no clue where they're going.

"Where did that girl go?" he asks.

"What?"

Todd repeats his question.

"Stop, I can't make out anything you say when you're walking," Daniel says, halting him by tugging at his arm.

"Sorry. Where did your girl go?"

"Who? Shauna?"

"I don't know her name." Todd shrugs. "The one you danced with."

"Shauna," Daniel confirms. "She went home."

"I thought she was coming with you." He blames his bluntness on the alcohol.

"Coming with me?" Daniel squints at him—definitely also drunk. "*You're* coming with me."

Resisting the urge to roll his eyes, Todd elaborates, "You know what I mean."

"The answer is still the same—" The rest of the world disappears; Todd thinks he means something else entirely, until Daniel continues. "—It's not like I'm taking someone home with me if you and my sister are there."

"Maybe next time?" Todd tries, ignoring the way the heaviness in his stomach has disappeared, and starts walking backward again.

Daniel snorts, rolls his eyes, and grabs Todd's arm, when he almost backward-walks straight into the hood of a car. "Maybe."

It doesn't sound as though he means it.

Todd still has the music in his ears in the car ride back to Daniel's place. His body is dead tired, but his head is still buzzing with energy.

"Did you have a good time?" Daniel asks, and Todd tears his gaze away from the city outside to turn toward him in his seat.

Daniel's face is flushed, and his hair, darkened from sweat, is curled at the temples. Todd resists the urge to put it back in order.

"I really did." As he says the words, warmth spreads through his chest like hot water spilled on fabric. It's the best night he's had in a long, long while. "Did you?"

"Very." Daniel smiles. It's tired in the best way, as if he's spent all his energy on having a good time. "I saw your dance-off with Gemma."

"Her ugly dancing was way better than mine."

"I'd say it was a pretty even competition until she brought out the Carson moves."

Todd laughs. That was definitely the final blow.

"I'm a pretty terrible dancer, so I go for ugly dancing. That way people will think it's intentional."

"Smart move."

"You looked like you were having a good time." Todd meets his gaze and bites his tongue.

"I can't really hear the music that well anymore. I can hear and feel the beats." He pauses. "I wouldn't be able to hear something played in here, but sometimes, at clubs, it can work."

"But you can't hear the lyrics?" Todd asks.

"No. Ten years back, maybe, but not anymore."

"Sorry for asking."

"I don't mind." Daniel's gaze slips to the window, then returns to Todd. "It feels nice when you want to know more about me and who I am."

Todd's gaze drops to his hands before he looks up.

"I always want to know more about you," he says before he can stop himself. "Would you share something with me?"

Daniel is quiet for a long while, just looking at him. "I'm scared all the time."

Blinking, Todd moves a little closer, as far as the seatbelt allows him. "About what?"

"Making choices. How do you know if you're making the right one?"

"I don't know." Todd shrugs and chews his bottom lip. "Maybe you just feel it? Like a sense of home?"

"Sorry?"

He reaches out, pressing a hand to Daniel's chest. "I think you feel it. Here."

Biting his lip, Daniel looks at Todd's hand. "And what if you don't? What if you feel like you don't belong anywhere?"

"Everyone belongs somewhere," Todd says. *Maybe it's a lie? It's better than saying that perhaps some people are bound to be lost.* He doesn't want to believe that, because it scares him. He's always thought he had his home in the gallery. Now, that's threatening to slip through his fingers. But what if he never had a chance to experience all of this?

"I hope you're right." Daniel covers Todd's hand with his own. His palm is warm and a little sweaty. Then he smiles, and whatever existed between them is gone.

A while later, when they're in the kitchen getting water bottles, Todd taps Daniel's arm.

"I just… thanks for letting me stay with you."

"It's no trouble."

"I wouldn't have wanted to miss out on this for any reason." He pauses. "Your friends are really cool."

Daniel squeezes his shoulder, but Todd would rather have a hug. Daniel pulls away before he can ask. "Glad to hear that. And that you had a good time."

Todd lies in the bed in the guestroom after brushing his teeth and washing the dried sweat from his body. It's already dawn. If someone had told him a month ago that he would be spending the night at Daniel's house, he would've laughed at them. On the other hand, if someone had told him the same thing at the end of August, he would have tingled all over.

Todd can't shake the feeling he got when Daniel tried to help him with ideas for the gallery and how he shared his own insecurities, how he offered thoughts and ideas although he would benefit from the gallery closing, and how he trusted Todd with something he probably doesn't tell a lot of people.

If Todd's being perfectly honest with himself—and since he's alone in the guestroom, staring up at the ceiling, he can be—he isn't sure that he would have been able to do the same thing for Daniel.

Rolling over on his side, he closes his hand around the corner of the pillow, pushing away the thoughts of Daniel holding it as they were pushing through the crowd.

Friends. He's messed this up once already. He's not going to do it again.

Chapter Five

Todd wakes around eleven when his phone buzzes on the night-stand. Groaning, he reaches for it and blinks until his vision clears. It's from Daniel.

> **Let me know when you're up and we'll have breakfast.**

Todd breathes deep, scanning his body before he attempts any bigger movements. His head is a bit heavy and cottony, but other than that, he feels better than he probably should, considering how much he drank last night.

< **I'm just gonna reconnect to reality. Gimme ten.**

He doesn't receive a reply but gets out of bed a few minutes later. At least he was smart enough to bring sweatpants, as his jeans probably smell like spilled beer and smoke machine.

The door to Daniel's room is open. Rocking back and forth on his feet, Todd decides to check if Daniel's left for the kitchen already.

He stops in the doorway, hovering, because Daniel is there pulling a shirt over his head.

It's nothing he hasn't seen, but it's more naked and intimate now when Daniel is in soft-looking pants and not his swimwear.

Daniel notices him as soon as the shirt is past his face.

"Morning," he greets. He looks a bit tired, too, as though last night's escapades will wear on him for the rest of the day. Todd can relate. He's drained, as if he's used his energy resources for the next couple of days already.

"Morning," Todd echoes. "Feeling okay?"

Daniel nods. "Woke up with a bit of a headache, but I took painkillers an hour ago."

"Good call."

"My biggest problem now is that my mouth feels like I've been chewing sand." Daniel grimaces.

Todd can definitely relate. "I'm feeling much better than I deserve."

Smiling, Daniel jerks his head toward the door. "Are you hungry?"

"I think starving is a better word."

"Starving?" Todd nods. "Great, because so am I."

The kitchen is empty when they get there, and there's a calm to the house that Todd didn't expect. The kitchen is kind of homey, with the sunlight flooding through the windows.

"Where's Ava?"

"She's at a friend's. She woke me up before she left."

Todd is secretly relieved; she clearly wasn't thrilled about him.

"I suspect it had less to do with her wanting me to know where she was going and more about her wanting to check if you were in my room."

Todd's face heats. He doesn't know why, since he really did sleep in the guestroom. He can't blame Ava for her hesitance toward him either, but it's a lot more comfortable to be around Daniel when he's not constantly reminded of his own behavior. Mom would probably say that means it would be well to be reminded of it, however.

He watches in silence as Daniel makes omelets, and he helps with making coffee, careful not to make it as strong as he usually does. He expected not being able to have a conversation would be awkward, because it's practically impossible for Daniel to keep up with one while cooking. It's not, though.

"Are your last midterms this week?" Daniel asks, as he plates the omelets.

Todd waits until Daniel has put the pan down and is able to look at him again.

"Yeah, Wednesday and Thursday. When's your last?"

"Friday."

"Are you feeling prepared?"

"Do I ever?" Daniel sighs; he has a strained look Todd hasn't seen before. "I've studied, though. Last night is the first in a long time that I've gone out instead of staying home to study."

Todd admires that kind of self-discipline. For a long while he thought that people were lying when they said that they studied several hours every day. After getting to college, he realized that's the rule more than the exception. "Everyone needs a break once in a while."

"That's true," Daniel agrees, but he doesn't look convinced. "But if I don't get the grades I want in my classes, I'll blame myself."

Law school probably doesn't care about everyone needing a break, either.

"You shouldn't. It's not gonna depend on whether you studied or went out last night. You were having a good time. It's a good way to motivate yourself to study more now."

"How's that?"

Well, Todd made that up, but he's not going to confess. "Lots of positive energy. Endorphins. You'll be able to concentrate better."

Daniel smiles; his face is soft and warm, as if he hasn't quite woken up yet. "I'm ninety-nine percent sure that you're making this up, but it makes me feel better, so I'm going to buy it."

"I would never."

Daniel scoffs. "Don't make me regret this."

Todd glares at him and fails spectacularly at anger, as he digs into his omelet.

"Is this heaven?" He resists the urge to lie down on the counter and cry.

"What?" Daniel has confusion written all over his face.

"This food. It's heaven." The omelet melts on his tongue, and Todd is torn between shoving it all into his mouth right away and eating slowly to savor every bite.

"I'm glad you like it."

"I don't think *like* is the right word."

Daniel smirks, but he holds his head a little higher.

"I could marry you just to have this for breakfast for the rest of my life

"You'd grow tired of it."

"I really wouldn't."

Todd has three cups of coffee. It's mostly an excuse to not have to leave the counter or the conversation. Things are so relaxed between them now, and he wants to wallow in it.

Daniel checks his watch two hours later, and Todd is instantly reminded of Daniel's midterm stress.

"Oh shit, I'm totally overstaying my welcome here, right?"

Daniel blinks at him.

"I mean, you'd rather study?"

That makes Daniel grimace. "I don't know if I'd *rather* study, but you're right. I probably should."

"Thanks again for letting me stay over," Todd says later, when he slings the bag over his shoulder at the front door.

"It was my pleasure."

"I mean, if you're ever going out in Brooklyn and need somewhere to stay, you're always welcome."

It's meant as a joke mostly, because what would Daniel do in Brooklyn that would require a sleepover? To Todd's surprise, Daniel smiles as though he appreciates the offer.

"I'll definitely let you know."

"Unless you're allergic to bunnies," Todd hurries to add. It would be just like him to give Daniel anaphylactic shock. "I have a pet bunny."

Daniel looks at him with a frown and disbelief in his eyes, his smile is uncertain, but he doesn't ask a question, just squeezes Todd's shoulder in goodbye.

When Todd gets home, he has a missed call from Evan. And what the hell, things are okay right now. He might be successful in mending this too.

Taking a deep breath, ignoring the way his ribcage seems to shrink and his chest pull tighter, Todd presses Evan's name in the list of missed calls.

It takes five painfully long rings before the call is picked up.

"Hello?"

Evan's voice is achingly familiar and yet foreign to his ears. It's been a year and a half.

"Todd?"

He struggles for something to say but comes up empty.

"Todd, is that you?"

Panic bubbles in his chest. He hangs up. He has no clue what to tell Evan or why he's trembling all over now. It's his *brother*.

When his phone buzzes in his hand with an incoming call, he jerks hard, almost dropping it. Evan's calling him back. Todd mutes the call and hides the phone under his pillow. Picking up Sandwich, he hugs her close as he tries to think of something positive.

"Well, I fucked up again," he tells her.

She twitches her nose.

A while later, Dad knocks on the door and finds Todd huddled on the bed with Sandwich pressed to his chest. She rarely lets him hold her this long, but maybe she can sense that he needs it right now.

"Evan called," is the first thing Dad says.

"When does he not?" Todd mutters.

"He told me that *you* called."

Oh, crap. "Butt-dialed."

"Uh-huh," Dad says, unimpressed. "When are we going to talk about this?"

"Preferably never."

To Todd's surprise, the mattress dips as Dad sits, and Todd is forced to look up from Sandwich's soft ears.

"Why won't you talk to him?"

Todd shrugs and lets Sandwich go with some reluctance. She hops toward Dad.

"I don't know. It's not like he wanted to talk to me when it mattered."

Dad sighs. "Well, it won't solve itself. You need to talk to him."

"I'm not ready."

"Sometimes you never are." Dad hesitates, but then he gives a little shrug and changes the subject. "How was last night?"

Relieved, Todd rolls onto his back. "It was really good. I went out with some friends in Manhattan."

"Mela?" Dad brightens considerably.

"Yeah, she was one of them."

"And you slept there?"

Of course, Dad has to ask about that.

"Nah, she slept at her boyfriend's."

Dad's not going to drop it, obviously. He never does. Mom says it's because he's a *worrier*. Todd's pretty sure that he's just nosy. "Who did you stay with, then?"

"His name's Daniel." Todd clears his throat and avoids looking at Dad. "He's friends with Mela's boyfriend and let me crash there so I wouldn't have to take the night train."

There's a moment of silence. "How nice of him."

"Yeah." Todd shifts. "We're not that close, though."

"Uh-huh," Dad says again, voice just as flat as before.

"I'm serious."

"Uh-huh," Dad says for the third time, completely exaggerating.

Todd throws a pillow at him. "I don't even know why I try talking to you."

"I'm your dad."

"Exactly."

Dad ruffles his hair. "Let me know when this friend of yours is coming over for dinner."

He leaves before Todd has a chance to protest. It would be one thing if Daniel really was something other than a tentative friend, but he's not.

Before going to bed, he checks his phone and pretends not to see the missed calls from Evan. There are seven. Instead he focuses on the text waiting for him from Daniel.

> **You forgot your sweats here. Also thanks for a great night out.**

Todd looks through his bag, and, yes, they're definitely missing.

< **Crap. Sorry! When do you want me to come grab them?**

Daniel's reply comes almost instantly.

> **When do you need them?**

Need them? Is there anyone who ever has an actual need *for sweatpants?*

< **No rush. Just want to relieve you from their burden**

> **Please, they're just lying on my chair. I'll bring them next time I see you?**

Todd pretends that he isn't happy about the fact that there will definitely be a next time.

< **Sure, don't stress about it when you have midterms to focus on. I have more sweats to lose at people's houses before I'm going to demand to get them back.**

> **I'm picturing a protest outside my house. Signs and all.**

Todd snorts and now he's picturing this too.

< **Free the sweats!**

> **I think this is getting out of hand.**

> **Admittedly I'm having fun.**

Todd bites his lip at the second text in a row from Daniel. It reminds him of the night they met.

< **I promise that there will be no protest outside your house. I'll send a petition though**

> **It does sound like the most peaceful option.**

< **Don't think that I don't get that you're procrastinating studying right now**

> **I'm that easy to figure out, am I? I'll get back to it. Going to let my sister hide my phone again. Sleep well!**

Curling on his side, Todd smiles to himself as he sets the alarm for tomorrow. Maybe they can end up being good friends. God, he hopes so.

✳   ✳   ✳

> **Were you serious with** the offer of having me over if I had business in Brooklyn?

Todd never expected Daniel to take him up on the offer to stay the night whenever he's in Brooklyn and doesn't want to go back to Manhattan. Todd thinks that he should know better by now, considering that everything he does seem to come back to bite him eventually. It's only been two weeks since they saw each other, but as soon as he reads the text, his stomach starts swirling.

< **Sure, when?**

> **Fri-Sat?**

He sighs in relief. His parents are going to D.C. over the weekend. His dad would never let this go.

< **That works. I don't have a guestroom to offer, but you can have my bed if you're okay with that?**

He quickly pushes away any thought of Daniel in his bed. Friends don't think of friends like that.

> **If it's too much trouble I'll find another solution. Don't worry.**

Daniel needs to use smileys. If Todd didn't know that he's the most polite person he's ever met, he'd think Daniel was being passive-aggressive.

< **It's not, unless you're not comfortable with sleeping in my bed :)**

> **I don't mind sharing your bed.**

Todd swallows, and types as quickly as he can. *Thank god for autocorrect.*

< **You don't have to share it with me. I'll take my parents' bed or crash on the couch**

> **I can sleep on the couch.**

Todd rolls his eyes. Jesus Christ.

< **No. My bed is comfy. You don't wanna miss out on this opportunity. Believe me**

> **Fine. I'll bring your sweats back to their natural habitat as a thanks.**

< Wow, your generosity knows no limits

It takes the kids in art class five minutes to notice that he's distracted that Thursday. His brain jumps between having Daniel in his home and the future of the gallery looking darker every day.

"But we're *not* talking cubism," Clara points out for the second time in half an hour when Todd has mixed up his facts—again.

"Sorry." He scrubs a hand over his face. *Get a grip*. With a twinge between his ribs, he looks at their eager, patient faces. If this is the last semester he has with them, he's going to make it count.

"You're absolutely right, Clara. So back to Fauvism. You're going to like this one, Jamal—it's all about colors."

When other kids have left. Logan peers at Todd over the front desk, biting his lip.

"Why are you sad?"

Of all the questions Todd thought he would come up with, this isn't it. "What do you mean?"

"You look sad. Why?"

"Sometimes I have a lot on my mind that worries me. I'm trying to make it right, but I don't know if I can, you know? So I'm sad."

Logan rests his chin on the desk and rolls an abandoned pen back and forth with his middle finger. After a moment he says: "It's okay if you tried your bestest, though."

Todd swallows the lump in his throat as he watches Logan leave with his dad. Trying doesn't really count in this particular situation. How is he going to spend his Thursday evenings if he doesn't have them?

On Friday, he meets Daniel outside the coffee shop. It's almost midnight, and Todd has been spending his evening with a few people from his modern art class. Usually he'd prefer to stay home alone, but the idea of just sitting around waiting for Daniel to text him was too anxiety-inducing, so he caved when he got the invitation.

Daniel looks amazing where he stands waiting, glowing in the light from the street lamp above him. His cheeks are a bit ruddy from the cool night air, and his face lights up, eyes bright, when he spots Todd.

He's wearing a jacket and a knitted sweater underneath it. Todd wants to stick his nose in it and take a few breaths. It's that kind of sweater.

"Hey, how's your night?"

Daniel's smile widens. "Good so far. How's yours?"

"Great! I don't live far from here, so maybe we should go before I freeze to death."

"It's fifty degrees," Daniel snorts.

"Don't be like that."

The walk is short. It's cold, but the lit windows are glowing like a thousand portals into other lives, and sometimes he wonders about the people who live behind them. Daniel's shoulder bumps against his, their arms graze, and Todd's heart jitters in his chest. His fingers itch to grab Daniel's hand.

Letting Daniel through the front door, Todd sees his home with new eyes. He takes in the earthy colors of the wood and all the greens and browns in the interior. Books are piled everywhere—a tell of his mom—next to items Dad has brought with him from one of his many trips home to Mexico. Todd's favorites are the patterned clay pots in the cabinet with glass doors. The many plants scattered all over the place and the large blankets on furniture calm him whenever he comes home from a busy day. All in all, it's a stark contrast to the whiteness, marble, and sleek steel in Daniel's home.

He watches as Daniel looks around with open curiosity. There's a tiny smile on his lips, and his gaze sweeps over the items in the hallway and what he can see of the living room.

"Where are your parents?" is the first thing he says, after turning toward Todd.

"Away in D.C. for the weekend. They left a couple of hours ago."

Daniel nods, seemingly confirming something to himself. "Can I look around?"

"Sure. Go ahead." Todd starts to gesture in invitation to do just that, but then he lets his arm fall limp to his side. "It's not exactly like your house."

"No," Daniel agrees, but it doesn't sound as if he's disapproving, and Todd follows him through the kitchen, where he stops. The newspaper is still on the kitchen table and there's a used napkin crumpled on the counter.

Todd winces. He should've cleaned up.

"It actually looks like someone lives here," Daniel comments. His eyes are bright, and his fingers trace the patterns in the surface of the table. Todd remembers carving them there with a table knife many years ago. He'd been furious that Evan got to go to the movies without him. He had been in so much trouble, but his parents kept the table.

"It's home." Todd shrugs.

"Can I see your room?"

"Yeah, of course. You're going to sleep there."

He pushes his hands deep into his pockets after pushing the door open. Everything in there is so predictable, from the multicolored string lights, to the collage on the walls. Most are made by his classmates, but some are his own.

Someone that doesn't quite fit in, though, is Sandwich. She's on the floor, ignoring the unknown visitor in favor of spreading hay all over the rag rug.

Todd groans. She isn't exactly helping with the first impression of their home.

"Sorry about the mess," he says, but Daniel doesn't notice.

All his focus is on Sandwich, and he crouches, puts his bag against the wall, and extends a hand toward her. He freezes halfway and looks up at Todd.

"Can I pet it?"

"Sure. She doesn't bite." Todd shifts his weight from one foot to the other. "She might pee on you if she likes you, though."

At that, Daniel shrugs and fully extends his hand. Sandwich pauses in her hay chewing and eyes Daniel's fingers. Then, she hops closer, pausing a few times as if to check that Daniel isn't making her hop all that way for nothing.

Todd has a hard time determining who's more pleased when she finally gets to sniff his fingers and then allows him to pet her between the ears. Daniel slowly strokes her back and sides and touches her big feet.

When Daniel looks up at him again, Todd makes a go-ahead gesture.

"You can pick her up. Don't say I didn't warn you about the peeing, though."

Daniel doesn't seem to mind the risk of getting peed on, because he sits cross-legged on the floor and scoops Sandwich into his hands. She looks surprisingly small. He holds her face-level, and then to his chest and lets her ears touch his chin.

"What's her name?" he asks, voice softer than Todd has ever heard it.

"Sandwich."

"What?"

"Sandwich," Todd repeats.

Daniel frowns, pausing as if he's trying to puzzle something out. "I'm sorry, but I can't make that out at all."

"I can fingerspell it?" Todd offers, because he knows the alphabet by now.

Daniel's eyes light up in a way that makes Todd's chest ache. "That'd be great."

Fighting the urge to chicken out when stage fright hits him, Todd slowly spells out S-A-N-D-W-I-C-H and mouths it as he works his way through the word.

Daniel bites his lip, clearly holding back a smile. "Sandwich?" he asks, checking.

"Yeah, I didn't name her."

"Spell it out again." Daniel scoots closer across the floor. When Todd gets to the N, Daniel reaches over with his free hand, and gently nudges his fingers, so that the tip of his thumb sticks out between his middle and ring finger instead of his ring finger and pinky.

Crap, he mixed up the M and the N again.

"There you go," Daniel says, voice gentle. Then he gives Todd a funny look. "Why Sandwich? It's a bunny."

Todd's used to the reaction.

"I found her in a pet store, and she bit anyone who tried to touch her, so the owner said that she was going to be snake food."

"Snake food?"

"Yes. He called her snake sandwich. I had to buy her, I mean, for obvious reasons. She won't listen to anything but Sandwich, though. Don't think I didn't try with any cute name I could come up with."

Daniel chuckles and presses his nose to Sandwich's head briefly before he puts her on the floor. She sticks close to him, apparently no longer in an overwhelming need to eat her hay all over the place. The risk of Daniel getting peed on just increased.

"You don't come off as a bunny person."

"I wasn't until I couldn't let her get eaten by a snake."

"I support that decision."

Todd looks at Sandwich. It's easier than looking at Daniel. "On the plus side," he says, "you won't be sleeping in here alone."

"What?"

"You won't be sleeping in here alone," Todd repeats.

"Changed your mind about the couch?"

Todd's face heats. "No, I meant that you'll have Sandwich here with you."

"Oh, of course." Daniel gives her a quick glance. "I'm sure she's great company."

Todd sits on his desk chair. "So, how come you're in Brooklyn?"

"I did an interview." Daniel shrugs. "About being an athlete who's hard of hearing. The journalist didn't have time until nine and I suspected that it would take a while."

Todd frowns. "The journalist didn't have time until *nine*?"

"It's a friend of mine. I wanted to do him a favor and I had to finish practice before I could go."

"Oh, I see. That's nice." Todd digs his fingers into his thigh. "Did it go well?"

"Sure. If I get my name out there in a positive way, it'll increase my chances. I mean, my average and the LSAT are more important, but you know how it is."

Todd doesn't, but he nods anyway. "That's really cool."

Silence falls between them, and Todd racks his brain for something to say, but he gets caught in the way Daniel sits on his rug, seemingly relaxed and at ease—in Todd's room.

"Thanks for letting me stay over," Daniel says suddenly, bringing Todd out of his thoughts. "I finished my midterms yesterday and seeing another human being outside of school is a welcome break."

Todd's heart stumbles. "It's no problem. Sorry I can't quite offer the same luxury you gave me."

"Just getting to hang out is more than enough."

Todd has to remind himself that it's not *him*. Daniel would have felt the same way about getting to spend time with anyone right now. Todd is just conveniently close by.

"Same. I met up with some people from one of my classes earlier, and it was exactly what I needed." He continues quickly as he realizes how that might come off to Daniel. "Having you over's definitely making that even better."

Daniel smirks as if Todd's momentary panic is obvious to him. Instead of replying, he scans the room.

"Except for Sandwich, this is everything I would've imagined your bedroom to look like."

Todd rolls his eyes. "I'm predictable, I know."

"Most of you isn't." Daniel looks at him for a long moment. "At least not what's under the surface."

Daniel comes to stand beside him and looks at the canvas on his desk.

"Did you make this?" Daniel asks reaching out as if to touch, and Todd has to grab his hand to stop him.

"Sorry," he says, when Daniel looks at him. "The paint hasn't dried yet."

"What?"

"The paint hasn't dried yet."

"How long does that take?"

"Almost a day, I'd say. It's usually touch-dry within twenty hours." Todd shrugs. "And yeah, I made it. It's just a new technique I'm trying."

He glances at the vivid colors. He used almost every bright color he has, but maybe he's been a little excessive with the yellows and reds. It's supposed to be an abandoned parkway, surrounded by autumn trees. Like most of his works, it's best observed from a little distance.

"What kind of technique?" Daniel asks, and Todd has to wait with his answer, until Daniel looks away from the painting. "I'm sorry, I just really like it."

"I've started using knives instead of brushes. I think the effects are pretty cool." He skips the nerdy talk of why he prefers the metal painting knives over plastic ones and how he found his current set by chance in a thrift shop.

Daniel's gaze flicks back to the painting and then to Todd's face again. "I haven't seen anything like this before."

Todd resists snorting. Clearly, Daniel hasn't ever heard of Afremov. Todd could stare it his works for days. "I'll show you some really cool ones, if you want?"

He expects Daniel to say no, because giving Todd a compliment isn't the same as having an actual interest, but he nods.

Opening his laptop, Todd brings up his folder with some of his favorite Afremov paintings. They're vivid, and his technique is refined compared to Todd's own clumsy work. He shifts on his chair, wanting to point out the richness of the colors, when he finds Daniel completely enraptured, eyes fixed on the screen.

Todd, his core growing warm and turning to liquid, nudges him with his elbow until Daniel looks at him. "I'll text you his name if you want to look into him more?"

Daniel's gaze falls to Todd's painting before they lock eyes again. "Do you sell these?"

"Oh, no, definitely not that one." *Selling his work?* That's for people with more talent than he has.

"That's a shame, I would've liked to buy it." Daniel scrutinizes him before he adds, "Let me know if you change your mind."

Todd stares at him and then at his painting. When he looks back, Daniel is checking the time. It's got to be super late by now. Here's a chance for him to leave this subject. He taps Daniel's arm to get his attention.

"Do you wanna go to bed or maybe watch some Netflix or something?"

"Netflix sounds nice."

They curl up on Todd's bed with his laptop on the desk chair in front of them with the captions turned on. Todd can't quite pay attention to the show Daniel picked. It's a crime show, but Daniel seems to find it entertaining.

Todd soaks in the warmth Daniel's body is radiating. It seeps through his clothes and his skin, down to the marrow of his bones. He aches a little when he looks at Daniel. He's close enough to touch, but at the same time light-years away. *God.* Todd knows he's messed up so bad.

"Another episode?" Daniel asks suddenly.

Todd blinks and nods. He hasn't noticed that they've finished one already.

At some time during the third episode, when his body grows heavy and his brain slows , he has to get up to brush his teeth and switch to sweatpants.

When he returns, Daniel has changed clothes, too, and is holding his toothbrush in one hand. Todd shows him the bathroom.

He locks Sandwich into her cage while Daniel is gone. Usually she can hop around freely in his room while he's at home, but he isn't sure if Daniel is comfortable with the risk of stepping on her in the morning.

"Do you want to finish the episode?" Daniel asks as he enters the room again.

To be fair, Todd doesn't remember much about the plot, but he likes this. *Hanging out.* So he nods.

He curls up against Daniel's side, pulls one leg to his chest, and stares with unseeing eyes at the screen as he allows himself to be distracted by Daniel's body heat once again.

"Are you tired?"

Todd nods against his knee. "Yeah, you?"

"Sorry?"

Swearing internally, Todd straightens and turns toward Daniel. "Sorry. I said yeah and asked if you're tired too?"

"A bit," Daniel confesses. "I kind of like the show we're watching, though, that's why I'm forcing myself to stay awake."

Because he hasn't hung out with anyone in a long time. Because of midterms. "We can hang out tomorrow as well, unless you have to leave early."

Daniel shrugs. "Around lunch. I have afternoon practice."

"Oh, okay." Todd glances at Daniel's wristwatch, wondering if it's a good idea to be awake at three-thirty in the morning the day before practice. Daniel probably knows, though, so he doesn't comment on it.

Todd lies on his side after a while, with his head resting just *nothing* away from Daniel's thigh.

Netflix's combined curse and blessing is the automatic continuation of the episodes, but tonight Todd doesn't mind when a new one starts.

"Do you want to watch another one?" Daniel asks. He's leaning back against the wall now, and Todd suspects that he's getting pretty sleepy as well.

Todd, too tired to lift his head and speak, reaches up and squeezes Daniel's forearm once.

"Is that a yes?"

Todd squeezes again.

There's a moment of silence before Daniel says, "Okay, if that meant no, I can't tell."

Todd snorts. He probably should just sit up and speak the way he's fully capable of doing, but then Daniel continues:

"Do it again if it means yes."

Todd squeezes once.

"How efficiently we communicate." Daniel sounds amused.

Smiling to himself, Todd doesn't withdraw his hand from Daniel's arm.

He has no clue when he falls asleep, but it's amidst a bunch of onscreen murders. When he wakes, he's partially covered by his duvet, and his face is pressed against something solid and warm.

Alarmed, Todd bolts upright so fast that his vision blurs. When it clears, he takes in Daniel's barely-awake form. He's blinking, probably woken up by Todd's commotion.

The laptop is placed on the nightstand. Todd must have fallen asleep, and Daniel must have decided not to wake him up or perhaps he tried and failed.

"Shit, I'm sorry," Todd says without thinking. He doesn't remember that there's no use, until Daniel's reply doesn't come.

When he starts to get out of bed and give Daniel his promised space, Daniel reaches out to stop him.

"God, just go back to sleep."

It takes Todd a second to decode Daniel's words and then he sighs. He *is* tired and he doesn't feel like putting sheets on the couch and finding a spare blanket. If Daniel doesn't mind, then neither will he. He's shared a bed with Mela a billion times. *It's no biggie.*

He turns over and ignores the overwhelming heat beneath the covers. He goes back to sleep with his back pressed against Daniel's arm.

* * *

THE NEXT TIME TODD WAKES, it's light outside, and Daniel is still asleep. He's on his back, with his light hair barely a contrast against the white pillowcase. His eyelashes are fanned against his high cheekbones, and his lips are slightly parted.

He's gorgeous.

Todd swallows and nudges him gently. It's probably already close to lunch, and if Daniel is supposed to make it to practice, he might not want to sleep all day.

Daniel only groans and tries to turn away. After a few nudges, he slowly blinks awake. The next moment is one Todd's going to store away for a long time.

Daniel's eyes search, unfocused and aimless with sleep. Todd watches the small crease form between his eyebrows, as if he can't place the string lights or the wall art. And then, Daniel's eyes find his face and take in the state of Todd's hair, sweep down to his lips, and finally connect with Todd's gaze. Then, a smile slowly spreads across his face, and the crease between his eyebrows smooths out.

"Hi," he says, voice soft, and the way he looks at Todd makes him want to kiss him.

"Morning," he replies, unable to keep himself from smiling back. "Will you teach me how to sign that?"

The question is out before he can stop himself. It's not Daniel's job to teach him. Worried that he has ruined the moment, Todd sits back on his haunches.

"I'm sorry."

Daniel frowns, and Todd wants to smack himself for making that smile disappear. Instead of replying, Daniel reaches over to the bedside table and gets his hearing aids. Todd watches him close the battery door and then put them in.

"Come again?"

"I'm sorry."

"For what?"

"I know that it's not your job to teach me. There are classes for that."

"Can you repeat that?"

Todd does, doing his best to say the exact same thing.

"I don't think there's an entire class for teaching you how to say good morning." Daniel grasps his wrist gently. "You need to stop apologizing so much. Asking me to teach you one sign isn't the same thing as asking me to teach you the entire language, and I've already told you that I'm fine with you asking me things. I'm capable of saying no, you know."

Todd relaxes, concentrating on Daniel's fingers on his skin.

"I don't speak for anyone but myself, though."

"All right," Todd says.

"Was it *good morning*?" Daniel asks.

"Yes." Todd does his best to concentrate on Daniel's hands and arms as they move. He has obviously slowed the movements for Todd's sake.

"One more time?" Todd leans forward on his knees to see better.

Daniel smiles and does it again. He says the words as he signs them, and that definitely makes it easier.

Todd shuts off the part of his brain that's terrified of failing and tries to mimic the hand movements.

"No, wait," he says, immediately knowing where he went wrong, and tries again.

"Good." Daniel reaches up to adjust where Todd's hands meet slightly, so that his fingers don't touch his palm, but the fingers of his other hand. He smiles when Todd tries again and nods his approval.

"Thanks for teaching me."

"It's my pleasure."

Todd smiles to himself and does the sign a few more times, just to practice. Daniel's watching him the entire time, with an odd look on his face that Todd can't place.

"Did you sleep well?" he asks then.

"What?"

"Did you sleep well?"

"I did." Daniel's face is still so soft and open. "You were right. I really didn't want to miss out on your bed."

"Well, you got the unexpected addition of me in it."

"Which was nice," Daniel says, as though sensing that Todd is about to apologize again. "Otherwise I would've tried harder to wake you up."

Todd has to admit to himself that waking up with Daniel definitely is one of the better things he's done in a while.

"It was a good night."

"Yes." Daniel smiles. "It was."

Todd looks at him, while his gaze has drifted off to look at the knickknacks in Todd's bookcase again. He's freaking gorgeous, and he's in Todd's bed, and *nothing* happened. It's somehow both a disappointment and a relief. He taps Daniel's arm to get his attention.

"Are you hungry?" he asks, to distract himself from Daniel's naked chest and stomach as he sits up. When he looks around, he finds that the sweatpants he forgot at Daniel's last week are lying neatly folded on his chair under the closed laptop.

"I'm always hungry."

"Do you like pancakes?"

Daniel stares at him. "*Like* isn't a strong enough word."

Todd snorts at the unexpected excitement on Daniel's face. "I make mean pancakes."

Watching Daniel eating pancakes is the most distracting thing Todd has ever been through, and he once took a croquis class with nude models. Daniel eats more pancakes than anyone Todd knows and he eats them with such enthusiasm that Todd suspects he doesn't do it very often.

"Don't they let you eat pancakes when you're a swimmer?" he asks, with a bite of pancake pushed into his cheek.

Daniel frowns, then shakes his head. "It's really difficult to read your lips when you have something in your mouth. The way you shape your mouth changes."

"Sorry, I'm just gonna—" Todd points to his mouth and gulps down the last of his pancake, wincing when he can feel it go all the way to his stomach. He chugs some juice and then wipes his mouth on a paper towel. When he looks up again, Daniel is smiling slightly.

"What I said was: Don't they let you eat pancakes when you're a swimmer?"

"Come again?"

Todd repeats the question.

"If I can eat pancakes?"

Nodding, Todd adds: "Because you're a swimmer?"

Daniel licks syrup from his bottom lip. "I can. I just rarely let myself, because it's not very healthy."

"I have pancakes at least once a week."

The look of disbelief Daniel gives him makes Todd laugh.

"That's so unfair."

"The only one stopping you from doing the same is you," Todd can't help but point out.

"I'd sink like a stone if I did."

"No, you wouldn't." He sips his coffee but remembers to put his mug down before he continues. "Besides, I read somewhere that muscles weigh more than fat."

"What?"

"Muscles weigh more than fat."

Daniel kicks his foot under the table. "Stop it. Don't enable me."

Biting his lip, Todd suppresses a smile. Like this, Daniel is like any other friend, except for the way he makes Todd's skin tingle and his world narrow to whatever space they're in.

"Can I ask you something?" Daniel asks, making Todd look up.

"Sure."

"It's about your brother," Daniel says tentatively.

Evan also has a way of making Todd's chest too tight, but in a very different way. This isn't a moment Todd wants to spend talking about Evan.

"Go ahead," he says anyway.

"He called you when we met for coffee, if you remember?" Daniel speaks in a careful way that reminds Todd of when he was a kid and tried to get a snack from the fridge while his parents were still sleeping. He still knows which floorboards creak.

"Yeah."

"You said that you weren't going to call him back, and I got the impression that it wasn't just because you didn't have time then and there." Daniel pauses. "Was my impression correct?"

Looking away, Todd licks his dry lips as he tries to find his voice. "Yes."

"You have to face me."

He turns toward Daniel as much as he can. "I'm sorry. I said yes."

"Can I ask why?"

Daniel scoots his chair closer, and Todd gets flashbacks of the first time they met. Once again, he's fascinated by the size difference of their thighs.

"You don't have to tell me," Daniel says, pulling him back from his thoughts.

"It's okay." Todd swallows and digs his fingers into his own thigh. "It's not that big of a deal, really."

At that, Daniel keeps quiet, watching him intently, and Todd takes a breath before he continues. He hasn't talked to anyone except Mela about this.

"Evan's four years older than me and he's always been the good one, you know? He was great in school, valedictorian and everything. He's pretty great at anything, really." Todd shrugs, and there's bitterness in his tone now.

"What did you say after *school*?" Daniel asks.

"Valedictorian."

Frowning, Daniel seems to puzzle over it, but Todd starts finger-spelling, reaching the I before Daniel's sighs at himself.

"Valedictorian? Of course. Keep going."

"I looked up to him a lot when I was younger. I did everything I could to be like him, but I never quite… managed. Um, school hasn't been very easy for me. I have trouble concentrating and theoretical stuff takes a long time for me to learn. It mostly just goes in one ear and out the other."

"Theory is difficult for you?" Daniel checks in.

Nodding, Todd continues. "The last few years, I've discovered ways that make it easier for me, like using flashcards—" He digs his phone out to show Daniel his app. "—but, Evan, he's amazing at everything he tries, and everyone who meets him loves him. He went to school in L.A., and he was great there too. Naturally."

Scratching his knee, Todd swallows the unwelcome lump in his throat.

"We got along much better when he was there, and we talked on the phone a lot. I kind of came to accept not being able to be him, so I decided to be me instead. I got my own interests and group of friends."

"Wait, you're speaking really fast, can you slow down for me?" Daniel stops his fingers where they're scratching at his sweats. "And repeat what you said after telling me that you spoke on the phone a lot."

It's easier talking fast. That way he gets away from the subject sooner. Speaking fast now, however, excludes Daniel from whatever he's saying, and that's the last thing he wants. So he slows to his normal pace and, even though it burns a little more to repeat his words now when he can't rush them, he sticks to it.

"Okay, keep going."

"I sort of had my own thing, with the art and stuff. It was a really great time, actually." He glances up at Daniel, who's still looking at him with intense focus, as if he doesn't want to miss a single word. "As I said, it's not really a big thing. He did an internship in L.A. and then moved to Vancouver to work with TV show production and he stopped caring, I guess."

"Come again with the last bit? Where did he move?"

"Vancouver. He works with TV show productions. And then he stopped caring."

Daniel nods.

"It was kind of a drawn-out process, where he forgot promises and to call or things that mattered to me. He never understood my interests, and I think he's thought of it like I'm wasting time and education on something useless. After a while I guess I just gave up on caring too."

He doesn't feel like talking about Evan's endless promises to come home for a visit and never actually showing up or forgetting Todd's birthday two years in row or how he canceled last minute on Todd visiting him, forcing Todd to leave the airport with his packed bags. He doesn't want to mention the constant comments on Todd's choice of college and his love for art. They aren't big deals one by one, but after a year of constant letdowns and then not being told about the move to Vancouver until it was already happening, Todd decided he'd had enough.

Staring at his own hand for a long while, Todd wonders what Daniel is thinking. He's so quiet. Then, slowly, as if to give Todd a chance to pull away, Daniel's hand moves from his own knee to Todd's, squeezing gently.

"Can I say something?" His voice is so soft that Todd can barely hear it.

When he looks up, he finds Daniel's gaze and the concern on his face. "Yeah."

"Is this the first time he's called you since he moved to Vancouver?"

Shaking his head, Todd threads his fingers together to stop himself from putting his hand over Daniel's. "No, he calls at least once a week nowadays."

"And you don't pick up?"

"No."

Daniel's quiet, and Todd can tell that he's trying to find the right words. "If he calls you once a week, do you really think he's stopped caring?"

Beginning to pull away, Todd swallows the acidic taste in his mouth, but he stops pulling away when Daniel squeezes his knee again.

"I don't mean it like that. Not like a criticism of you." He untwists the knots of Todd's fingers and rubs his thumb over Todd's knuckles. "There's nothing wrong with how you feel. If you don't want to talk to him ever again, then don't. I just want to put it out there, that if you want to reconnect with him, I really think he's trying to reach out to you."

"I doubt he thinks he's done anything wrong," Todd mutters.

"What?"

"I doubt he thinks he's done anything wrong," Todd repeats.

"You won't know if you don't give him a chance to prove you wrong."

"Or right," Todd adds.

"Or right," Daniel agrees. "It seems like it's wearing on you. Maybe you'll be able to close that box for good if he really doesn't want to talk it out. Maybe you won't need a box at all if he does."

Todd takes a breath and allows himself to meet Daniel's gaze for a long moment. He looks honest, as if he really does want the best for Todd.

"Okay," Todd says finally. "I'll think about it."

In return, he gets a smile almost identical to the one he got when Daniel woke up.

Soon Daniel leaves for practice. Todd wishes he had an excuse to hug him when they say goodbye at the front door.

Chapter Six

TODD TRIES TO FOCUS ON preparations for his classes, he really does, but his thoughts always return to Evan and the conversation he had with Daniel this morning. Now, it's obvious that Evan's been trying to get a hold of him. Mom and Dad have gotten involved during the last few months, and, if Todd's honest with himself, he *knows* that Evan wants to talk to him. No one calls this often unless they want someone to pick up.

It doesn't matter that he's been trying to tell himself otherwise—he misses Evan. He has been for a while.

Closing the lid to his laptop, Todd scrolls through the contacts on his phone instead of searching, just to buy himself a bit more time. He hovers his thumb over Evan's name before he puts one earbud in his ear and presses the CALL button.

His heart is racing. He's about to cancel on the seventh ring, when he hears, "Todd?"

Todd tries to find his voice. It takes a couple of attempts, and he panics. "Yes," he manages finally.

There's a sound on the other end that he can't place and then, barely more than a whisper, "You called me back."

"Yeah." He clears his throat, trying to ignore the lump in his throat. "Yeah, I did."

Evan breathes on the other end. It sounds unsteady and strained.

"Are you crying?" Todd whispers.

There's another sound, high-pitched, so, *yeah, Evan's definitely crying.*

"Why are you crying?" he asks, trying to make his voice as soft as Daniel's was earlier.

"I'm just really happy," Evan says eventually, voice wavering, "that you called."

That's all it takes to make Todd's tears roll too.

Evan's happy that he called.

It takes a long, long while before they're able to actually talk to each other. For almost half an hour, Evan starts sobbing as soon as Todd tries to say anything, and Todd's heart swings between feather-light and aching.

"How are you?" Todd wipes his face with the hem of his T-shirt. His cheeks are stiff; the skin is dry from crying, but it doesn't matter right now.

"I'm okay," Evan tells him. "Better now. I've been trying to get to talk to you for so long."

"I know." Todd blinks at the ceiling, taking in the familiar sound of Evan's voice. It's as if they spoke just yesterday, because he knows it so well. The only difference is the slight change in his accent.

"I didn't think you wanted to talk to me."

Taking a breath, Todd decides to be honest. "I didn't."

"I can understand that."

"It would've been better if I had told you instead of shutting you off." He's known this all along, but whenever he gets hurt, it's as if the grayscale disappears from his brain and everything is just black and white.

"I'm not sure I would've gotten it if you had. It took me almost six months to realize that we weren't talking anymore. I was too busy with everything else."

Evan's voice is as easy to read as Todd's face. It always gives him away and right now it's so full of shame and regret that Todd's stomach aches.

"I was really angry and hurt."

Evan takes a slow breath on the other end. "You have every right to be."

"I might be willing to consider forgiving you."

"That's all I ask for." Evan clears his throat, and Todd hears someone else's voice on the other end.

"Is this a bad time?"

"I'm at work, but I don't care." Evan has never said that, so Todd decides to believe him.

"It's okay, we can talk later."

"Don't worry about it. They can do without me the last hour before I get off."

"I mean it. You can call me when you're home, all right?"

Someone speaks on the other end again, and Evan pauses. "Promise to pick up?"

"Pinky swear."

"I'll call you in two hours tops, okay?"

"Yes. Go."

When Evan hangs up, Todd stares at his phone. Evan was happy that he called. The realization makes his stomach contract so hard that he has to hunch over. Evan has missed him.

The next two hours are a strange mix of emotions. At first, Todd can't wait to talk to Evan again—they have a lot of catching up to do. Then, the doubts start. *What if Evan doesn't call?* He's made promises before and never kept them. When there's forty minutes left of Evan's two-hour window, Todd's convinced that this was their only phone call for the coming year and a half as well.

Five minutes before the two-hour mark is up, Todd's phone rings. He lets out his breath in a rush when the display lights up with Evan's name.

"Hello?" he answers.

"Hi." Evan's voice is quieter than Todd remembers it, but his relief is obvious. "Are you free to talk?"

"Yeah, I'm just home doing nothing." Todd scoops up Sandwich from the floor and places her on the bed before he sits down himself. He might need some emotional support for this. "Are you home?"

"Just got to my apartment. The traffic was crazy."

"Was it bad?"

"There was an accident, so I had to take another route." Evan pauses, and Todd reaches out for Sandwich. "I wasn't sure you were going to pick up."

"I wasn't sure that you'd even call," Todd replies.

Evan takes a breath. It's a bit noisy through the phone, as if he's holding it too close to his mouth. "I want to apologize for how I've behaved, for making you promises and then not keeping them and saying things about the choices you've made."

"You really hurt me," Todd whispers, and then the words tumble out of his mouth. "Especially when I was going to come see you. I was in the line to check in and everything, and then I had to leave, and everyone saw. I felt like a freaking idiot for crying in an airport and having to get a cab. The driver asked me where I'd been, and I had to lie, because I couldn't tell him that I hadn't been *anywhere*."

"Todd." Evan's voice cracks over his name. "I'm so sorry."

"Yeah, you really should be." Sandwich nips at his thumb. "But I'm sorry too. I should've talked to you instead of just shutting you out. It wasn't fair, either."

"In your defense, I'm not sure I would've wanted to talk to me about it either," Evan says. "I got a big head and it took me a while to get it out of my ass."

Todd snorts. "You've always had a big head."

"It was worse than usual there for a while." It sounds as if there's more to that story, and Todd is way too curious to let it go.

"What happened?"

"I almost got fired and had to get my shit together."

"You almost got fired?" Todd echoes, just to be sure. Evan almost getting fired sounds like a really terrible lie that no one would believe.

"Imagine that, huh?"

"I'm having difficulty, honestly. You're the last person I could ever see getting fired."

"That's what happens when you get a big head for no reason." Evan clears his throat. "I was lucky, because I got a second chance and had to realize that I can learn a lot from other people."

Todd hums. He doesn't have words that can describe his thoughts, so that's all he's got.

"So," Evan says after a longer pause. "What's up with you?"

Where to start? "I have a whole bunch of weird things going on right now."

"Like what?"

"I don't know where to begin." Todd lets Sandwich go when she struggles in his grip. He decides to go for the quick summary option. "I still have my job at the gallery that I really like, but I found out a while back that it's not doing that great financially and we're having problems finding artists that will attract a younger crowd."

"I see. And then what?"

"Well, then I went to this party with Mela and I met this dude, his name is Daniel, and we got along really well."

"Did you go home with him?"

"No," Todd sputters. As if he's ever going to talk to Evan about that anyway. "Shut up; let me finish."

Evan chuckles. "Fine."

Todd explains Daniel wanting the gallery's space for his club, and how Todd lied to postpone dealing with the situation. "I felt so bad when he found out, and then we had to meet several times anyway, because Mela is dating his friend Jesse."

"So you're talking now?"

"Yeah," Todd says slowly. "I think we're sort of friends. I stayed at his place last week when we went out in Manhattan, and he stayed over last night."

Evan whistles, and Todd really wants to hang up on him. Evan's been hanging out with jocks and popular kids too much all his life.

"Shut up. It's not like that. We're friends."

"Is that what you keep telling yourselves?"

"We *are*. I was a dick to him and I'm just really happy that he even wants to be friends with me." Todd looks at Sandwich where she's sniffing at his feet. "He's really great."

"Tell me more about him."

Todd clears his throat to get rid of the weird fluttering in his chest. "He's a jock. I mean, super-jock. He's on the swim team and he's really great, which he's *very* aware of. He goes to Columbia and he wants to go to Harvard Law when he's done this year."

"Wow," Evan commends. "Ambitious guy."

"Yeah, but he's also down to earth in a weird way. Like, he's cocky at times, because he knows that he's good, and I'm pretty sure he knows that he's hot too. But he's really cool and, even though he wants the gallery's space, he helped me out with some business ideas that I really like." Todd chews his bottom lip. "And he's hard of hearing, so I've been trying to learn some ASL, but it's really difficult."

"Have you used an app?" Evan asks, and it's the last thing Todd expected him to say.

"I have two, but I keep forgetting everything the moment I close them."

"Maybe you can try the same thing you did in high school?" Evan suggests. "Putting notes on everything? Or make flashcards?"

Todd can't believe he hasn't thought of that himself.

"I think there are cards you can buy too," Evan continues. "We got some for the office, when we had an intern who's hard of hearing. I think the cards are for kids, but you can learn basic vocabulary, which might help."

Todd makes a mental note for himself as he looks at Sandwich, who's lying against his thigh. He really wants to make it easier for Daniel to be around him and to do his part for their friendship. However, Evan and Dad are equally nosy, and Todd doesn't want to say too much, so he switches the subject. "Are you coming home for Christmas?"

"I might," Evan says. "I'll see if I can get some time off. I can't make any promises, though."

It should be disappointing, but Todd is *relieved*. "No promises" means that Evan can't break them.

"If you want…" Evan begins and then hesitates. "If you want, I can check with some of my contacts about having their art in your gallery."

"Exhibiting," Todd corrects as his heartbeat picks up.

"Yes, that. I've met a few artists through work events and I can make a few calls if you want me to?"

His pride says no, says that he doesn't need *Evan's* help when he's been distant for such a long time. Especially not since he's been criticizing Todd's love for art since the dawn of time. However, the rational part of his brain says *yes*, because he needs all the help he can get. He can't be picky.

"Can I think about it?" he asks, knowing all too well a quick answer is going to give him anxiety in a few hours, no matter what answer he gives.

"Sure. Call me or text me when you've decided."

They talk about TV shows and YouTube videos, until Dad knocks on Todd's door to let him know dinner is ready. Evan promises to call within the next couple of weeks. Todd wishes that the spark behind his ribs didn't ignite so easily, but he wants Evan to be true to his word.

"Was it that friend of yours?" Dad asks him, as he hands Todd a full plate.

"No, it was Evan."

Both Mom and Dad pause, and it's as though there's no sound and no time passing.

"You talked to Evan?" Mom asks finally.

"Yeah." Todd clears his throat and pushes his rice around on the plate. "I figured it was about time."

"Oh, honey," Mom whispers, and there are tears in her eyes. She looks as if she's going to come around the table to hug him, but before Todd can stop her, Dad has wrapped him into a crushing embrace that's hurting his ribs. And he's five years old again, hugged by them both, as Mom wraps an arm around his back and kisses his cheek.

Todd clutches his fork convulsively and blinks until his vision clears. Mom can't stop saying *oh, honey*, and Dad doesn't say anything, but the way his hands tremble as he lets Todd go says everything.

"Did you know he almost got fired?" Todd blurts, overwhelmed by the urge to put the focus elsewhere.

✳   ✳   ✳

BETWEEN CLASSES AND WORK, TODD creates flashcards and notes he can put on furniture. Most of the signs requires several… *steps*, so he's putting a lot of mini squares on the cards, with arrows. Mostly they work as a reminder to practice the signs, and he uses the app when he doesn't remember how to do them. Mom raises her eyebrows when she finds him taping a card on the fridge next to the shopping list.

"What's going on?" Her eyebrows climb even higher as she squints at the card. "Why are you learning ASL?"

"It's for a friend. I want to be able to communicate better," Todd explains and points at the stack of cards he's placed on the kitchen table.

Mom looks at him. "Give me half, and I'll help you put them up."

They tape cards everywhere. Todd assumes that she explains to Dad, because he doesn't ask Todd about them.

He uses the flashcards to learn the basic words and the app for simple phrases and repeats whatever word he comes across in the apartment.

He's cleaning the front desk at work when he's interrupted by a text from Daniel.

> **Having Jesse and Mela over on Friday. Do you want to come?**

Todd suspects that it's not just Mela and Jesse that Daniel will have over, but who sends the entire guest list in a text anyway?

< **Sure :) That sounds fun**

> **Naturally you're welcome to stay over if you don't have anywhere else to sleep.**

Todd doesn't ask Mela about sleeping over. She would probably say yes, but staying over at Daniel's was *fine* then and it's not going to be worse this time. They're a little more comfortable around each other now.

< That makes things a lot easier. Thank you!

Dad gives him an all too knowing look when Todd tells his parents that he's going to be in Manhattan Friday to Saturday. Todd doesn't call him out on it, since Mom seems oblivious and he really doesn't want them *both* asking him questions.

Daniel meets him at the subway station. He looks casual in fall jacket and dark jeans, and the damp look of his hair tells Todd that it's started to rain during his train ride.

"Hey," he says when he stops in front of Daniel. "Thanks for meeting me."

With a smile, Daniel nods toward the nearest exit. "It's no problem. I don't expect you to find the way by yourself yet."

Yet.

"My phone has a GPS, and there are a whole bunch of map apps."

"Come again?"

"I have a GPS and map apps on my phone." Todd holds it up for emphasis.

"Remind me of that next time, so I won't have to suffer an involuntary outdoor shower."

"Well, you're about to have another." Todd laughs when Daniel bumps his shoulder as they start walking.

It's a short walk, and Todd is grateful for that, since it's in silence. He's also grateful for his beanie, because the rain would completely mess up his hair.

Daniel's house is quiet.

"Where's your family?" Todd asks, after removing his shoes and jacket and tapping Daniel's shoulder for his attention.

"My parents are away, and Ava is at our grandma's."

"Didn't you want to go?"

"I can't. I have extra practice on Sunday that I can't miss." Daniel shrugs as if it doesn't really matter to him.

"Does your grandma live close by?"

Daniel smiles at that and takes him to the kitchen. It seems to be their first stop, whenever Todd's here. "Occasionally. She's usually in Germany, but she's got a place in D.C. too."

Todd's just about to ask about Germany when his gaze locks on the family photo on the wall. When he was here before, it seemed too personal to look too closely at the family photos. It hits him now that he knows the two people behind Daniel and Ava, and he doesn't know how he didn't recognize them at the gallery.

The man, Daniel's dad, is Mark Berger, former football star and now his Dad's favorite television sports commentator. Daniel's mom is Elizabeth Berger, whose face is on at least two cookbooks and whose name is on a whole bunch of kitchenware in Todd's home. He doesn't know what boggles his mind more: that these people are Daniel's parents or that they're *married*.

"Oh, my god," he says to himself and then turns to Daniel, who's watching him with interest. "Why didn't you tell me?"

He remembers Daniel's reaction when Todd asked if his mom was an interior designer, as if he wasn't sure if Todd was joking. That makes a lot more sense now.

"Tell you what?" Daniel asks, stepping closer.

"That these people are your parents."

"To be fair, sometimes I'm not entirely sure myself."

Todd glares at him. "It's not funny. I feel like an idiot."

"Why? I don't expect everyone to know who they are. It was a nice change."

"My dad *loves* your dad," Todd tells him and glances at the picture again just to make sure.

"Well, I guess someone has to." Daniel grimaces, and Todd is immediately brought out of his starstruck state.

"I'm sorry. I didn't know it's a sensitive subject." *Foot in mouth, a story by Todd Navarro.*

"It's not. He's well aware I'm not his biggest fan."

Todd bites his tongue on the *why?* that's dying to slip out. Daniel doesn't look as if he wants to talk about it, judging by the squared shoulders and the pinched eyebrows.

"Can I help you prepare anything?" he asks, and his chest expands at the way Daniel's shoulders relax.

"No, they're bringing the food, and we'll put the snacks out later."

"What's the plan anyway?"

"Sorry?"

"What's the plan?"

"For the evening?"

Todd nods.

"Hanging out and board games."

Todd has always enjoyed board games. He's a lot better at them than athletics. "How many are you expecting to show up?"

Daniel frowns. "Just the four of us?"

Oh. So there's not a massive guest list. Daniel was really just having Mela and Jesse over and asked if Todd wanted to come too. That makes sense; Todd wouldn't want to hang out with a couple either.

"Is that a problem?" Daniel asks, as if he's heard Todd's internal conversation.

"No, of course not. I just sort of assumed that it would be a big crowd."

"It's easier with fewer people," Daniel says, and Todd looks at him, waiting him out. "Well, frankly, four people is not exactly ideal. I'm expected to converse with everyone and I can't. Jesse's going to help me out with interpreting."

"We'll try to figure it out."

"I'll be around people who know me and what I need, so it's different from when I'm with a group of people I'm not close to. It's easy to forget that I need things from the people around me." Daniel shrugs. "I think I told you before, but I had better hearing when I was younger, and it took me a long time to be comfortable asking people for what I need."

"It shouldn't have to be like that," Todd says.

Daniel eyes him. "You forget sometimes too."

"I know," Todd frowns at his hands before looking up again. "I'm trying to do better. I wish it wasn't something I have to think about consciously. I'm working on it."

"Sorry?"

Todd repeats himself.

"I know."

"I'm sorry."

"I know that too." Daniel smiles slightly. "It wasn't until I started spending time with other people with hearing loss that I stopped feeling like I was the odd piece in the puzzle somehow. Most of them are like me: We've grown up with hearing parents and siblings and friends, in hearing culture. I didn't even know about Deaf culture until quite recently. How messed up is that?"

Todd can't think of anything to say that doesn't sound like an empty cliché, but Daniel doesn't seem to need his input.

"When I hang out with other people like me, it's a lot easier than when I'm spending time with hearing people. Sometimes, especially in large groups, it's easy for people to forget to not have several conversations at the same time or interrupt each other. It's tiring to read lips and it's difficult it is for me to hang out with people in bars or restaurants because of all the distractions."

Todd swallows strokes the back of Daniel's hand, which is resting on the counter. His skin is a bit dry. "That must be difficult."

"Yes. It takes up a lot of my concentration, and afterward I'm beat, you know? I have my hearing aids, but they're not magical. I can't even use them all the time. Some of my closer friends learned to sign to make it easier for me, Jesse for example. We're about equally fluent. We started learning together."

I'm learning too, he wants to say, but he's far from getting there, despite practicing every day. It would be false advertising.

Daniel takes a slow breath, then gives a small shrug and says, "I'm proud of who I am, but it really blows when other people *forget* who I am."

That statement feels final. That's okay. It's up to Daniel to decide when or where he wants to share.

"Anyway," Daniel says. "Let's go upstairs for a bit."

Todd sits on Daniel's bed after an indecisive moment of awkward lingering. He watches as Daniel straightens some notes on his desk. His shoulders visibly relax with every second that passes, and he scoots a little to the left when Daniel comes to sit opposite him.

Hugging his legs to his chest, Todd looks at him. "So, how are you?"

"Good." The pause makes Todd wait, and Daniel looks away. "I took the LSAT a while back."

"When?"

"Around midterms."

Todd had no clue about that, but he should've asked. "How did it go?"

"I should find out any day now."

"How did it *feel?*"

"What?"

"How did it feel?"

Daniel lets out a sigh. "I really have no clue. Right there, it felt okay, which is usually a good sign. I've started doubting my answers more now and I just know that I didn't get the score I need."

He looks weary all of a sudden, as if all the air has left him, but softer and more vulnerable than ever. Todd digs his fingers into his arms.

"You don't know that yet."

"I'm not even sure I want the score to get in," Daniel admits, and his voice is so quiet that Todd can barely make out the words.

"Why not?"

"That way I don't have to make a choice."

"And you don't want to go to Harvard?"

Daniel shrugs and stares at Todd's hands for a long while. "I don't know, honestly."

The urge to comfort is so strong that Todd has to bite his lip to keep from saying anything. He waits and waits until Daniel looks up at him again.

"My grandfather always said that I would be great at law, and my mom thinks so too." Daniel takes a deep, slow breath that reminds Todd so much of how he tries to calm his own racing heart when his brain starts working at high speed.

"What do you think?" he asks, trying to make his voice gentle.

Daniel blinks. "Come again?"

"What do you think?"

"I've always known that I didn't want to go into sports, like my dad. I've always assumed that I wanted to go into law. It's just now, when I might have to make that choice…" He takes another breath and lets it out through his nose. It's loud in the silence. "What if I make the wrong one?"

"You can always make a new choice," Todd says. "Maybe you can't change the one you've already made, but you can make a new one."

Daniel nods, but he doesn't look convinced. "I always figured, you know, that your occupation should be your purpose in life."

"Do you still think so?"

"Sorry?"

"Do you still think that?"

"I don't know anymore." Clearing his throat, Daniel looks at the duvet and then up again; his cheeks have some color to them now. "I'm thinking that maybe the project, the one I told you about, maybe that's what I'm supposed to do."

"Can't it be?"

Daniel shrugs again. "I don't know. Is it a failure if I choose the wrong thing?"

"No, definitely not." Todd squeezes his knee. "I think failure is when you choose the wrong thing and then don't try to do anything about it, even if you can."

"What? I didn't catch the part after choosing the wrong thing."

"If you don't do anything about it, even if you can, I think that's a failure." Todd looks at him. "Not just making the wrong choice. That's just part of life."

"So how do I know what to choose?"

"Maybe you have to ask yourself if you will regret not giving it a try?"

That brings out a tiny smile. "Maybe you're right."

"You're one of the smartest people I know, even if I don't know you that well yet. You'll figure it out when you get there."

"You know me pretty well," Daniel tells him. "You had me all figured out from the start, remember?"

Todd grimaces, remembering that conversation so well. *Has it really only been a few months? It feels as though it's been years.* "Don't remind me."

"Why not? I had a great night."

Biting his lips, Todd has to look away from Daniel's gaze. The part of him that sometimes wonders what things would've been like if he hadn't messed up is always louder when they're alone like this.

"So did I." He offers finally. "You were really cocky."

He looks up when Daniel lifts his chin with a warm hand. "Come again?"

"So did I," Todd repeats. "You were really cocky."

"I was not," Daniel scoffs.

"Yes, you were. You just bragged about how great you were at swimming and that you're *so* smart."

Daniel gapes, but a glint in his eyes makes Todd's stomach lurch and his skin crawl in anticipation. "Liar. You're the one who *asked* if I was a good swimmer, and I *confirmed.*"

"You *bragged,*" Todd protests.

"I did not. You were judging me so hard, and I had to defend myself."

"I did not judge you!"

"No?" Daniel smirks. "Am I imagining all the comments about me being typical Ivy League and me being a stereotypical jock?"

Todd somehow manages to get his stupid grin under control and does his best to give Daniel his most serious nod. "Yes, I think you might want to get that memory of yours checked up."

When Daniel doesn't reply, but just looks at him with that glint still in his eyes, Todd cracks under the anticipation. Grabbing a pillow, he throws it in Daniel's direction and immediately regrets it when Daniel catches it and pushes him down on the bed with it in two seconds flat. His arms are locked against his chest and Todd can't stop laughing, making it impossible for him to find enough strength to fight back.

"Let me go," he whimpers, and his cheeks ache.

"What?"

"Let me go," Todd says again.

"Giving up already?" Daniel puts the pillow aside, but his hand locks around Todd's wrists, keeping him in place.

Todd stares up at him, struck by the way Daniel looks at him. His grin is warm and wide, and he's so close, leaning over Todd on the bed. The air between them goes from fun to tense in the best of ways, and Todd just *knows* that they're going to kiss.

Licking his lips, his eyes drop to Daniel's mouth.

"Wanna help me set the table?" Daniel asks.

Blinking, Todd forces himself to meet Daniel's gaze and suddenly he's hot all over for a completely different reason. God, he's so *stupid*. There was never going to be a kiss. They're *friends*.

"Yeah, sure," Todd says.

Daniel climbs off the bed and Todd is left awkwardly disentangling himself from pillows and sheets to go after him down the stairs. His beanie has slipped off, and his hair looks a little wild when he walks past the mirror on Daniel's open closet door, but he leaves the hat on Daniel's bed anyway. Mom always nags him about not wearing it indoors.

In the kitchen, Daniel is already grabbing glasses from the cabinets and there are plates on the counter. He taps Daniel on the shoulder.

"Where are we gonna sit?" Todd asks him, once Daniel has put the glasses down. His gaze lingers on Todd's hair, and there's a new kind of smile on his lips for a second.

"Sorry?"

Todd repeats the question.

"What do you think? Dining room or kitchen?"

Todd shrugs. "Maybe kitchen? If we're gonna eat and play games. I'm gonna get intimidated in the dining room."

Daniel snorts at that. "You're not, but I see your point. Kitchen it is. The table is smaller."

It's round with six chairs, and Todd thinks it will be easier for Daniel to sit here, especially with Jesse helping. They set the table together in silence, and Todd puts the glasses on the wrong side, but Daniel just rearranges them.

Todd notices weird little things, like the way Daniel bites the inside of his cheek when he's considering where to put the vase with fresh flowers or how he lines up the plates and bowls of snacks on the counter hesitantly, as though he's worried that Todd thinks he's overdone it— which he totally has, because there's snacks for twenty people, but it's sweet. Why Daniel prepares the snacks already, Todd has no idea, but it's not like Cheez Doodles go bad anyway.

"I don't know what you like," Daniel confesses.

"I like everything that's edible."

Daniel turns away, but Todd catches the smile.

Mela and Jesse arrive shortly after that, and Todd is stiff with surprise when Jesse hugs him instead of giving his usual shoulder-squeeze.

For a group that hasn't been hanging out together regularly, they're oddly comfortable and in sync. When they team up for the board games, Todd automatically teams up with Daniel and doesn't think twice about it until it's two a.m. and his stomach hurts from too much laughing. That's when he looks away from Mela and Jesse sitting close together on one of the living room couches and realizes that his own feet are under Daniel's thigh on the other.

He takes in Daniel, who's looking at his cards in deep concentration, but his arm is resting on Todd's knees, using them as an armrest. Todd wiggles his toes experimentally. Daniel doesn't look away from his cards when he reaches down to squeeze Todd's calf and says, with a laugh in his voice, "Stop, I'm concentrating."

Todd *knows* that it's nothing on Daniel's side, since he definitely backed away from a perfect moment to kiss, but it stings a little bit how easy and unproblematic affection seems to be to Daniel. It's as though it's not even *that*, as though touching someone this way doesn't have a deeper meaning to him. In comparison, Todd is warm and pliant and comfortable this close to him. *It's not just the wine.*

"What?"

Todd looks away from where his feet have disappeared under Daniel's thigh and finds Daniel looking at him, obviously having noticed his staring.

"I'm just thinking about my next move," Todd lies.

"Did you forget the rules again?" Daniel smirks.

"I never forgot the rules! You just use the wrong ones."

Mela and Jesse leave an hour later, and Todd loads the dishwasher while Daniel lets them out. It's not until he's grabbed the dishrag to wipe the counter that he notices Daniel watching him from the doorway. A sudden rush of insecurity washes over him, and he puts it down.

"Sorry," he says, realizing that he's taken some liberties.

"For what?"

Todd holds up the dishrag.

"For cleaning up?" Daniel steps closer. His shirt is rumpled, and his hair is disheveled from a long night. He looks tired in a warm, pleased way.

"I kind of did it from habit."

"Thanks. That's really nice of you."

Todd smiles and puts the dishrag down for the second time. "Did you have a good time?"

"I did. Did you?"

"Yeah, it was great." *It was a freaking double date, but with only one couple and two people where one is oblivious, and the other is pining.*

"Do you want to go to bed?"

"Yeah. I think the wine glasses are still on the coffee table, though."

"Come again?"

"I think the wine glasses are still on the coffee table."

"I'll deal with them tomorrow." Daniel nods toward the door. "Come on, let's get to bed."

"Can we maybe watch Netflix first?" Todd asks when they reach Daniel's floor. He's not ready to part ways.

"Sure."

Todd changes into sweats and a T-shirt, then goes to Daniel's room. Daniel is already in bed, covers tucked up to his waist, and he's not wearing a shirt. Todd is proud of himself for managing not to look, as he curls up against the headboard next to Daniel.

"Wanna continue the one we watched last time?"

"Yeah."

Todd breathes in the smell of Daniel's skin and closes his eyes. Maybe it's cologne or just his body wash, but he smells nice despite having a long day, and Todd's chest *aches*. Because this, this feels a lot like falling in love, and he knows that he shouldn't.

He opens his eyes when the mattress moves. Daniel is out of bed putting the laptop on the desk, and Todd must have fallen asleep sitting up with his head uncomfortably against the headboard. His neck aches.

Groaning, Todd rubs his eyes and musters his strength to get out of Daniel's bed and make the short walk to the guestroom.

"Stay if you want." Daniel's words take him by surprise.

"Sorry for falling asleep."

"It's fine. I figured we've shared a bed before."

"It's always because I fall asleep on you."

"Can you repeat that?"

"It's always because I fall asleep on you."

Daniel smiles. "Yes. You can go back to sleep again as soon as you're under the covers."

"You don't mind?" Todd asks, just to make sure. He knows it's a bad idea, knows because he's already too attached.

"No." With a shrug, Daniel gets in bed and reaches for the bedside lamp. "When I turn the lights out, we're out of ways to communicate."

"Gimme a second." Todd kicks off his sweats and drags his T-shirt over his head before he can think too much about it. He's already warm. The sheets are tepid when he gets in, but they're so soft. "Okay."

Daniel turns the lights out.

"Goodnight," Daniel says, and Todd reaches out to squeeze his arm. It's not exactly something you say *yes* to, but he thinks Daniel will understand.

He's fast asleep before he can fret about it.

⁀ ⁀ ⁀

TODD WAKES WHEN FINGERS STROKE his hair. Blinking slowly, his eyes focus on Daniel leaning over him in bed.

"Morning," he says and removes his hand.

After a second of hesitation, Todd signs *good morning* and hopes that he remembers the movements correctly. Judging by the way Daniel's smile widens, he does.

"Did you sleep well?"

Todd nods and squints at the sunlight flooding into the room. "What time is it?"

"Eleven."

"And you're awake? You're *smiling* and awake?" he grouses.

"Have been for almost half an hour."

"Oh, my god, go away." Todd pushes at him without any effort behind it. He'd much rather grab Daniel's hand and put his fingers back in his hair, but he doesn't, for obvious reasons.

"I've made coffee."

"I've changed my mind. You can stay."

Daniel smacks Todd's bare thigh where it's been exposed, as he gets off the bed. "You might want to drink it before it gets cold."

He turns away and disappears out the door before Todd can reply, but the promise of coffee makes him force himself out of bed and into his T-shirt and sweats to pad downstairs.

Daniel has made toast, too, and there's a steaming mug waiting for Todd at the table, along with a plate. He doesn't think hunger is the only reason that his stomach contracts, but he'd rather not think about that.

"Wow!" He sits and nudges Daniel's foot with his. "What did I do to deserve this?"

"Sorry?"

Todd repeats the question.

Daniel smirks. "Probably nothing."

"Rude." Todd tries glaring, but the coffee smells way too good. He hugs the mug with his hands and watches as Daniel cuts his toast and stirs milk into his coffee.

The silence between them stretches, but Todd finds it comforting. He drinks his coffee and scrolls through the news on his phone, and Daniel is reading an actual newspaper he's spread out on the table. The toast is incredible, but Todd is too distracted by the way Daniel refills his mug without asking that he forgets to enjoy the bite in his mouth.

Chewing on the crust, Todd puts his phone down and glances at the page Daniel's reading. It's finance stuff. Why is he surprised? He gives Daniel a gentle nudge with his foot to get his attention.

When Daniel looks up at him, Todd forgets his question.

"When do you want me to leave?" he asks.

With a shrug, Daniel sips his coffee. "When do you need to be elsewhere?"

"Tomorrow night," Todd snorts, because that's when Dad wants them to have family dinner again.

"Okay."

That's definitely not the reaction Todd expected, and he has to nudge Daniel under the table again when he returns his attention to the newspaper.

"I was kidding. I can't stay until tomorrow."

"Why not?"

"You don't want me to stay for two nights?" he puts it as a question, because Daniel seems completely fine with the idea.

"Why not? I'm home alone. Company is always nice. I have practice in a couple of hours, but you can come with or stay here if you like."

Todd's throat makes a weird sound. This is something he'd say to a boyfriend if he had one or to Mela. When Daniel says it, it sounds so simple and easy. Still, Todd's heart is freaking out as if he's been proposed to over coffee.

"Uh." He taps his fingertips against the table. "Okay, sure. I didn't bring any extra clothes, though."

"What?"

"I didn't bring any extra clothes."

"I guess you have a tough choice to make. Either borrow something from me or stick to nudity."

"You joke about it like I would never walk around naked in your house."

Daniel quirks an eyebrow, and Todd caves immediately.

"You're right, I wouldn't."

"I hope you're never captured if there's a war. You'd crack in two seconds."

Todd makes a face. He's not going to dignify that with an answer—he would do *great*.

"So," he begins when he remembers talking to Evan. "I called my brother."

Instantly serious, Daniel stops with his mug halfway to his mouth before he puts it on the table. "How did that go?"

Chewing his lip, trying to find the right words, Todd watches as Daniel folds the newspaper and pushes it away before he angles his chair toward Todd's.

"It went… surprisingly well, actually."

"How so?"

Todd has to divert his gaze to gather his thoughts. The crumbs on his plate are less distracting than Daniel's eyes.

"I mean, at first there was a whole lot of crying." He tries to say it as a joke, but when he looks up again, Daniel has that crease between his eyebrows and freaking *concern* written all over his face. "After that, well, we sort of talked it out a bit. He apologized. I'm sort of working on forgiving him."

"There's no rush, is there?"

"To forgive him?"

Daniel nods.

"No, I guess not."

"I think you're really brave for calling him."

Todd squirms in his chair. "Did I mention the crying?"

Daniel smiles. "It doesn't make it any less brave."

"Says the guy who confronted my lies right away," Todd mutters.

"Sorry, I didn't catch that."

"I said—" Todd straightens up and mentally slaps himself for not speaking clearly. "That you're the one who confronted me about my lies in the coffee shop when you found out. I waited forever to do talk to Evan."

"To be fair," Daniel says. "We had met two times before that. This is your brother. I imagine that there are a lot more hurt feelings involved."

"Yeah." Todd hesitates, knowing that he's already apologized once and that they're friends now. "I'm still really sorry for how I behaved."

"I know. We're okay now."

Todd claws at his face, but makes sure to uncover his mouth when he says, "Jesus Christ, why are you so *nice*?"

Daniel barks out a laugh. "Would it make you feel better if I punched you?"

Todd eyes Daniel's arms through his fingers. "Probably not."

The smirk on Daniel's face fades into something more serious. "What did your parents say about you not talking to your brother?"

Todd hugs his knees to his chest. "I mean, they know me, so I don't think they were too surprised that I shut him out. My mom wants everyone to get along, so she tried to make me talk to him. Family is important to my dad, and I think it worried him that we weren't talking, but he didn't express it the same way."

"Your mom wants you to get along, and family is important to your dad?" Daniel checks.

"Exactly." With a shrug, Todd diverts his gaze, careful to keep his face turned toward Daniel. "I don't know. Sometimes I think his obsession with family dinners and spending time together and snooping around in my life comes from him leaving his entire family and, you know, culture behind in Monterrey. He had an entire life he left there, and then his kids were fighting, and I was annoyed with him."

"Where? Can you spell that out?"

"Oh, sure, sorry." Todd is incredibly proud of himself for managing to get the M and N right this time around.

"Monterrey, that's in Mexico, right?"

"Yeah." Todd nods against his knees. "He moved here for my mom, when he was just done with college."

"How did they meet?"

"She was on vacation, and my dad worked at a bar at the hotel where she stayed. He told me he proposed to her on the first night."

Daniel smiles. "Wow."

"She said no." Todd snorts. "He had to propose four more times and then he gave up. She proposed to him a year later."

That makes Daniel smile, and Todd can't help but do the same. His parents might be annoying at times, but they could be a lot worse, for sure. He expects Daniel to mention something about his own parents, but he keeps questioning Todd.

"Is your brother your only sibling?"

"Yeah, thankfully. Are you hiding any others than Ava around here?"

"I think she's enough to handle." Daniel grimaces as though he remembers something.

"I think she might've learned from her brother," Todd says innocently.

"From what I've heard, her brother is actually pretty great," Daniel tells him.

Fighting to keep a straight face, Todd shrugs, hoping that it looks nonchalant. "When he makes an effort, maybe."

Daniel nudges him with his foot. "You okay?"

"Yeah, I was joking about that she got it from you," Todd says hurriedly.

"No, I meant after talking to your brother."

"I think so." He studies Daniel and sees his attention, as if he really cares about what Todd has to say. After so many conversations, Todd doesn't know why that still blows him away. "I guess I'm kind of scared that he'll get right back to his old ways in no time."

"That's a valid fear." Hearing that makes the guilt in Todd's belly ease somewhat. "Have you talked to him about it?"

"No. We didn't talk for that long."

"Do you want to talk to him about it?"

Taking a breath, Todd nods. "I think I should."

"Do you want a hug?" Daniel sounds hesitant. *Maybe he doesn't offer hugs that often.*

"From you?"

"I mean, if you'd rather have one from someone else, I'm sure I can find a random person on the street who's willing."

Todd snorts, but he's freaking out a little bit. With the exception of Daniel using his legs as an armrest and that calf squeeze last night, their only physical interaction was when they kissed the first time they met. Todd imagines that Daniel's hugs are firm and warm, but he's scared to find out.

"I'd like a hug, thanks."

And it's awkward to get to his feet when Daniel does, just to get a hug. It's almost a formal thing, as if he's greeting his boss. But when Daniel envelops him, wrapping him up in his arms, Todd can't do anything but melt against him. Strangely, not being able to communicate like this makes hugging easier. He doesn't have to say anything. Instead, he puts his chin on Daniel's shoulder and digs his fingertips into the soft fabric of his shirt at the small of his back. There's a low whistling sound coming from Daniel's hearing aid, but it stops when Todd moves his head away just a bit. Daniel is both solid and soft against him; his body is well-toned, but his embrace is gentle.

It seems like a long time, but probably isn't more than a minute, when Daniel's hold loosens and Todd has to step away.

"Thanks," he says, because *how the hell does one express gratitude for a hug?* "I needed that."

"Anytime." Daniel smiles, but then he busies himself with clearing the table and Todd helps in silence.

He brings his phone to Daniel's practice and a book he picked from Daniel's bookcase. He'd rather sacrifice his hair to the humidity of the pool than be found hanging out alone in Daniel's room if his parents came home unexpectedly.

Swim practice seems utterly boring. They're doing laps upon laps, and Daniel is wearing shorts instead of his usual suit. Todd's going to have to ask about that later. He's in the bleachers, several rows up, because he doesn't want Daniel's teammates to get the wrong idea.

He checks social media and then starts on the book Daniel lent him. The background noises of the water and people talking are soothing. He suspects that he could've gotten a lot of school work done if he had brought it here, because there would be nothing else to do, nothing to distract him.

"Ready to go?"

Todd straightens with a jerk and finds Daniel standing in front of him, wearing his regular clothes. His hair is wet, probably after the shower, and he looks pretty tired.

"Sure. I didn't even notice that you were done."

"Just fifteen minutes ago or so."

When they reach the doors together, Jesse catches up to them, places a gentle hand on Daniel's shoulder, and stops them both in their tracks.

"Hey, Todd," he greets, signing as he speaks, smiling in the same way he's done since the night Todd first met him. "How's it going?"

"Good thanks. You?"

Jesse's smile grows wider. "Good, good. Staying for practice, huh?"

"I didn't have anything else to do," he explains, his neck growing hot.

"He's staying until tomorrow," Daniel fills in. *Doesn't he realize that that's just making things even worse?*

"Cool," is all Jesse says, but his grin makes Todd want to create a sign saying *We're only friends* and staple it to his forehead. "See you guys around."

"Bye," Todd tells his back.

"Hungry?" Daniel asks him.

"Very."

"Do you like pasta?"

"Are there people who don't like pasta?"

"Too many."

"God, who allowed them to exist?" Todd says and then heaves a sigh for effect, proud of the way his words make Daniel smile.

That night, they curl up on the couch on Daniel's floor and watch TV for several hours. It's mostly reality shows that don't engage them. Todd's chest burns with the way they're so close together, without actually touching much. Daniel's arm brushes against his every now and then, when he reaches for his drink or the popcorn that almost set off the fire alarm. Half of the bag is in the sink, burnt into a black mess, but Todd managed to save the rest of it. It tastes like soot, but that doesn't matter.

He nudges Daniel's arm, and waits while Daniel turns off the TV and turns toward him on the couch.

"Why do you want to be a judge?"

"A judge?" Daniel checks, and, when Todd nods, he's silent and his gaze grows distant before he looks at Todd again. "My grandfather told me I'd make a good one."

It's the same explanation Todd got the first time they met.

"Do *you* think you'd make a good one?"

"I hope so," Daniel says, after hesitating again. "I looked up to him when I was a kid. He died when I was fourteen, lung cancer, but he's the only one who's always told me I can be anything I want. That I can do anything I want."

"He must've been great."

"He was," Daniel nods. "A product of his own generation in a lot of ways, I guess, but he was always willing to learn. He's the one who took me to my first swim practice and he's the one I told that I'm bisexual before anyone else. I was terrified. He was dying in a hospital, and I felt like I'd been lying to him, because I hadn't told him. I guess I was scared that he wouldn't approve, you know?"

Todd knows that feeling. Even though he knows his family, before he told them he felt an ounce of fear that they'd turn out to be strangers, people he didn't actually know. "What did he say?"

"I had to explain what it meant, and he just asked me: *That's it? I thought you were going to confess a murder.*" Daniel smiles to himself, his gaze far away, as if he's back in the hospital with his grandfather. "He told me that I can be anything I want to be, because of who I am. Not despite, *because.*"

"I'm glad you had someone like him," Todd says, when Daniel focuses on him again. "He sounds like a great person."

"I honestly can't imagine where I'd be without him. I know it sounds cliché, but he made all the difference for me." Daniel's gaze flicks to the black TV screen and then back to Todd. "I don't remember what's going on in the show we're watching."

The trip to the past is over for today. "Someone died and now they're trying to find the murderer," Todd says, laughing when Daniel shoves him, causing him to topple over on the couch.

He sticks his feet under Daniel's thigh and proceeds to watch the rest of the episode lying down. Daniel doesn't comment, and the silence between them is just as comfortable as last night.

An hour later, Daniel stretches, and Todd blinks sleepily at the screen.

"Are you ready to go to bed?"

"Are we sharing?" Todd asks, just to make sure. He isn't usually this direct, but Daniel is pretty straightforward most of the time, and it makes things really simple.

"Sure," Daniel says with a shrug. "We obviously managed last night."

"We did."

In a way, it is stranger going to bed with Daniel tonight, when they don't have a TV show to watch together in bed. However, it's a lot easier to just curl up under the covers than pretend to pay attention to the show on screen.

"Today was nice," Todd tells Daniel, when he's under the covers and turned toward him. The lamp on the bedside table is still lit, so communication still works.

"It was. I hope you didn't mind the practice."

"Not at all. I was kind of surprised of how nice it was there."

"Come again?"

Okay, so the lighting might not be ideal. Todd grabs his phone from the nightstand and taps out his reply in the notes before he holds it out to Daniel.

"Thinking about taking up swimming?"

Todd snorts, and erases his first reply, only to type again. **Are you kidding? I can barely swim like a normal person, let alone the shoulder-dislocating thing you do.**

"Butterfly," Daniel informs him, smiling more with his eyes than his mouth.

"Is it difficult?" Todd tries, angling his head so the bedside lamp shines on his face.

"Difficult?" Daniel shrugs. "I mean, it's sometimes hard pushing yourself. I find butterfly the easiest for me, but there are some people who find it the hardest. It's really just about what you're good at and what you enjoy."

There's clearly a science to swimming. Todd isn't stupid; a lot of time and effort goes into something like that. "I think I'd be great at sinking."

Daniel smirks and rolls his eyes. "I doubt it."

"I almost die every time I have to walk up these stairs. I'd drown before I got to the other end of the pool."

"What?"

Todd types it out on his phone again.

Daniel laughs as he reads. "I'm sure there are arm floaties in your size."

Todd pushes at him under the covers. "How considerate."

"I'm always *really* considerate."

Todd wants to agree with that, because Daniel has considered his needs and his situation. He's probably raised that way. But they're teasing now, so there's no room for being nice.

"Who said that? Because I've only ever heard *you* say that and I don't think it counts."

"Wait," Daniel says, and chucks a paperback from his side of the bed, hitting the light switch, and Todd is momentarily blinded by the sudden light. "Sorry. It became too difficult for me. Can you repeat please?"

"I said: Who said that? Because I've only ever heard *you* say that, and I don't think it counts."

"It's my house. I decide if it counts or not."

"Oh, my god, is this not a free country?"

Daniel smirks. "It's free if you agree."

A part of Todd wants to move closer and press his face to the place where Daniel's shoulder and neck meet. He doesn't. He gives Daniel a gentle kick under the covers.

"When's your next competition?"

"Sorry?"

"When's your next competition?"

"Next week." Daniel eyes him. "Do you want to come?"

Yes. "Sure. Are you going to wear those shorts?"

His question makes Daniel frown, until his realization dawns. "Oh, that. No, it's called a drag suit. It's to create more drag when you're practicing, so that you're faster when you compete."

"Huh." Todd blinks. So there *is* an entire science to this. "Does drag mean that it's heavier?"

"Basically, yes. The suits we compete in create much less water resistance."

Stifling a yawn, Todd eyes him. "I think I like the ones you wore today better."

"Remind me to get you a pair."

"I don't think it's the right season for swimwear," Todd points out, and his chest is warmer than it's been in a long time, if ever.

"You're hanging out with the wrong people then." Daniel chucks another paperback at the light switch.

Chapter Seven

NATURALLY, BECAUSE THINGS ARE GOING great, they have to turn to shit.

Todd is working, going over their shortlist of artists that are about to exhibit when Cruella sweeps through the doors. She's wearing fur, per usual, but considering the fall weather outside, it's more legitimate this time around.

"Todd," she greets, flinging her arms out.

Todd resists rolling his eyes as he closes the folder with the list. "Gloria."

"I'm so sorry about what happened," she says in a tone that doesn't make her sound sorry at all. "You know how it is with competition. Sometimes you have to seize an opportunity when you see it."

Unease crawls up his spine as he scrutinizes her. She has made things up before, just to make herself sound better, but there's something about the pleased expression on her face that makes him suspect that this time there's something behind her words.

"What do you mean?" He hates giving her an advantage, but there's nothing else he can do. He needs to need to know what she's up to.

"Giselle. Such a talented girl. I know she's your friend, but sometimes money speaks louder than friendship." Gloria gestures airily, and Todd tries to remember if he's ever told her about Giselle and her upcoming exhibition. He doesn't think he has, which makes this even more worrying.

"What about her?"

"I offered her money up front, not only commission from sales. I'm so sorry, darling, but that's business for you, right?"

He doesn't point out that the norm is for new artists to get commission from sales. She's always done things differently.

Taking her word that Giselle decided to exhibit somewhere else would be stupid. He's going to have to ask Giselle directly, but his stomach is tight with worry and suspicion.

"I don't really care," he says, because he comes up with nothing else. He doesn't want to ask too much or give away anything. She doesn't need to know about their financial trouble.

"I just wanted to apologize personally."

"Sure. We appreciate it. Have a good day."

Pressing her lips together, Cruella sweeps out the door. As soon as she is out of sight, he grabs his phone and types a text to Giselle, asking her if she's still planning to showcase with them. This could be just another of Cruella's lies, and, if it is, Giselle shouldn't be pulled into the drama.

When his shift is over, Giselle still hasn't replied. There could be any number of logical reasons for that, that doesn't have *anything* to do with her choosing another gallery. *But… it can't be this difficult to reply with just a quick yes, can it? Even if she's working, or painting, she should've been able to reply.* It occupies his mind on his way home, and he's almost run over twice when crossing the streets.

His parents aren't around when he gets home. *Crap.* He could've used the distraction of talking to Dad or having Mom entertain him with stories from work. He focuses on studying for finals and finishing a school project. Giselle still hasn't replied when he's finished, and the voice at the back of his mind telling him they've lost her, grows more and more insistent.

It takes three days to get an answer, and that's only because he spots Giselle outside one of his classrooms.

"Giselle!" he calls.

The crestfallen look on her face tells him everything, even before he has the chance to catch up to her.

"So, it's true?" He stops in front of her with his heart somehow both sinking and racing.

"She offered me a lot of money," Giselle whispers. She doesn't quite look him in the eye, and color is rising to her cheeks. "I'm really sorry, Todd. I appreciate the fact that you reached out to me, but I have to think about myself and I want to make a living out with my art."

Anger coils, hot and prickly, in his stomach. *How freaking difficult could it be to just say this right away?* But instead of giving in to the urge to say something rude really loudly, Todd takes a deep breath, pushes away the worry about how they're going to keep the gallery afloat now, and mentally counts to ten. Despite his anger, a part of him can understand her. Most of the people he's surrounded with every day are in the same position: worried about leaving college and wondering if they're going to be one of those who succeed or one of those who don't. He can't blame her for seizing a better opportunity. However, he does blame her for handling it utterly crappily and putting him in a terrible position.

"No, I get it," he sighs. "But you should've told me."

"I'm really sorry." She looks as if she's about to cry.

"I probably would've done the same." Shrugging, Todd shoves his hands into his pockets. "I hope it will be a success."

He doesn't. He wants to, but he doesn't.

"You're not mad?"

"I am, but I can't blame you. We're all trying to make it out of here with some kind of success, right?"

"I'll call Mrs. Floral today."

"You should. She deserves to hear it from you."

Giselle nods, visibly swallowing, before she hoists her bag up farther on her shoulder. "I'll see you around, Todd."

✳   ✳   ✳

MAYBE GISELLE ALONE WOULDN'T BE so bad, but several of the other artists also decide to leave. They're her friends and naturally they're going to hear about getting paid better next door. Todd can't blame them, either.

He's not surprised when he's met by Mrs. Floral's pale face the next time he comes to work. In just a few days, things have turned from carefully hopeful to a black hole, swallowing up anything that even resembles hope.

The gallery is empty now, compared to only six months ago. The walls seem bare.

"We're going to have to close," she says, and Todd sinks down in the nearest chair.

"All right." It's as if he's a balloon, deflating with every second that passes, as the cold, hard truth about their situation dawns on him.

"We did our best, honey, but sometimes it doesn't work out no matter how hard you try."

"I really thought it was going to work out," he whispers.

Mrs. Floral pats his cheek, as if *he's* the one in need of comfort. "You did an amazing job. I would never have come this far without you."

"How long do we have?"

"We'll close up after Christmas."

"I'll have to tell the kids."

It's the worst thing Todd can remember doing in a while. His stomach aches as he stands in front of them. He's supposed to tell them about Dadaism, but he can't pretend his mind isn't elsewhere, that everything is going to be okay.

"So, I have something to tell you."

"Are you dying?" Logan blurts and Clara shrieks.

"No!" Todd hurries to say. "No, I'm not dying. *No one's* dying."

"My grandma's dog is dying," Raina says. "She has cancer."

Wow, that came out of nowhere. "I'm sorry about your grandma's dog, Raina."

"It's sad, but she's in pain now, so it's better." It's matter of fact, as if she's repeating words her parents have told her fifteen times already.

"It's okay to be sad anyway," Todd says, making his voice gentle. "Will you be okay when I tell you something else that's also sad?"

"Did someone else die?" Logan asks, eyes big and horrified.

"No Logan, no one died." Todd sighs and drags a hand over his face. *Jesus. This isn't going as planned.* "I don't have a good way to tell you this. I wish I didn't have to at all, but it's only fair that I tell you before I tell your parents. We're going to have to close the gallery, and *Kids & Canvas* won't continue next semester. I'm so sorry. I know you guys like being here and hanging out with you is the best part of my week."

There's a long, stretched-out silence. Jamal stares at the table, his hands wrapped hard together, knuckles turning white. Logan has collapsed backward in his chair, staring at the ceiling, and Clara looks at him as if he's cancelled Christmas.

"I'm sorry," Todd whispers. "I've been trying to fix this, but I *can't*. I'm so sorry."

Jamal doesn't say or do anything for the remaining thirty minutes. Todd wants to talk to him, but not in front of the other kids. He'd like to offer a hug, but he's the one who failed them.

When the gallery is empty and the kids have been picked up by their parents, he sits on the too-low, pink plastic stool in their room and cries.

He can't fix this.

At home that night, he sits on the floor trying to make Sandwich jump the obstacle. The fact that she refuses has very little to do with Todd still wanting to cry. So he calls Mela.

"The gallery is closing," he greets.

There's a moment of silence before she says, "What?"

"Cruella stole some of our artists." He picks at a rip in his jeans. They're worn, and should probably go into the trash, but they're his most comfortable pair. "All of them, actually. She offered them more money than we can, any money, to be honest, where we only pay commission. There's nothing we can do about it. The kids' program is gone as well."

"That sucks," she says, voice quiet. "I'm really sorry. I know how hard you've been working."

"It really does suck," Todd agrees. "What the hell do I do now?"

"You find another job."

She's right, of course. He needs the money, like every other college kid, and he needs something to put on his resume. A gap wouldn't look good at all. But the kids? For them there are not a lot of other options. For some, there are none.

It sounds as if she's opening the squeaking doors to her closet.

"I'm coming over, all right? Let's hang out tonight."

It's not really a question. First of all, Todd's never going to say no to hanging out with her. It's been a while. Second, even if he did, she would've showed up anyway. She never lets him wallow alone.

An hour later, the doorbell rings, and Todd can hear Dad's overjoyed, "Mela!"

They've been friends for so long that Dad considers her a part of the family. It's as if his favorite child is coming home whenever she visits.

The next moment, his bedroom door opens, and Mela enters in bright green pants and a polka-dot shirt.

"Heya," she says and walks over to him, where he's still sitting on the floor. She crouches and hugs him, presses her cheek to the top of his head, and digs her fingers into his upper arm. "Do you wanna play cards?"

They do—that silly game they came up with when they were eight that doesn't make all that much sense—and Mela wins every round, but Todd doesn't care. He's just grateful that she's here.

"Did you have to cancel anything important?"

She meets his gaze over the cards. "This is the most important thing right now."

"Playing cards?"

"Beating your sorry ass so hard that you forget about being sad."

Todd snorts, but his chest is warming. "Gee, thanks."

"And I've missed you a lot lately. Any excuse to hang out is a good one."

"Jesse won't be annoyed?"

"If Jesse gets annoyed about me wanting to be there for my best friend when he's having a rough time, he's not a guy I want to date."

Biting back a smile, Todd takes his turn and picks a card. "Did you tell him as much?"

"I didn't have to. I told him I had to be with you today and he was A-okay with that."

"God, how is he so great?" Todd sighs dramatically. He means every word, but she doesn't need his approval.

"He also gossips a lot, so I happen to know that you spent an extra night at Daniel's."

Instead of looking at her, Todd focuses on his terrible hand. "Do you have any reliable sources for that?"

"I have you, and the way you're totally avoiding this question tells me everything." Mela smirks, as she wins another round. "Did you bang, or what?"

"Who the hell uses that expression anymore?" *Or ever.*

She points at herself and pauses as if she's about to mic drop. "Me."

"No, we didn't *bang*. We're friends."

At that, she shrugs. "Sometimes you can be friends who bang."

"We're just friends without the banging." He flicks his hand of cards at her.

"Do you like him, though?"

He doesn't know why the thought of denying it crosses his mind. "Yeah. I think I do."

"Maybe tell him that."

"No." His palms grow sweaty from the thought. "There was this moment where we were joking around and having fun, when I was so sure that we were gonna kiss. It was the perfect opportunity. And we didn't."

"So?"

It's Todd's turn to shrug now. "So clearly he doesn't feel that way."

"It's not like you kissed him and he turned you down. Maybe he thought the same thing about you."

"He's the one who stepped back, not me."

"The fact is still that *you* were the one to turn him down, if you recall? It's only logical that you also reach out to him if you've changed your mind."

"I'm not logical," Todd sighs. "I'm a *coward*."

"A coward with pride issues," Mela amends, and Todd suspects that it might be the most accurate description of him of all time.

"I'm working on both."

"I know. I still love your proud, coward ass."

Laughing, Todd leans back against the side of the bed and rests his head on the mattress. The paint on the ceiling is cracked only when stared at. Maybe he needs to stop looking for the cracks.

"When are you guys getting married?" he asks, steering the conversation to Mela and Jesse.

"God, stop that. We haven't even been dating for six months."

Collecting the cards and putting the drying rubber band around them, Todd leans back against the bed. "Lots of celebrities marry after a month or two."

"They also tend to get divorced within less than a week."

"So maybe you guys could make it to two."

"You're terrible. I'm gonna give you away to Daniel, and he'll have to take care of your sorry butt."

That doesn't sound entirely terrible, but thinking about Daniel takes his mind to weird places where it really shouldn't be.

"Are you staying for dinner, though?" he asks instead of indulging in that subject.

"Of course I'm staying for dinner. I'm staying the night."

Todd chest swells until he's sure that his ribs are going to crack. He might be losing his job, but he still has her. Whatever happens, he'll *always* have her.

Dad and Mom are thrilled to have Mela over for dinner. Todd doesn't mind their focus on her. Perhaps they won't notice he's down.

"So, Daniel told me that you're coming to the meet on Saturday?" Mela asks him later when they're sitting on his bed with Sandwich between them.

"He asked me if I wanted to come, and I figured why not?"

"I'm glad that you're hanging out by yourselves."

"He's fun, and I'm just happy that he wanted to forgive me."

Mela looks at him. "So, you're really not going to tell him that you like him?"

Shaking his head, Todd reaches for Sandwich. "I don't think so. I think that would ruin everything all over again."

"I don't think it would," Mela says, nudging his foot with hers. "But it has to be your choice."

"I think I'm just setting myself up for another failure."

"It's not a failure," she protests. "I'm also convinced that Daniel wouldn't stop hanging out with you if you told him and he said that he wasn't interested."

"I think *I* would, though. It'd feel like he just did it to be nice." Todd takes a breath and decides to steer the conversation elsewhere. "Did you know that his parents are famous, by the way?"

"Yes, I've been to his house."

Todd grimaces. "I literally only realized the other day. I'm such an idiot."

Tipping her head back, Mela laughs. "Didn't you *meet* his parents when they came to the gallery?"

"I did! I think I must've been too confused and stressed, because his dad was *right in front of me* and not *once* did I think 'Hey, aren't you the guy my dad gushes over at least once a week?'"

"I don't know how you function in modern society."

"Once I even asked him, a hundred percent serious, if his mom was an interior designer, and I thought he looked at me a little weirdly, but it didn't make sense until the other day."

Mela hides her face in a pillow and she's laughing so hard that she's honking. Todd's okay with that; he thinks he was pretty stupid too.

"I talked to Evan," he says after a long silence while Mela braided her hair and Todd beat his streak on his latest phone game obsession.

Mela pauses. "You did?"

"Yeah, called him." Out of the corner of his eye, he can see her straighten up.

"How did it go?"

"Okay, I guess. We talked for a bit. He said that he would call me back soon, but it's been over a week." Admitting that he's worried about being brushed off again is difficult. Deciding to call Evan was hard enough, and now he's thinking that maybe it was all in vain. They might be back where they started.

"Did you call him?"

"No, but I wasn't the one making promises and then breaking them."

She reaches over to squeeze his hand. "Okay. I see why you're hesitant. Wait a couple of more days and then send him a text?"

"I might." Evan is the only person who can make him feel angry and guilty at the same time.

"I figured we should have brunch after the meet," Mela says then, as though sensing that Todd isn't in the best place to talk further about Evan.

"Maybe that French place we went to for my birthday?"

"Oh, yes." She nods eagerly. "I don't know if they like French food, but they'll have to starve if they don't."

"Seems fair, considering they've been the ones competing," Todd snorts.

"Definitely fair."

✳   ✳   ✳

EVAN CALLS HIM TWO DAYS later and Todd's thumb trembles over the ACCEPT CALL button for several rings before he manages to pick up.

"Hello?"

"Todd?"

"Hi."

"Hi."

Evan sounds just as relieved as the lightness in Todd's chest. The tension leaving his shoulders makes him sag in his desk chair.

"Is this a bad time?"

"No, I'm just studying. I could use a break."

"Okay."

The break turns into an hour of talking movies and Evan's current job, which is the production of a pretty cool superhero TV show that Todd thinks that he might need to start watching.

Still, he's at peace when they hang up. *Baby steps*, he tells himself.

Going to the meet that Saturday is a welcome break from studying. Todd is familiar with the place now and climbs the stairs with Mela to find decent seats. He still doesn't know when Daniel or Jesse will be swimming, and Mela doesn't seem to know either.

To his surprise, Ava is climbing the stairs with two people he now recognizes easily. Daniel really does look a lot like his dad, and his mom is talking on the phone.

Both Daniel and Jesse win all of their heats, and Todd doesn't know why he's sitting on needles the entire time they're in the pool. They seem to move through water so effortlessly, as if they belong there.

However, when they go to lunch afterward, Daniel is quiet and closed off in a way that Todd hasn't seen him since they weren't friends. He looks… drained. Todd suspects that it has something to do with him, but he can't for the world understand why. He tries to think over the last time they met or talked, but there's nothing he can think of that could have made Daniel angry. On the other hand, he's come to accept that he's pretty good at doing and saying hurtful things without realizing it. He should probably ask.

Jesse and Mela talk as though nothing's going on while they look through their menus. Todd focuses on his own, making half-assed attempts to sign the fruits in the smoothies under the table, just for practice. He can't fully sign them, of course; even the sign for *fruit* requires him to put the ASL sign for F to his cheek. He's been trying repeat the signs for words he knows when he comes across them. He wonders if there's something wrong with his hand anatomy, because some things he just can't get right.

He's signing "berry" when a prickling feeling at his neck makes him look up and he wants to sink through the floor when he notices Daniel watching him. There's something definitely off with him, and Todd lets his hands fall into his lap; his nails dig into his palms as his face grows hot. He doesn't know if he should apologize or say something else, but the waiter saves him when he saunters over.

"Ready to order?" he asks.

Jesse and Mela order in an instant, and Todd picks the first thing on the menu that catches his eye. To his surprise, Daniel doesn't say anything, but gives Jesse a nod. Clearly, Jesse knows exactly what he means, because he says, "He'll take the same as me, please."

Daniel keeps quiet during lunch and is either checking something on his phone or concentrating on his food, and Todd leaves with an itch under his skin. He's sure that he's messed something up, but he doesn't know what or how.

At home, Mom and Dad are cooking together. He's surprised to hear them speak Spanish, since Dad has almost stopped doing that. It makes his throat go a little tight.

"Hey," he says, as he walks past. "I wanna be alone for a bit. Let me know when dinner's ready."

Mom tries to say something, but he shakes his head and heads to his room. Sandwich is fed, and her cage has been cleaned. It's probably Dad's work. He does that a lot, though he likes to pretend that Sandwich is nothing but a messy pet that eats a lot of pellets.

If he's done something to offend Daniel, he wants to apologize, but he wants to know *what* he's done so that he can avoid doing it again. However, he's definitely risking coming off as an insensitive dick for not even knowing what he's done wrong. On the other hand there's no way he can make anything better if he doesn't ask and then apologize. Before he can decide what to do, his phone buzzes with an incoming text from Daniel.

> **Can I stay at your place tonight? I'm having a bad day and my dad is around.**

Todd starts typing a reply, but then hesitates.

< **Definitely. My parents are home, but you're more than welcome**

> **Are you sure?**

< **100%**

> **Can you tell them that I'm HoH? I'd normally do it myself, but I don't have any energy.**

< **Of course!**

Going out in the kitchen again, pulse picking up, he clears his throat. "I'm having a friend over for dinner tonight, and he's staying."

"Is it the Daniel friend?" Dad asks.

Todd sighs. "Yes, and we're really nothing but friends."

"What did I miss?" Mom looks at them as if she expects an answer.

"I have a friend whose name's Daniel," Todd says, speaking fast to make sure Dad doesn't get a say. "Dad thinks he's my boyfriend, and he's not. He's had a bad day and he wants to get away from home for a bit."

Mom looks as if she wants to ask, but apparently something in his expression makes her change her mind. "Of course, honey. We have plenty of food and we have a spare bed in Evan's room."

Todd's shoulders sag. "Thanks. He's hard of hearing, so make sure to face him when you talk and don't interrupt each other, so he can read your lips."

Dad nods, and his gaze grows distant the way it always does when he makes a mental note of something. "Okay, is there anything else we can do?"

"He's usually okay with telling you what he needs himself, from my experience, but I don't know how he feels about that today."

"It's going to be fine," Mom says, radiating calm. "We'll make it work together."

Todd wants to hug them, but instead he pulls his phone out and types.

< Just talked to them. You're more than welcome to stay for dinner and then stay the night. When will you be over?

The reply is almost instant.

> When can I come?

< As soon as you're ready

> I'll be there in an hour tops

Todd tidies the worst of the mess in his room and shoves some of his dirty clothes under his bed. Mom is going to kill him if she finds out, but the important thing is for Daniel to have someplace he feels okay. Todd will hand over his bed and sleep on the couch or in Evan's room. Mom probably meant for Daniel to sleep there, but that doesn't seem right.

Daniel shows up fifty-three minutes later—it's not as though Todd kept track or anything—with a bouquet of flowers in one hand, a bottle of wine in the other, and a bag over his shoulder. He looks less closed off, but wearier, as if someone's dumped a bunch of worries on his back.

"Hey," Todd says, stepping aside. "Are you okay?"

Daniel smiles and nods, but it doesn't look entirely genuine. "Sorry for dropping myself on you without a warning."

"I did get a warning," Todd protests. "And it's definitely nothing you should apologize for. I'm happy that you're here."

"So, your parents," Daniel says, gaze flickering around as though he expects them to appear at any moment. "Do they know that I need to read lips? It might be trouble for them, especially tonight, because the battery for one of my hearing aids just died on the way over, and I forgot to bring a spare."

Todd thinks his chest is going to crack. *Trouble?* "They know. I just didn't want it to be more difficult for you than necessary. And you're never *trouble*. We'll make it work."

"Thank you." Daniel's smile is small, but at least it looks as if he means it.

"If it's too difficult, I got a big text app," Todd says, frowning as he holds up his phone to show what app he's talking about. He waits until Daniel looks at him again. "So we can type instead?"

"Great. Thank you."

"I just want you to be comfortable," Todd blurts, and his face grows hot instantly.

"I know. Come on," Daniel says, voice soft. "Introduce me to your parents so I can hand over these."

Todd holds the flowers and the bottle while Daniel removes his coat and his bag, leaving them both in the hallway. Maybe Todd aches for an entirely different reason, when Mom and Dad turn around to greet them when they enter the kitchen. Mom gushes over the flowers and Dad compliments the wine way too much, but the tension bleeds out of Daniel's shoulders.

A moment later, he wants to bury himself in the nearest pot, because as Daniel looks around, he realizes that the cards he's made to practice signing are taped up all over the place. When their eyes meet, Daniel's gaze is hot, and there's a barely there smile on his lips. He doesn't comment, but it doesn't seem he disapproves.

Todd's chest is on the verge of bursting throughout dinner, with the way his parents really make an effort, not interrupting and talking over each other as they usually do. Tonight, they make sure to look Daniel in the eye and take turns. Dad doesn't turn away even once when he speaks. Dad's accent makes it more difficult for Daniel to read his lips, but Dad just asks for a good app when Daniel gets frustrated, and Daniel helps him put it on his phone. He and Daniel talk about accounting. Dad types and types and types in his slow, one-fingered way, and Todd just watches with a lump in his throat.

Daniel, for his part, is super-polite and he has hidden his troubles under a smiling mask. A month ago, Todd wouldn't have been able to tell, but he can see the cracks in that mask now.

"We'll be in my room," Todd tells them after dinner.

"Thank you for dinner, Mr. and Mrs. Navarro," Daniel says, smiling as he stands up. "It was lovely."

"Thank you for joining us, honey," Mom replies, voice warm. "And for the beautiful flowers."

Dad, on the other hand, gets up from his chair and does this thing where he clasps Daniel's shoulder and squeezes slightly. Daniel blinks and his cheeks grow pink, and Todd wants to be embarrassed, but this is his dad caring.

"You're welcome here anytime you want, son."

"You can go to my room. I'll get your bag," Todd tells him and he's a little surprised that Daniel only nods and does as he suggests.

Mom and Dad are filling the dishwasher when he walks past the kitchen. They talk in quiet voices and don't seem to notice him. Todd stops in the doorway, clutching the strap to Daniel's bag.

"Thanks," he tells them, and they straighten with their hands full of dirty dishes. "For being great. And stuff. That means a lot."

Mom looks as though she's going to say something, but Todd smiles and continues to his room. It's not a discussion they need to have. He just wants them to know that he's noticed and that he cares. Before he closes the door after him, he hears Dad say, "I'm the great, and you're the stuff." Mom bursts out laughing.

Back in his room, he finds Daniel on the floor with Sandwich cradled against his chest. He looks worn out, as if he's run fifty miles uphill and hasn't stopped to take a break—until now.

"Hey," he says, stepping into the room.

Daniel looks up. "Sorry," he says, gesturing at Sandwich. "I came in here and when I sat down, she came up to me on her own."

"No need to apologize." Todd shakes his head and drops Daniel's bag next to him on the floor. In reality he's pretty happy to see them getting along. It usually takes a lot of edible bribes for her to like new people. Daniel must have a magic touch. "She wouldn't let you hold her if she didn't want you to, believe me."

Daniel smiles then, and Todd thinks his ribs are going to crack when he sticks his nose into the soft fur between her long ears. Putting Sandwich on his lap, Daniel reaches for his bag and puts a small case on the floor next to him. Then he opens pockets, rummaging around.

"I'm looking for spare batteries," Daniel tells him without looking up, so he's not expecting a reply. "I usually have spares in my bags, but I couldn't find any on the way here, but I know I should—" With a triumphant noise, Daniel holds up batteries. He switches out the dead one, then puts the aids in his ears. Some whistling and scraping sounds come from them before Daniel gets them right, and he looks up at Todd with a smile. "There we go. Thanks for letting me come over." Daniel is silent for a long while, but Todd can sense something else is coming. "Your parents are really great."

"Sometimes they're not," Todd confesses. "Sometimes they're nosy, and my dad tends to forget that I'm my own person."

"Why's that?"

"Well, he wants me to take accounting, and I don't want to be like him."

"Because he's an accountant?"

"Accounting manager. He's really proud of his profession." Todd shrugs. Being an accountant is nothing compared to being a sports commentator on TV or owning a huge kitchenware and cookbooks brand. "My mom's a librarian."

"That sounds really cool. I wish my parents had more normal jobs. Especially my dad." Daniel sighs. "I think he'd be easier to deal with."

"Are you okay?" Todd asks. "If you don't want to, we don't have to talk about it. I just want to make sure that you're okay."

"I will be," Daniel says, shrugging. "I'm sorry I was rude at lunch."

"You weren't rude."

"Not socializing around other people is rude."

"Sometimes you don't feel like talking to anyone. That's okay. I was glad you were there to begin with."

Daniel smiles. "I was pissed because the starting official at the meet refused to use hand signals, even though he *has* to. It made my start late, and I got behind."

"But you won." Todd knows, because he was there. Judging by the grimace on Daniel's face, it's the wrong thing to say.

"This time. Maybe I won't next time if it happens again." Daniel clears his throat. "It's not as much the fact that I got behind in a heat I won anyway. It's more the fact that he refused to accommodate me, even though he knows I don't wear my hearing aids while swimming. It's been a while since that happened. It always makes me feel like I'm an odd piece in the puzzle. That I'm not *really* supposed to be there."

Todd sits opposite him; their knees touch. "That's not fair. For you to feel that way, I mean."

Daniel shrugs.

"But you're *really* supposed to be there. I mean, I don't know anything about swimming, but just watching you compete I can tell that you're great. *Anyone* can see that. It's like you were *born* to be there." He squeezes Daniel's knee, the way he got his own squeezed such a long time ago. "You shouldn't have to put up with that treatment. It's not right. But please don't feel like you're the faulty piece and not him. He's the one who's somewhere he shouldn't be. You're *exactly* where you're supposed to be. Being discriminated against can never be your fault."

Daniel looks down, and Todd swallows when he presses his nose into Sandwich's fur. For several breaths, Todd thinks he's messed up. When Daniel looks up, his eyes are glassy. Todd's hands itch to reach out in a hug.

"I think I would've been okay with that on some level, if it wasn't for my dad being an asshole when I got home after the meet."

Todd hesitates. "Do you want to talk about what happened?"

"There's not much to say, really. He basically told me that I shouldn't make such a big deal out of things that are bound to happen." He takes a breath. "Not with those words exactly, but that's the meaning of it. He doesn't mean it like that, and I know it. I think it's his way of encouraging me, and he thinks he's making me stronger by saying that. But my hearing loss isn't a burden to other people."

"No, it goddamn isn't." Todd squeezes Daniel's knee harder. He has no clue what else to say, but Daniel continues anyway.

"Sometimes I can just brush it off, but at times like today, I just can't stand him. I felt like I had to get out of there." Daniel lets Sandwich go when she starts to struggle against his grip. Without her, he looks more vulnerable. "I really appreciate this. That you could have me over with such short notice."

"Any time. My parents love you." Todd hesitates, because he also knows that his dad can be limitless when it comes to certain things. "I tried to explain to my dad that you're not my boyfriend, but I'm not entirely sure that he believed it. Just so you know, if you talk to him at some point and he says something weird."

"Come again?" Daniel says. "You explained what?"

"That you're not my boyfriend. I don't think he believed me. I wanted to tell you in case he says something weird."

To his surprise, Daniel's face splits into a grin. It's the most genuine thing Todd has seen all night. "Don't worry about it. He seems like a cool guy."

"When he wants to be," Todd amends, because compared to what Daniel's dad said, his own is definitely great. Then, he remembers Daniel catching him signing under the table at the restaurant where they had lunch. "So, um, I don't know if it was tactless of me, what you saw in the restaurant earlier and, um, the cards all over my home."

Daniel's eyebrows climb. "The what?"

"My bad attempt of practicing signing under the table and trying to learn."

"Why would you have to apologize for that?"

"I don't know. It's a habit I've developed, to practice the few words I know when I come across the objects. I've discovered that menus are really good for that."

"Todd," Daniel says. "You don't have to apologize for learning how to sign. I appreciate that you do that. You don't have to do it under the table in a restaurant to hide it from me."

"I just felt stupid. I'm not very good."

"Well, if I tried to learn Spanish right now, I doubt I'd be very good at it either. It takes practice and a lot of patience."

Todd nods, but Daniel needs to know that there's a little more to it than that. "I did tell you that I don't have the easiest time with theoretical stuff, right?"

"Sorry?"

Todd repeats the question.

"Right," Daniel confirms.

"So, I've been trying to learn for a while. I want to do my part. It takes a lot of time for me, and I don't want you to think that I'm not trying, because I *am*, it's just—"

"Todd," Daniel interrupts. He squeezes Todd's fingers; his gaze grows warm. "You're not trying to make me someone I'm not, and I'm okay with you the way you are too. Today, seeing you practice some signs and seeing these cards that you've made… It makes me really happy. Really, really happy. It's okay that some things take time."

Relief punches through him. He wishes he could kiss Daniel right now. He wants to. He squeezes Daniel's fingers back instead. "I just want you to know that I'm doing my best."

"That's more than enough."

For a moment, they only look at each other, and Todd wants to kiss, touch, *anything*. But he can't. When Daniel's gaze falls on something behind his back, Todd lets out a breath.

"You still have the painting," Daniel points out, and, when Todd looks over his shoulder, there's the oil canvas he was working on the last time Daniel was here.

"Yep," he says, after turning back to Daniel. "Why?"

"You still won't let me buy it?"

Shaking his head, Todd smiles at Daniel's disappointed frown. He won't sell it to him, but he'll definitely give it as a Christmas gift.

They don't talk much after that. Daniel is pale, dead tired from a bad day and having to concentrate so hard on reading lips, and Todd really can't blame him for that at all. He has days when he doesn't want to see another human being's face.

Daniel plays with Sandwich, and Todd tries to finish up some last-minute flashcards for his studying for finals. It's late when he looks up and finds Daniel dead to the world on the floor with Sandwich curled on his chest.

Oh, god. Taking pictures of people sleeping is way too creepy, but if it wasn't, he would, so that he could capture this moment with a good conscience. Instead he allows himself to look for a while, to take in the rise and fall of Daniel's ribcage and the way Sandwich's nose twitches in her sleep. Carefully, he removes her from Daniel and puts her into her cage. She's so tired after all the playing that she barely opens her eyes before she goes back to sleep.

Daniel, on the other hand, blinks rapidly as soon as Todd's fingers touch his shoulder. It's less intimate than touching his cheek.

"Hey," Todd says and can't help but smile when Daniel's eyes find his. "I think my bed's more comfortable than the floor."

Daniel looks around as though he hadn't realized that he's on the floor. Then he nods.

"Come on." Todd helps him to his feet, and Daniel winces when he stretches his legs. He undresses swiftly and apparently doesn't care that he hasn't brushed his teeth. Todd knows that level of exhaustion.

He watches as Daniel slides under the covers, and suddenly his own body aches to go to sleep. "I'll be on the couch," he tells Daniel, smiling, when their eyes meet.

Daniel frowns and pats the empty spot next to him. "Get in."

"It's really not a bother," Todd says, but then Daniel folds down the duvet on the side closest to Todd and pats the mattress again, and

Todd *knows* that it's okay. They've shared a bed before. He just had to make sure that Daniel really is okay with it today too.

"Okay, I'll be there in a minute."

When he comes back after brushing his teeth, Daniel is asleep again. The case for his hearing aids and his wristwatch are on Todd's nightstand. He shifts, still unconscious, when Todd gets in. The bed is already warm and welcoming after the cold, hardwood floors. Just as he's drifting off, Daniel mumbles something under his breath, probably in his sleep, and Todd smiles to himself.

When he wakes again, Daniel's face is pressed against his neck, and hot breath is tickling his ear. Todd swallows. He's woken up with his own face pressed against Daniel's arm, sure, but this is so intimate.

Glancing at Daniel's wristwatch lying on his bedside table, he finds that it's still way too early to get up and decides to go back to sleep despite Daniel spooning him.

In the morning, Daniel wakes first and Todd wakes a second later when Daniel moves away from him and then reaches across him. There's the sound of something snapping shut, and then the sounds from Daniel's hearing aids before he's gotten them in place. Blinking, he finds Daniel sitting up in bed, hair in disarray, and with marks from the sheet on the side of his belly.

"Good morning," Todd says, and signs it at the same time. Daniel smiles as he signs it back to him.

"Did you sleep well?" Todd asks.

"Yes. Did you?"

"I did. I was really tired, so it wasn't like I had trouble falling asleep."

"Me either, apparently," Daniel snorts. "I can't believe I fell asleep on your floor."

"It's happened to me more times than I can count," Todd says. He stretches under the sheets, loving the way his spine pops and limbs protest. "I hope I didn't kick you while I slept."

"What?"

"I hope I didn't kick you."

"You kick me at least twice every night," Daniel tells him and then he smirks. "But it's not too bad."

Todd has to look away when Daniel stretches his arms over his head. When he turns back, Daniel is still looking at him.

"You should know," Todd says. "We've shared a bed several times."

Daniel smiles, then. "Why spend time on making extra beds and more laundry, when this is completely fine?"

"You're not the worst bed partner I've had." Todd does his best to keep a straight face.

"Do I even want to know?"

"Probably not, honestly." Todd specifically remembers the time in high school when they had five people in a queen bed after a horror movie marathon. The bones in his back must have aged ten years during that night.

"I'm glad to hear that though. Sadly, you're probably the worst one *I've* ever had."

"Oh, my god," Todd groans and shoves a pillow at him. "You're the worst."

"I'm also not serious."

"You're lucky or I'd let you go home without breakfast."

"Do you have plans today?" Daniel asks.

"Just covering for Mrs. Floral for a couple of hours at the gallery, but other than that, nothing."

"Working?"

Todd nods. "For a couple of hours."

"Do you mind if I stick around?"

Todd looks at him. *Is this about his dad or does he just want to hang out more?* Either way, he's always up for spending more time around Daniel. "Sure. You can either come with me to work or stay here. It's your call. My parents will probably be around if you stay here, though."

"What?"

"You can come with me to the gallery or stay here. But my parents will be around."

"I'll stay here. I'm sure Sandwich can use a friend."

"Don't say I didn't warn you about her peeing, though."

"I'm starting to think you made that up."

Todd wants to be around when Sandwich pees on him the first time. It's going to be wonderful. It's really not a question of if, but *when*.

They eat breakfast alone at first, but Dad shows up for a third cup of coffee and lingers. He seems to enjoy talking to Daniel.

"So you're going to Harvard?" he asks, which is apparently something he caught in yesterday's conversation and types something on his phone before showing it to Daniel. It must be the same question he just asked, because Daniel replies,

"I hope I'm going to Harvard, but I don't actually know yet."

Dad types on his phone again, and Todd manages to catch a **They'd be happy to have you**.

Daniel looks at the screen, and a small, almost shy smile spreads across his lips. "Thanks."

It's strange leaving Daniel behind when he goes to work. The gallery is slow per usual, but Todd has grown to appreciate it in a new way. In a few weeks, he won't be able to come back here. Is Daniel still interested in the space? If they can't keep the gallery, making it into a meeting spot for kids who are deaf or hard of hearing is the best option Todd can think of.

With a lump in his throat, he welcomes a patron. His copy of *History of Modern Art* is lying on the counter. He should bring it home. It's been here since just before midterms. He hasn't had use for it since, with all his flashcards and notes from his classes, but it's the newest edition, a good eight hundred pages, and it cost him a freaking fortune. There's no way he's leaving it behind.

The bell over the door chimes fifteen minutes before he's off duty, and he assumes that it's Mrs. Floral until he glances up and finds Daniel strolling through the doors. Compared to how weary and tired he was last night, this is a completely different person. He's smiling; the air around him is carefree. He signs *hello* when he steps inside the door, and Todd repeats it.

"Sorry to bother you at work," Daniel says and leans against the counter with both arms. "I just figured that the weather is nice, and I could maybe pick you up and treat you to lunch?"

"Not a lot happening here anyway." Todd gestures around the empty reception area. "Lunch sounds great, but you don't have to treat me."

Daniel's cheeks are red, but right now, Todd doesn't think it's just because of the cold outside. "It's a thanks. For yesterday."

Todd resists the urge to touch him. "You don't have to thank me. I don't mind being there for you if you need someone. Actually, I'm happy to help."

Daniel smiles then. He's got such a great smile. If he had an excuse to see Daniel more often, he would, just to talk and see him smile. He's brought back to reality when Mrs. Floral comes in, waving to them over a takeaway mug. She beelines for the office with a smile that makes Todd want to blush.

"Has this been here since last time I was here?"

Turning back to Daniel, Todd finds him holding his book. *Was the gallery tour around midterms? Possibly.* "I think so. I studied for that midterm here with the book and then just used my notes before the actual test. I should probably sell it back. We only used it for the first half of the semester. Such a waste of money."

"I didn't catch what you said after selling it back."

"We only used it for the first half of the semester. It was such a waste of money."

The expression on Daniel's face is unreadable, and Todd wants to ask, but he doesn't know how. *Why was your face doing that weird thing just now?* doesn't seem like a good way to put it.

"What do you want for lunch?" Daniel asks before Todd has a chance to get his brain in order.

"I know this tiny burger place that's really good." Just as they're about to leave, Todd having grabbed his coat, he adds, "We couldn't save the gallery."

A second later Daniel wraps him into a hug so tight that his bones protest, but Todd doesn't mind. He thinks that maybe, eventually, things will be okay.

Chapter Eight

Todd can't quite let go of what Daniel said before they parted that Sunday.

"Have you asked anyone for help?"

He hasn't. Mom and Dad don't know. Actually, no one knows except Mela and Daniel, and Evan knows a little. It's possible that either one or both of them have told Jesse, but he doesn't know for sure. Asking for help is the last thing he wants to do. That's letting everyone know that he can't do it on his own. It's admitting defeat, isn't it?

He kicks a stone as he walks down the sidewalk, having just left the gallery. It's so empty now, the walls naked and bare, and the kids are upset a lot of the time.

It's getting dark, as the coming winter has made the days shorter and the evening come faster. He pulls his coat tighter around himself and picks up the pace. It wasn't this cold this early last year, was it?

Mom and Dad aren't around when he comes home. He has a vague memory of them mentioning going away for a few days, but he's been sweating over finals whenever he's home, so he hasn't been paying attention lately.

He suspects that asking for help now would be useless anyway. What could anyone help him with? The gallery is closing, and that's that. Still, it would suck if he found out later that there was something he could have done. He knows himself well enough by now; something like that would break him, and he wouldn't be able to let it go.

He doesn't know how many times Mela has told him to stop letting his stupid pride get in the way. So maybe it's time.

He sends a group text to Mela and Daniel.

< **Hey, so the gallery is most likely going to close up as you already know. A bunch of artists left us for another gallery. Do you guys have any ideas of what we can do to save it? I don't want this to be happening.**

He tries to not sound desperate, but he isn't sure if he succeeds. In less than a minute, Mela replies.

> **They're in swim practice for another hour, but let's set up a crisis meeting at my place and we'll brainstorm until we have a master plan**

Todd swallows the lump in his throat, because he knows that she'll do her utmost. But he also knows that she has finals, too, and she's putting that aside for him.

He calls her immediately.

"Can you come over right away?" Mela asks as a greeting.

"Yeah, but is it okay? I know you have finals."

"It's fine. I actually plan my studying."

Todd rolls his eyes, but it's really just to keep himself from being too mushy. "Okay, I'll be there."

"I'm sure Daniel and Jesse will turn up after practice."

"It's okay if they don't."

"Don't be silly," she says, voice warm. "Despite all their aspirations to run the world, they'll make time for this, I'm sure of it."

Todd isn't as convinced, because he knows how much Daniel is stressing over his finals, and if Jesse is planning a political career, then he's probably in the same boat. However, thirty minutes after he gets to Mela's, the doorbell rings, and a moment later there are two familiar voices in the hallway.

Todd shuts his eyes and then straightens as their voices grow stronger, coming closer.

"Thank you," is all he comes up with, when Jesse and Daniel enter the kitchen. They look as though they've come straight from practice, with Daniel's hair still wet, and they smell faintly of chlorine. Jesse clasps his shoulder hard, but Todd thinks that maybe it's his way of being reassuring. Daniel, on the other hand, just sits on the chair next to him and squeezes his knee.

"You needed our help?" Jesse prompts, signing as he talks. His eyes are bright and he's rubbing his hands together as if he can't wait to get started.

Todd swallows his knee-jerk reaction to deny that he needs their help. He's brought them here instead of letting them study. He can at least be honest about needing their help.

"Yeah." He scratches his knee through his jeans. "We had a plan to save our gallery and managed to get a bunch of people from school to agree to exhibit. There are some really talented students graduating this year, and I thought it would be our only shot."

Jesse nods, interpreting while Todd talks, and Todd is momentarily brought out of his explanation when Jesse holds up his hand as if asking him to pause, pulls out a notepad, and scribbles on it.

When Jesse nods, having put the pen down, he continues.

"Um, and it seemed to be working. I mean, the gallery wouldn't make a lot of money, but maybe it could be a way for us to at least stay afloat until we got something better, you know? But then, I find out that the gallery next door has offered them money up front, whereas we could just offer them commission."

He shrugs, trying to shake the heaviness from his shoulders.

"I just don't want to give up yet, but I don't know what to do."

There's a silence around the table, until Jesse has finished translating and then taking a couple of minutes to jot down some notes. He puts his pen down. "So, what kind of assets do we have among the four of us?"

Todd blinks. *What does that even mean?*

"My mom has press contacts," Daniel says immediately. "If we had a story to sell them, she can get it out there."

"Same here." Jesse nods. "It's definitely important to reach out. It doesn't matter how great the gallery is if no one knows it exists."

"I don't really have a story to sell them," Todd says.

"Do you remember when we discussed this the first time you stayed over at my house?" Daniel asks. "That you could brand it as a gallery that would be a great platform for graduating art students from your college, because it's Brooklyn-local and add more famous artists."

He does remember that. There's just one problem. "I think I could get the students if we had the more famous artists, but we don't."

"In reality," Jesse says. "You'd probably only need one or two. That way, we could get the word out. You could have a reopening with this new concept, and we could let local news sites and papers know about it. After that, it shouldn't be too difficult for you to get of new artists."

"I don't even have one or two." It's ridiculous that he's an art student, but he has zero contacts in the industry. If he'd been more like Evan, he probably would've had a hundred names to pick from.

"But you know someone who does," Mela points out, just as Todd realizes the same thing.

"I can't ask him," he mutters.

"Why not?" Mela asks. "He already offered, and you do talk again. Letting Evan help you isn't a bad thing, Todd. If you need his help to succeed, it won't make your success any less."

"I agree." Daniel squeezes Todd's knee again. "It's still your thing. You still did this, even if you had help."

Todd is quiet for a long while, his head spinning with doubts. Asking Evan for help is admitting that he's better even at something that's Todd's. However, if he doesn't ask Evan for help, there won't be anything that's his in a couple of months.

"All right," he sighs and picks up his phone. "I'll call him."

"Do it, and we'll see if we can come up with a less-vague idea." Mela nods at him, smiling, and he pretends his stomach doesn't hurt as he closes the door to her bedroom and presses Evan's name.

He picks up on the second ring.

"Hello?"

"It's me," Todd says. "Is this a bad time?"

"No, of course not." He can hear a door closing on the other end and a lock turning. "I just got home."

"I need to ask you a favor. You're free to say no, but you're kind of my only hope. I wouldn't ask if you hadn't already offered."

"What is it?"

"The gallery is about to close, but I don't want to give up. I've got this idea that my friends helped me with, but we need someone who's famous, so we could actually get the media to care."

"So, artists?"

"Yeah. If you know anyone?"

Evans hums. "I know several people. How much time do I have?"

"Well, as little time as you can manage."

Evan laughs. "Give me a week and I'll get back to you."

Todd's throat is so tight that he can barely get the words out. "Thank you. Are you coming home for Christmas?"

"Can I? I managed to get some time off."

"Yeah. I think I'd like that."

There's silence on Evan's end, until he clears his throat and says, "Then I'll be there."

In the kitchen, Jesse is scribbling on his notepad, and Daniel and Mela are both leaning over his shoulders to look. As soon as he steps through the door, all their focus is on him, though.

"He'll do it."

Jesse punches the air as if he's just won a heat, and Mela rounds the table to hug him. It looks as though Daniel is on his way out of his chair, too, but Mela reaches him first.

"Talk to Mrs. Floral," she says. "I think we have people to contact at most of the important platforms you could use to get this out. These guys have hooks out all over this city."

"Thank you," Todd says, and his cheeks hurt from how big his smile is. "You guys are the best."

※　　※　　※

"I'M NOT SURE WE HAVE finances to stay afloat that long," Mrs. Floral says, and Todd's good spirits plummet in an instant. "I have to admit, I'm not that knowledgeable, but I've managed this place for a long time now."

He's asked Evan for help. *Evan*. He can ask Dad too.

"Can I borrow the books? My dad's an accountant. Maybe he can take a look." Todd shrugs. He knows nothing about accounting and finances. There might not be any use for his dad to take a look, but it's worth asking him.

"Of course, honey." Mrs. Floral pats his cheek, her fingers trembling. "If you manage to do this, and I hope you do, you can consider this your own gallery when I retire."

"You're not allowed to retire," he says immediately, but the idea of it vibrates between his ribs, making his fingertips tingle as he grabs the books from the desk. "I'll let you know tomorrow."

"There's no rush, honey."

Oh, but there is.

Dad's having his evening coffee in front of the TV when Todd barges in. Daniel's dad is on the screen, talking about tactics or something, and it's a bit too weird to wrap his head around.

"Can you help me with something?" he asks, and Dad looks up as if Todd has just told him that he's seen a dragon outside.

"Help you?" Dad asks, as if he wants to make sure.

"The gallery isn't doing well, and I'm trying really hard to save it. I've got this plan that my friends and Evan helped me with, but Mrs. Floral doesn't think we have the finances to keep the place open long enough to make it happen." Todd holds the books in his hands; his fingers are stiff from clasping them too hard.

Dad looks at them. "She does it by hand?"

"Uh. Apparently?"

"Jesus. Okay, hand them over and let me have a look." He heaves a sigh when Todd puts the books on the coffee table. "This might take a while. Put some more coffee on, will you?"

Todd hovers; for the second time this week, he isn't sure if he's going to cry or break open.

"Did you want something else?" Dad asks as he grabs his glasses from the table.

"Just to give you a hug," Todd says before he knows what he's saying. The stricken look on Dad's face says everything about how long it's been since Todd offered him a hug. Feeling as though he's five years old again, Todd wraps his arms around him and slouches a little so that he can press his face against Dad's shoulder.

"Thank you," he whispers. "You're the best dad."

"And you—" Dad begins, voice thick. "—are one of the two best kids out there."

"Sap."

"You're the one crying, not me."

But when Todd backs away, wiping his cheeks with the back of his hand, Dad's eyes are wet too.

"Now get that coffee going and leave me alone." Dad doesn't pull off looking stern, but Todd does what he says anyway, and he sends a text update to Mela, Daniel, and Jesse.

It takes hours. Todd refills Dad's cup more times than he can count, but he doesn't dare interrupt the concentrated look on Dad's face. There are notes that Todd doesn't understand, and Dad's muttering under his breath. He doesn't seem to notice that Todd is in the room.

He's scrolling through every social media site he can think of for the fifth time, when Dad finally appears in the open door to his room.

"I have good news."

Todd almost drops his phone as he jerks upright in bed. "You do?"

"Yes, there are some cuts you can make that haven't already been made. I don't know how much time that will buy you, but it's something." Dad hands over a bunch of papers. They don't make a lot of sense to Todd, but he hopes that they will to Mrs. Floral.

"Thanks. This… Thanks." Todd clutches the papers.

"Can we talk about something else?" Dad asks and sits on the edge of Todd's bed.

"Um, yeah, sure." After putting the papers in his bag, he sits next to Dad.

"It's about Daniel."

Todd rolls his eyes, because *god*. "He's not my boyfriend. I already told you!"

"But he wants to be," Dad says with a smile. "And you want him to be. So why isn't he?"

"No, he doesn't." Todd sighs. "Maybe back in September, but not anymore."

Dad shakes his head. "He does. I've seen the way he looks at you."

"That's just his personality. He's like that with everyone."

"Todd, I've been around a lot longer than you. He wants to be more than just your friend. You didn't even sleep in separate rooms when he was here."

These ideas aren't welcome right now. There's no room for them. The only thing that's keeping him from falling for Daniel completely is reminding himself of that Daniel doesn't feel the same way. Dad shouldn't be telling him this.

"It's not going to happen. I'm trying to accept it."

Dad ruffles his hair. "You've been stepping out of your comfort zone a lot lately. I'm proud of you. I'm not going to push you, but you should think about talking to him."

"Thanks, Dad." Todd rests his head against his shoulder, allowing himself to take that to heart.

✳   ✳   ✳

TODD HAS FINISHED TWO OF his finals when they have another meeting at Mela's. Her parents are rarely home, living the life of a successful doctor and a scientist making groundbreaking discoveries in cancer treatment, so it's the easiest spot to gather.

"I talked to Mrs. Floral after asking my dad for help," Todd says, waiting for Jesse to interpret before he continues. "And she doesn't think the extra money will last that long."

"So we need a donation," Mela states.

Todd grimaces. "Yeah."

"My mom will make one," Daniel says easily, as soon as Jesse has interpreted for him, as if it's not a big deal, and Todd frowns at him. Daniel gives him a small shrug before he continues, "If we can get this thing to happen, there will be media exposure. If she makes a donation, her name will be connected to something positive, and she'll get exposure in return. It's a win-win and not a lot of money for her in comparison to buying an ad."

Jesse nods. "For sure. Talk to her. If she isn't up for it, I'll talk to my parents."

"It's that easy for you?" Todd asks, and he wonders if he's the only one with his mind boggling. It's as though they're talking about who's going to buy the coffee, not donate *actual money*.

"It's all business," Daniel explains. "My mom's great at business. She'll see the opportunity and take it."

"It feels a bit like charity to me."

"It will definitely look like my mom did a nice thing for the gallery and art students, but it's a cheap way of getting publicity *and* doing something positive."

"Wow, there's really no good in the world," Todd snorts, making the rest of them laugh.

"Not when it comes to making money," Daniel agrees. "But sometimes you can make it work in your favor, right?"

"If you can make it happen, I'll be forever grateful."

Daniel does make it happen. Two days later, Todd gets a text from him.

> **My mom wants to have you over for dinner and talk about the gallery. Already made sure you get a donation, though. I think she just wants to know what to tell people when they ask.**

Todd winces. Meeting the parents? Daniel has already met his, but that was different. His parents are *normal* people. Daniel's parents are people who are somehow untouchable, people you see on TV but who don't actually exist in real life.

< **Oh god. When? What do I wear?**

> **Are you free on Friday?**

< **Yeah. I'm gonna die**

He doesn't die, but he's nauseous as he rings the doorbell to Daniel's house. He's able to find the way on his own now, and there's a terrible wait while his brain tries to figure out how he should react if one of Daniel's parents opens the door.

To his relief, Daniel is on the other side when the door swings open. *"Hello,"* he signs. *"How are you?"*

Todd only remembers how to sign that he's doing good, so that's what he does, and Daniel's grin totally calls his lie.

"Is this okay?" he asks, gesturing at his button-up with zebra stripes and his dark jeans. Mom wanted him to go super-formal, but that would suffocate him.

"You look great. You really don't have to be nervous at all."

Todd gives him a flat look. That's easy for Daniel to say, since they're his parents. They changed his diapers. *It's not the same thing!*

"My mom is pretty chill." Daniel nods toward the staircase while Todd removes his shoes.

"Did *you* just say chill?"

Rolling his eyes, Daniel walks backward up the stairs. "Who do you think I am? Of course I say chill."

"This is probably the first time I've ever heard you say such a youthful word."

Daniel barks out a laugh. "I don't know why we're friends."

Elizabeth Berger is in the kitchen, looking like one of the stills from her cookbooks with her yellow dress and her light pink apron. Her hair is blond, but not as light as Daniel's and his dad's. When she notices

Todd, her face brightens in a smile that's so much like her son's that Todd is a bit overwhelmed.

"You must be Todd," she says. Her voice is smooth and warm, just the way Todd recognizes it from the commercials. She signs as she speaks. "I'm Elizabeth."

"Nice to meet you, Mrs. Berger," he says, shaking her hand.

"Please call me Elizabeth. Daniel tells me that you're trying to help art students." She releases him in favor of patting Daniel on the cheek, and Todd gets flashbacks from every time Mrs. Floral does that to him. "He gets invested in everything, this one. You're going to make a great lawyer."

Daniel's smile falters, and Todd hurries to say: "Yes, well, I work at this gallery, and we want to try a new approach."

"They want to create an opportunity for local art students to take the first step after graduating," Daniel fills in.

"It's really difficult to make a career in art," Todd explains. "If we can even help a few, it would be amazing."

"Oh, I completely agree." Elizabeth nods eagerly. "Let's discuss this more over dinner. Daniel, go get Ava and your dad."

Being left alone with Elizabeth Berger is almost as intimidating as it would be to be left alone with her husband. Just *almost*, and Todd is secretly grateful for that.

"It's so nice to finally meet you," she says, as she removes the pot from the stove. "Daniel has been talking *so* much about you, and I couldn't resist lending a helping hand when he asked me to. This dinner is really just to finally get a face to the name." She winks, and Todd doesn't know where to put his hands.

"Um, well, this is the face," he tries and is relieved when she laughs as if he was intentionally funny.

"I can definitely see why Daniel has been raving so much about you," she says, still signing. Maybe it's not even a conscious choice she makes anymore. That would make sense.

"I haven't been raving," comes a voice from behind Todd, and Daniel is back with Ava in tow.

"Hey, Todd," she says, signing as well, and this time she doesn't look as though she despises him. "What's up?"

"Did you teach Daniel to say chill? Because my mind was blown earlier," Todd says, and Ava gives Daniel a skeptical look.

"Can you even put it into context?" she asks.

"Why do you make it sound like I'm forty?"

"Duh," Ava says, exchanging a look with Todd that makes him feel as if he's winning. They're *bonding*.

Todd smirks at Daniel, who fails spectacularly at glaring. He's just about to say something, when a familiar man strides in as if he's walking on stage in front of a crowd.

"Todd!" he exclaims and grabs Todd's hand to shake it so fiercely that it feels as though his entire arm is going to come off. "It's so nice to meet you."

"It's nice to meet you too, Mr. Berger," he says, having to resist rubbing the life back into his fingers when his hand is released.

Mark Berger is a person who takes up a lot of space, not only because he's a tall guy with broad shoulders and definitely a hint of his old professional football career in his body, but also because he talks a lot and he talks so *loudly*. Todd's ears are sweaty after twenty minutes into their dinner. He's learned more about professional football than he has in his whole life.

"Todd, I have to tell you the story of how I got my nickname," Mark begins, and Ava groans. She's been interpreting for Daniel, for which Todd is grateful. He's noticed that Ava and Mrs. Berger sign constantly while speaking, but Mr. Berger only does it on occasion.

"You really don't. We've heard that story a thousand times, and no one cares."

Mark Berger has a nickname? Todd had no idea.

"It's a good story," Mark protests, but his brilliant TV smile has diminished.

"It's really not." Ava shakes her head and picks up a carrot with her fingers, ignoring her mom's *manners* as she puts it in her mouth. "It's actually a pretty terrible story."

Daniel snorts into his food, and Todd has to bite his lip hard to keep a straight face. He isn't sure if this is regular procedure in this family, or if he's witnessing the start of a war. When he glances at Elizabeth, however, it seems as if it's the former.

"You have been overruled, love," she says to her husband, and Todd suspects that they let him have his own show for a bit, probably not listening that intently, before they can ignore him with a good conscience. "Please tell me more about your gallery, Todd."

He swallows a too-big bite of food and winces at the way he can feel it go all the way to his stomach. *Smooth.* "What do you want to know?"

For the next two hours, he's asked questions he doesn't know how to answer. They sound so grown up and *professional*: about the business plan and if they've made a SWOT analysis. When Todd doesn't know how to answer, Daniel fills in for him, and apparently Jesse has done a whole bunch of things in that notepad of his, because Daniel has really great answers to most of the questions. All Todd has to do is explain why it's so important to him.

"I grew up in Brooklyn, and art has always been very prominent there. You can see it everywhere," he explains. "I'm sure you know that. The gallery where I work has been like a second home to me, and Mrs. Floral is such an important person in my life. For me, art was the only thing that made sense when nothing else did. I felt like there was a space for me there, when I couldn't find one anywhere else."

He takes a swig from his glass and sneaks a look at the people around him. He expects them to look politely bored, but there's actual interest on their faces.

"Mrs. Floral is one of those people who donates everything she can to people who need it more and she always tries to see the best in people. Working for her and getting to do one of the best things I know was a dream come true. I got to see the sometimes-nervous artists come look at their work hung up for people to see. For some of them it was maybe the first time anyone could look at their pieces, you know? And I've seen people find a chance to catch their breath in that gallery. Sometimes they come in and they're stressed out and then they disappear in the gallery for hours. When they leave, they're like new people.

"She just didn't have the best business plan, I guess," he continues. "And we realized too late that we weren't doing very well financially and that we were losing artists to our competition. Now, when we have a plan for how we want to do things, we don't have the funds to get the ball rolling."

"That's where I'm able to help," Elizabeth says, after exchanging a look with Daniel. "My company would like to donate. Art and opportunities for college graduates are two very important things, both to me and to our society in general. I would consider it an honor to give you a helping hand until you're able to get back on your feet."

Daniel had already told him that he would get the donation, but relief punches through him like a blow to the gut. It takes all he has to not sag on the chair.

"That… it— Thank you, Mrs. Berger, that would make a huge difference."

"It's Elizabeth to you, honey."

Mark hasn't said anything after being told off by Ava, and Todd isn't sure that he's listened to anything that's been said, but it doesn't really matter.

"Are you staying over, Todd?" Elizabeth asks, and Todd is instantly pulled from his thoughts.

"Um," he says, glancing at Daniel who gives him a nod-shrug combination that pretty much translates to *if you want to*. *Does he* want *to*? He probably shouldn't but being around Daniel is like scratching an itch these days. "If that would be okay."

"Of course!"

*   *   *

"I JUST REALIZED THAT I don't have any extra clothes," he says when Daniel has closed the bedroom door behind them. "I should probably catch a train home."

"I have clothes." Daniel shrugs.

"Can I borrow a shirt?"

"Sure. I'm sure we have extra toothbrushes as well."

Todd thinks about saying no anyway, but he likes hanging out with Daniel and now when his mom has offered to donate enough money to maybe save the gallery, it seems rude to leave.

"That would be nice, thanks."

To his surprise, they don't watch TV shows all night. They're lying on the bed, face to face, talking about really stupid things like Daniel's pet hamster that ran away at least a dozen times and once his mom had to have some of the floorboards in the living room removed to get it out. They mostly use the big text app on Todd's phone when things get long and complicated, since Daniel is tired, and Todd tries out a few signs he remembers. It's not a lot, but Daniel's eyes light up every time.

"Thanks for inviting me over," he says. "I'm glad Ava doesn't hate me anymore."

"She never did."

Todd kicks his foot.

"She didn't! But she's not angry with you anymore."

"I only have myself to blame," Todd says, and the fact that Ava wasn't too happy with him doesn't really matter now, when he seems to have been okayed. He deserved it, and now he's been better.

"That's old now," Daniel says. "We're beyond that."

They are. Todd knows that they are. He looks at Daniel, at the light color of his eyes and his hair, and how all of his attention is on Todd now. The way Daniel talks to him is sometimes so overwhelming. It's as if Todd really matters to him, to someone who's planning on going to Harvard Law and do great things in life. Todd can't get over the fact that it was *him* Daniel reached out to when he wanted somewhere to go that Saturday. Now he's here, in Daniel's bed and maybe he messed up several months ago now, but things are better this way, aren't they?

His chest tightens uncomfortably as he tries to push away the fact that he's got it so bad. He's going to get over it eventually. He's done that before. There's no way he's allowing himself to mess this up again, and here's Daniel in front of him, smiling.

"There's going to be smoke coming out of your ears if you don't stop thinking so much."

"That obvious, huh?"

"Has been since the first time I met you," Daniel tells him, his eyes warm as he looks at Todd. "The only thing missing is rolling subtitles on your forehead."

Todd laughs, only partially to hide his embarrassment. "I haven't mastered my poker face just yet."

"I like that." Daniel shifts on the bed. "I'm good at reading people, but I like that I can tell when you're annoyed with me."

Or when I'm trying to avoid you, Todd types out, trying to get away from the potential *I like that it's so obvious that you're crushing on me.*

"That wasn't for very long. To be fair I was just as keen on avoiding you."

Todd thinks back on the dinner at Mela's and how he escaped the balcony as soon as Daniel got there. **What happened with the girl at Mela's birthday dinner?**

Daniel's gaze grows distant as he frowns, as if he's trying to recall. "We went out to a club with everyone else."

"I thought you dated her," Todd confesses.

"What?" Daniel asks.

"I thought you dated her," Todd repeats.

"We talked at one dinner." Daniel snorts.

"And that makes it impossible?"

"I was being nice and polite. She was great to talk to, a lot of fun. That doesn't mean that I want to get in her pants."

Todd pretends he's not relieved. "I know it's none of my business, sorry."

"I'm not that surprised. I remember you running inside the first chance you got when I tried to talk to you."

"What were you going to say?"

"I don't know," Daniel says, biting his lip. "Maybe trying to see if that person I hung out with an entire evening and night was someone who existed for twenty-four hours only or if he was still there."

Todd thinks the room has grown warmer, or maybe it's just him. "Was he?"

"Someone who only existed for one night? No. I hang out with him a lot now."

Todd resists the urge to bury his face in the pillow and grin. "I'm really glad that we do."

"Me too."

"I'm really glad that we're friends."

"So am I."

He decides to change the subject to something safer. "What are your Christmas plans?"

Daniel shrugs. "Nothing except for sleeping and not studying. And practice, obviously."

"Jealous."

"You?"

"I think Evan's coming home."

"Can you repeat that?"

"I think Evan's coming home."

Daniel stills. "How do you feel about that?"

"Okay, I think." Todd wiggles his toes and unlocks his phone. **I'm nervous that it won't work out. That we've been not-talking for so long that we're just not going to be able to be around each other like normal siblings. But I miss him.**

"Of course you do," Daniel says softly. "He's your brother."

He types again, with more hesitation this time. **Yeah, and he's trying hard. I mean, so am I, but he's sort of the one having to prove a point, and I have to work on forgiving him.**

"I don't think either of those is easier than the other," Daniel tells him. "Forgiving someone can be hard, even when you know you should."

"Was it hard for you?" Todd asks.

"Not when you apologized," Daniel says. "I think I had already forgiven you at the time, and when you apologized to me, it felt like I was okay with moving on. You obviously meant what you said, and I could tell that it was hard for you."

"Do you think I should be ready to forgive him?"

"That can never be my call to make," Daniel says, nudging him. "It's also vastly different to be hurt by someone you've met once and someone who's your family and you should be able to trust with anything."

Todd stays quiet. Daniel is right. It's different for sure; Evan has been someone he's looked up to most of his life, and then he felt betrayed by him.

"What about you?" Todd asks then. "How are things with your dad?"

"Sorry?"

Todd types it out.

"Same as ever." Daniel shrugs. "You saw how he is. That's him on a good day. That's him making an effort."

Do you clash, or did something happen?

"I don't know." Daniel looks away, maybe choosing his words carefully. "He's never been that much of a parent, you know? At first it was football and then he was a TV personality all of a sudden. He wanted me to do football as well, but I didn't like it that much. I guess he's so used to being liked and a bit of a star, that he's just never understood that sometimes he has to make an effort."

"How come?"

"Aside from his obvious need to get attention, it's just really difficult to be around him. Whenever I point out that I'd like his support with things, like the project I have with my friends, he thinks I'm being ungrateful, and we don't talk for a few days. He keeps telling me that I only want to go to Harvard because my grandfather said so and because I don't want to be like him. And I'm scared that he's right."

Todd reaches for Daniel's hand before he can stop himself. Here he is complaining about his dad badgering him about classes, when some dads are like this.

You haven't considered moving out?

"I have and I'm going to if I get accepted. Sometimes I want it to work, though. Other days I've already given up and I feel like I could just as well stop talking to him altogether."

"Would he listen if you told him this?"

"I doubt it."

Todd squeezes his hand. "Then that's his goddamn loss."

Daniel gives him a tiny smile. "Thanks."

"You can share Sandwich's cage if you wanna move out."

"Come again?"

Todd types it on his phone.

"Wow, you're so generous."

Todd laughs as Daniel pushes a pillow in his face. Fighting it away, he says, "You love her."

"She's cute."

"You know what else was cute? When you two were sleeping on the floor."

Daniel grimaces. "I had so much back pain the next day."

"That's not because of the floor sleeping. That's because you're *old*."

"I think she peed on me," Daniel confesses with a grimace. "My shirt smelled weird when I got home."

Todd can't stop the laugh that bursts out of him, and the disappointed look Daniel gives him doesn't make anything better. "I *told* you!"

"I feel betrayed. I thought she was my friend," Daniel mutters, but his lips are twitching.

"I can't believe she peed on you, and you didn't even notice until the next day," Todd wheezes.

"I thought *you* were my friend too." Daniel snorts and kicks his leg. "Clearly I was wrong."

It takes Todd a while to sober up, but as he does, he feels unnaturally light. He watches Daniel lying on his back, carefully ignoring Todd's fit of laughter, and typing away on his phone with a concentrated look on his face. It's not even Christmas yet, but he knows from experience how quickly the spring semester passes. He reaches out to tap Daniel's arm to get his attention, and smiles when Daniel turns toward him.

"So, you're moving to Boston, then? When you get accepted."

"What?"

"You're moving to Boston when you get accepted?"

"If."

"When," Todd corrects.

"I think so. I think I want to go. It's close by, but I think it would do me good to be by myself for a while."

Todd nods and tries not to think about Daniel moving away. Boston really isn't very far, but sometimes Manhattan feels like the other side of the planet, and not just a train ride away. Boston is definitely farther. Travelling to Boston would require them to stay friends for that long, though.

"I'm gonna visit you if you move."

"I'm counting on it."

Todd smiles, his heart warming. "I might bring Sandwich, just for you."

"You sure know how to bribe someone."

Do you remember that time you got me that cold beer and you told me you had to kill a few people to get it?

To his surprise, Daniel's smile turns embarrassed. "Yes, but in reality, I just ran home and got one from our fridge."

Todd freezes as his brain tries to understand what Daniel just said.

"You did what?"

Daniel shrugs. "They were out of cold drinks, and it was just a couple of streets away. It was worth it."

"I think that's the nicest thing anyone has ever done for me," he breathes. "I mean, except for the fact that you guys skipped out on studying for your finals just to help me out with stuff."

"What?"

Todd repeats himself, less breathy this time.

"I'm too tired, can you write it down?"

He should've just typed it out from the start. He shows Daniel his screen; his cheeks warm as he watches Daniel read.

Daniel laughs. "Thank god you added that."

"Would you have taken all that back if I hadn't?"

"Definitely not. It was a good break. You would've done the same for me."

Todd's heart warms. "Yeah, for you I would've."

In an instant, Daniel becomes serious. "I have no doubt in my mind that you can pull this off."

"You don't? I doubt myself all the time."

"I think that's why you're going to succeed. You've worked so hard for this, made such an effort. It's going to work out."

He inhales deeply. **I just need an answer from Evan and I hope that I can actually put this plan in motion. If we have a good name to tell people, I'm sure more graduates would get interested.**

"That would definitely make it easier for you. Otherwise it would sound like a vague promise, and I think most people are cautious about those."

Todd nods. He would be too. Evan texted him yesterday to ask for more time, and that sucked, but right now giving Evan more time is his only option. A small voice at the back of his mind whispers that this is another empty promise, that Evan isn't going to call him and let him know if he found someone or not, that he's going to drop off the grid or shrug and say he was too busy to bother.

"You're disappearing into your head again," Daniel says, a little smile on his lips.

Todd grimaces and stretches on the bed. "Sorry, bad habit."

"It's going to be fine."

Todd is about to answer when the door bangs open. He jerks around, and Daniel turns a second later, reacting to Todd. His heart rate slows dramatically when he notices Ava in the doorway.

"Sorry," she says and signs, clearly not very sorry at all. "Were you making out?"

"What do you want?" Daniel sighs, and Todd remembers hearing the same question from Evan every time Todd barged through his bedroom door just to disturb. Evan's high school girlfriend hated him.

"I wanted to ask something, but I forgot what it was," Ava says.

"You wanted to snoop," Daniel states.

"Please, I already know." She rolls her eyes. "You might not wanna tell Mom and Dad, but duh, I'm not blind."

Todd wants to bury his face in his hands. God, he doesn't have much of a poker face, but he didn't think it was this obvious to people who don't know him that well. Apparently, his crush is visible as a freaking lighthouse in the night.

"Did you want something?" Daniel asks again, and he sounds sharper. Maybe he knows, too, and he doesn't want to embarrass Todd.

"Just your new Netflix password, since you changed it *again*."

"I'm not giving you my Netflix password."

"*Daniel.*"

"It's not going to happen."

"You're on my side, right, Todd?"

And then Ava's gaze is on him, and her eyes turn huge and innocent, as if she didn't just put his crush on her brother out there for everyone to see.

"Don't drag me into this," Todd says, holding his hands up. "I'm definitely not taking sides."

He smiles to himself as he leans back against the pillows, only half listening to their bickering. Daniel's home and his family are so well put together. They're perfectly fitting pieces to the same puzzle, and everyone has their part. Hearing them argue like real siblings, where Daniel is unreasonable and Ava sort of whiny and a bit spoiled, is definitely making them seem more human.

"Sorry," Daniel says when Ava bangs the door closed. "She's used to getting what she wants."

"Aren't you?" Todd asks, looking up at him from the pillow.

Daniel gives him a grin. "I always lose at home, so I'm only second place on the list of spoiled kids."

"Thank god, that makes it so much better." Todd rolls away, laughing, when Daniel throws a pillow at him.

"You're a terrible guest, insulting me like that."

"You obviously like having me here. You even let me sleep in your bed."

"It's clear that I need to work on my character," Daniel agrees and flops down next to him. "I do like having you here."

After a moment of silence, he adds: "I'm getting a serious headache from concentrating so much when we talk. It'd be great if we could just… not talk for a while. I'm pretty beat."

Daniel plays games on his phone, and Todd reads angry posts on social media and leans more heavily against Daniel with every scroll on his phone. He still smells so good.

The next morning, Todd wakes first, with his legs tangled with Daniel's. It's not that early, and he's definitely too awake to go back to sleep. Daniel looks as if he's far away still when Todd glances at him, and it doesn't seem right to wake him now when it's the weekend. Padding out from Daniel's room, Todd finds the remote and sinks down on one of the couches outside.

He turns the volume down so low that he almost can't hear anything, worried that it will disturb the rest of the family. However, since he's heard footsteps, at least someone else is up, but he's just too uncomfortable to go downstairs by himself.

After twenty minutes, there are steps in the stairs, and Ava's blond head comes into view. She waves at him over a glass of juice.

"Is he still sleeping?"

"Yeah, I didn't want to wake him."

She shrugs. "He's probably tired from studying. I thought I heard you get up—" Todd is just about to apologize when she adds, "—Daniel's never that quiet. Do you want breakfast?"

"Um, sure."

"Mom and Dad are already away. No need to worry about awkward parents."

Todd snorts. "Am I that easy to figure out?"

"Anyone who doesn't get anxious over talking to their kinda-boyfriend's parents is a liar or a sociopath."

"He's not my boyfriend," Todd sighs when they walk down the stairs together.

"I said kinda-boyfriend."

"He's not that either."

Ava slows for a step or two. "But you'd like that, right?"

"Um." *What's a polite way to tell someone that you're not comfortable talking with them about their brother?*

"I'm only asking because I already know that he's super up for that."

"He's not," Todd sighs. "I mean, really, he isn't."

In the kitchen, Ava hands him a bowl and gives him a skeptical look. "I took you for a smart dude, Todd, but I'm thinking I might have to take it all back."

"Ouch, thanks for that."

Ava opens her mouth to say something when a door bangs upstairs.

"I told you," she says. "You were way too quiet."

It's easy to follow Daniel's steps down the stairs and then to the kitchen. He appears in the doorway, hair messy and eyes merely sleepy squints. "Are you both already awake?"

"Even if we weren't before, we would've been now. It's like you're a cross between human and elephant."

Todd chokes on his coffee, and Daniel narrows his eyes at him.

"I definitely didn't catch that," Daniel says to Ava.

"I'll write you a note."

"Funny."

Todd watches and listens, as Ava and Daniel sign while speaking. By now, he's pretty sure that the signing is out of habit, but that the speaking is for him.

When Todd leaves a couple of hours later, Daniel hugs him in the hallway, and for some reason it feels like a goodbye. Todd aches as he pulls away, and the raw look on Daniel's face confuses him. *Why would they have to say goodbye?*

There's a lump in his throat the entire way home, as his brain tries to get a grasp of what's happened. *What if it has something to do with what Ava said when she barged in on them last night?* Maybe Daniel is at a point where he doesn't think he can ignore Todd's obvious crush anymore.

Todd sticks his hands in his pockets and walks home as fast as he can from the subway stop. He wishes he had mittens. *It wasn't this cold yesterday, was it?*

He pushes away any further thoughts of a possible goodbye as he bends over his books at home. He has two more finals and then he's done. He can do this.

Chapter Nine

EVAN CALLS HIM AFTER HIS second-to-last final.

"Hello?"

"I have some good news," Evan says, and Todd is instantly lightheaded with relief.

"You do?"

"Called in a couple of favors and I have two people for you to start with. You need to call them yourself, though, and talk to them. They're up for it. Maybe take a look at their work before you do—"

"Of course I will," Todd interrupts. "I'm not gonna call them without knowing what it is that they do."

"Of course not," Evan says quickly. "I'll text you their names in a bit."

Todd chews his lip; his hand trembles where he's clutching his phone. "Thank you, Evan. Really."

"I'm just happy to help." There's a pause. "I might not get it, but I've understood now that it's really important to you. I want to help where I can."

"It means a lot to me."

"I'm glad." Evan clears his throat. "Call them as quickly as you can. I think they have a lot on their tables right now."

Todd browses their websites that night. Renatta Fischer is a name he's heard. She was a student at his college five or six years ago and has since then made a name for herself with thread and rope creations in vivid colors and patterns. Todd looks at picture after picture; his chest grows tight with the amount of work in her pieces and how they catch his interest even without seeing them in real life. The second person is Emery Musayev, whom Todd thinks he met once during his first year in college. Most of his work is digital, and, from what Todd can tell from his website, his pieces are *massive*. One piece covers an entire wall, and the patterns are hypnotizing.

He thinks they'll fit, both with the gallery and each other, combining modern aspects of art and different mediums. Best of all, they've both already made names for themselves, and their work is frequently bought for quite a chunk of money. He'll call first thing tomorrow.

He's got his heart in his throat the next morning when he calls the first number Evan gave him.

"Fischer," comes the answer on the fourth ring.

Todd's voice gets stuck in his throat. "Hello, this is Todd Navarro. Um, I got your number from my brother—"

"—Evan, yes," she fills in for him, and there's instant recognition in her voice. *Thank god.* "How are you, Todd?"

"I'm good, thank you, how are you?"

"Splendid," Renatta says. "Are you calling about your gallery?"

"Yes," Todd says, relieved that Evan has at least told her that much. "I don't know how much he explained to you, but we're trying to combine exhibiting art from known artists with the work of college graduates to give them a step in the right direction after school."

"From what I understand, you're attending my old alma mater, right?"

"Yes."

"I think this is a great idea, Todd. Normally I don't stray from my idea of how to do my business, but this is for a good cause."

"If everything goes as planned," Todd says, almost tripping over his own words. "I think you'll have a lot of media exposure as well."

"And that is definitely worth a lot," she says. "When do you want to get this show on the road?"

"When are you available?"

"I can start tomorrow, but it will take me a couple of weeks before I have my work set up, and I will need access to the gallery."

Todd's pulse picks up, but it's not from nervousness or anxiety. "You got it."

"Meet me there at four, and we'll shake hands in person, okay?"

"I'll be there. Thank you so much."

"Pro tip for business in the future: Don't sound like I'm saving your ass. Say it like you're doing me a huge favor."

"But you *are* saving my ass," Todd whispers after she's hung up. The high of having a successful call makes it a lot easier to call Emery.

Evan must have had pretty big favors to call in from them, because Emery is also happy to help out.

Mrs. Floral is at the front desk when he gets to work that afternoon. She looks up at him and smiles as though his success is obvious. "It seems to me like you have good news to share."

"I have," he says. "We have a donation that will keep the gallery afloat until we can pull this off, and we also have two pretty cool artists that are interested."

Mrs. Floral's face softens into a brilliant smile, and the next moment tears roll down her cheeks. "Oh, honey, that's incredible."

She hugs him.

"We're going to make this happen," he says, patting her back. "You know that, right?"

"I knew it right from the start, hon. You've got it in you. All you have to do is put your mind to it."

Todd sucks in a breath, straightening where he stands, as if he's just grown a good foot from her words alone.

"We have so much to do," he tells her.

"And we will get right to it."

He sends a group text to Mela, Daniel, and Jesse, letting them know that the plan is a go.

Jesse and Daniel are going to handle the contacts with the media, and Mela is going to get the word out through social media. Todd, well, his job is to get some of his friends from school to agree to exhibit.

That Thursday, Todd's buzzing while he stands in front of the kids. They've lost their energy and their interest in the past few weeks, and he hasn't pushed art knowledge on them, when all they've wanted is to spend time together.

"So, I have some good and some bad news," he tells them, and Logan scrunches up his face as if he's going to start crying any second now, and Todd hurries to add: "Mostly good!"

"Why do you *hate us.*" Najwa sighs and flops her head down on her arms on the table.

"Come on, guys, just listen to me for a second." Todd crouches, resting his arms against the table too. "So, the good news is that the gallery isn't going to close. We're going to be here again next year, and *Kids & Canvas* is going to be here as well. Since we haven't had time to put the application for next semester on the website, you can all continue next semester if you want. I'll talk to your parents. *But,* we're going to have to close for a few weeks now, so we can open the place again next year, with a bang."

"With a *bang*?" Clara repeats and stares at him as if he's lost his mind.

"A reopening. We're going to make some changes to the rest of our work here, so we have to close up for a bit. But not *forever* and that's the important part, right?"

"We can stay?" Jamal asks, disbelief written all over his face as he stares at Todd.

"You can stay," Todd says, chest warming as Jamal bites the inside of his cheek and stares at the table.

They can stay, but so can he. Right here, where he belongs.

He bumps into Giselle after his last final. He's put his anxiety aside and is handing out flyers Mela gave him. That he stood in the bathroom on the verge of throwing up for twenty minutes before he got himself together is a different topic altogether.

"Hi," she says, stopping right in front of him. She's paler than usual, and there are dark circles under her eyes. Todd gets the impression that it isn't just because of finals.

"Hey," he says and expects to feel smug, but he finds himself only being able to feel sorry for her. "Are you okay?"

"Not really," she says and shrugs as if it isn't a big deal, but she looks as though she's about to break down in tears.

"What's going on?" Todd follows her when she steps off the path.

"I made a huge mistake by turning my back on you and Mrs. Floral for Ms. Sosa."

Huh. Todd has actually never heard Cruella's last name until now. "You don't have to feel bad about that. You were offered more money from her," he says, and it's easier now, when he knows that the gallery might actually make it, if all the pieces fall into place before January thirty-first, when they are going to have a reopening of the gallery.

"I'm actually not getting any money at all," Giselle sighs. "Apparently she doesn't have any. It's not just your gallery having a rough time, and when you and Mrs. Floral managed to make a one-eighty, Ms. Sosa has cut me off."

"She cut you off?" Todd gapes. He's dealt with Cruella before, but she's mostly appeared to be an overly dramatic woman who likes to make life hard for others in ways that are annoying, but not actually destructive. This is extreme.

"I don't know, she was pretty upset and said that I can't count on ever putting my work up on her walls." Giselle sighs. "I'm sorry. I just wanted you to know that I'm happy that things are going well for you. I'm sure it's going to be a huge hit. I'll definitely be there for the reopening. I've wanted to see both Fischer's and Musayev's work for years."

Todd hesitates. A bunch of people have applied for their student's spots, but he approached Giselle for a reason. She shouldn't have let them down. But he remembers his mom's words about holding a grudge: *People are fighting battles you don't know anything about.*

"I think you should be there because your art is on the wall, not as a patron," he says.

Giselle freezes. "What do you mean?"

"We all make mistakes, Giselle," he says. "I didn't approach you in the first place just because you're a good person, but because you're a great artist. I wouldn't be doing my job properly if I would pass up on having your art there for the reopening."

She looks as though she's going to protest, but then she closes her mouth. "This time, we'll sign a contract, all right? That way you won't have to worry."

"I'm not worried," he says, because he isn't. This time around, he's not dependent on her. He has something she wants, something to *offer*. It's the most amazing feeling.

*   *   *

EVAN COMES HOME THREE DAYS before Christmas. He stands in the hallway, looking as if he's aged at least five years since Todd last saw him, and at the same time as if nothing's changed. The strangest thing of all, he figures, is the fact that Evan is standing in the hallway *at all*. Todd hasn't believed that he'd actually be here. Well, until now, when he's standing right in front of him.

"Hey," he says, and the sound of his voice combined with the look on his face stabs Todd like a knife between the ribs.

He thinks that he's going to cry, but it's only the trembling in his body.

"Are you okay?" Evan asks, just as Dad comes out to the hallway from the kitchen.

Todd nods, then shakes his head, then nods again. Is he? *Maybe. Probably.* Seeing Evan like this, compared to speaking to him over the phone, makes all his old wounds raw again.

The next moment, Evan pulls him in for a hug, and Todd feels as if he's going to break open. He clutches Evan's shirt, hugging him for as long as he dares, before stepping back and wiping his eyes on his sleeve.

"Sorry."

"No, *I'm* sorry," Evan says, and his eyes are wet too.

"I know," Todd says quietly.

Thank god for Dad, because he wraps Evan into a hug, and Todd has a chance to escape to the kitchen to get some space.

Dad has made machaca con huevo, Evan's favorite, and Todd just observes. He knows that Mom and Dad have been to see Evan in Canada a few times, so it's not weird for them. To Todd, however, it's like there's a glitch in his brain when Evan takes his usual spot at the kitchen table. The last time someone sat on that chair was when Daniel came for dinner.

Todd hasn't seen him since the time he was at *Daniel's* for dinner, but they've texted since. Finals have gotten in the way, as well as planning for the reopening. Daniel and Jesse have been putting a lot of time into that in addition to studying and practice, so Todd hasn't wanted to bother him with asking if they can meet. Still, it gnaws within him, maybe there was something to his sense that they were saying goodbye. *But why would they?*

The longer he observes Evan, the more he comes to realize how much the same he is and so vastly different at the same time. He's got the same confident air, and he talks with an ease that Todd just never figured out. It's obvious that he's used to approaching people that he doesn't know. He's always been great at networking. However, where he sometimes was cocky, there's a humbleness to him now. He doesn't push his ideas where they're not wanted or offer his opinion where there's no room for it. He takes up space, but he doesn't steal it from anyone else. *So maybe almost getting fired was good for him.*

"When do I get to see your gallery?" Evan asks him when they're all in the living room later, playing board games.

Todd shrugs. "Tomorrow, if you want. I'm going there anyway to make sure that they have everything they need."

"Okay." Evan nods.

Todd's quiet for most of the evening. He thinks about texting Daniel but decides against it. He'll do it tomorrow.

✳   ✳   ✳

TOMORROW TURNS INTO AFTER CHRISTMAS, and then there's New Year's, and he's invited to Jesse's for dinner. Todd dresses to impress. He even wears *slacks* and a freaking bowtie. No suit jacket, though, because it's just really inconvenient at all times.

Evan has promised to pick him up afterward, which is nice. He's meeting some old friends, and Todd hasn't dared to ask Daniel if he can stay over. Mela is obviously going to stay with Jesse.

Mela meets him at the stop, and they walk together, huddled in their coats. The sidewalks are slippery, and Todd has to steady himself several times against lamp posts and other objects that won't topple over.

"The food is going to be amazing," Mela says. She has glitter on her eyelids and a really puffy skirt on her dress.

"Is he a good cook?"

She snorts. "He's terrible, but there will be a chef."

Todd almost slips. "A *chef*?"

"I know, ridiculous, right?" Mela rolls her eyes, and Todd wishes that he had brought a suit jacket anyway.

"Why can't he just order pizza?" he mutters. "Like normal people."

"Can't order pizza if you want to be the next president." It sounds as if Mela has had this discussion with Jesse before.

"I'd vote for a pizza kind of president."

"Me too."

Todd bites his lip. He doesn't want to ruin the evening, but he needs to talk to his best friend.

"Out with it," Mela says before he has the chance to say a word.

"I think Daniel is avoiding me."

"He's not," she says immediately.

"I think he is." Todd takes a breath. "Last time we were *alone*, he hugged me when I left, and it felt like he was saying goodbye."

"Have you talked to him?" Mela asks. Of course she has to ask *that*. Todd might have overcome a lot of things recently, especially regarding his pride. However, talking about his feelings with someone, particularly someone like *Daniel*, is still too scary for a coward like him.

"No."

"And you're not going to try?"

"Probably not," he sighs. "I'm all for personal development and stuff, but—"

Mela interrupts him with a loud snort. "I've missed you."

"I've missed you too."

"How about we hang out next weekend?"

"All weekend?" Todd asks, just to make sure.

"At least."

"I think that's exactly what I need."

Jesse's house is impressive, and Todd gets the feeling that Jesse's parents probably are well known to people who are into politics. Todd only knows the big names, but he doesn't know a whole lot about everyone else.

There are a couple of other people there that Todd doesn't recognize, but Jesse introduces him and makes him sound as if he's someone that matters.

"This is Todd Navarro; he's the driving force behind the nascent-artist project I told you about earlier."

And Todd shakes hands and smiles and makes sure to remember their names. Evan has told him that networking is important, and these people? They're the ones he should make connections with. He does his best not to feel like an idiot for being the only one who's not wearing a suit jacket. They're in *college* for Christ's sake.

"Um, thanks for that," he tells Jesse when the rest have moved on to talk sports. "For introducing me."

"Of course I'm going to introduce you to my other guests." Jesse clasps his shoulder. "I like the idea of bringing cool people together."

"Ugh, who made you this nice?" Todd groans, and Jesse laughs.

"Come on, Daniel is about to be here any minute."

Todd swallows and straightens his bowtie. He wishes he could have worn a beanie. It would make him less self-conscious about his hair.

He's talking to Mela in the dining room—it's all dark wood panels, open fireplaces and chandeliers—trying not to be intimidated by the number of forks on the table, when Daniel shows up with a guy in tow that Todd doesn't recognize. He's tall, and chubby, and his hair's a little on the long side of a surfer's cut. His face is kind, with round cheeks and laugh lines around his mouth and eyes.

Daniel has cut his hair, just a little bit, making him look polished in his suit. Todd's fingers itch with the urge to grab Daniel's tie and pull him in for a kiss. If only he were allowed to do that.

Daniel hugs Mela, and Todd expects things to be awkward, but then Daniel hugs him, too, and this time it doesn't feel like a goodbye.

"Nice to see you," Daniel says, smiling.

"Yes, you—yes," Todd manages, tearing his gaze away from Daniel's shoulders in the suit jacket. *Dear god.*

Daniel laughs, and then drags his palm from Todd's shoulder to his hand. It's brief, but so *there* that Todd is sure that he didn't imagine it. "This is Charlie, my interpreter for the evening," he explains and gestures to the guy next to him.

Todd shakes his hand, and Charlie smiles. "Nice to meet you."

He watches as Daniel moves on to the other guests, and this time Charlie takes part in the introductions, signing names and greetings, and Daniel replies. Todd notices some people seem confused. Maybe they have a difficult time putting together Daniel needing someone to sign for him, while preferring to speak for himself.

"I put you two beside each other," Mela says. "I know you're supposed to sit every other girl and boy, but there are more guys, and I figured you usually have a good time. Also who the hell is that orthodox anymore, anyway?"

Staring at the cutlery when they sit down, Todd wishes that he could google under the table to find out which one to use first. He wasn't born in a *barn*, but it seems to him there are at least a handful more than there should be.

When the first course is served—yes, *served*—he glances around. Much to his relief, Daniel's hand sneaks over and gently nudges the fork farthest from the plate.

Todd shoots him a grateful look before he digs in, and Mela was right, the food is amazing. The guy next to him, Jonah, is hoping to be an engineer, and he's so passionate about bridges that Todd's getting really into it, too, when he talks about construction and what types of bridges that are more favorable for what use. He didn't know that there were different kinds of bridges, except for the aesthetics, of course. How Jonah is able to say *advanced erection techniques* with a straight face, he doesn't know, but there's apparently a really impressive long span bridge in Hong Kong.

Whenever a new course arrives, Daniel subtly tells him what cutlery to use, and it doesn't take long for Todd to relax. He's in safe hands.

The wine makes him warm and less worried about doing and saying the wrong things. It also makes him wish that he was the one talking to Daniel and not the girl on the other side of him. Daniel is, per usual, very focused on her in their conversation, but it seems easier now, when Charlie is there to help out.

"Can I come to the reopening of your gallery?" Jonah asks, and Todd is grateful that Jonah's girlfriend is so busy talking to Jesse that Jonah bothers to talk to *him*.

"Would you want that?"

"It sounds very interesting, and I want to support the idea in any way I can. Can I bring Madeleine too?"

"Bring your entire family," Todd blurts, and Jonah laughs. "I'd love for you guys to come. It would be great to have familiar faces there."

"Madeleine is really into art. I don't understand it, really, but I'm all for more opportunities for college graduates."

After dinner, Todd is listening to a conversation about health insurance. Jesse's friends are a lot like Jesse: engaged in society, politics, well-read, and probably kind.

Todd leaves the group and looks around for someone else to talk to: Mela, Daniel, or even Jonah.

Daniel is talking to a guy in a gray suit—his name might be Eric—and Charlie isn't around. *Maybe he's in the bathroom.* Todd is about to sneak over to Mela instead, when Eric lets out a sigh, flings his arms out and leaves. When he breezes past, Todd hears him mutter: *repeating myself a hundred times.*

Todd freezes. Daniel has frustration written all over his face; his mouth is pinched, and his eyebrows are drawn together. Their eyes meet, and Todd racks his head for the phrases he's learned on YouTube.

"You okay?"

Daniel's face softens, and he nods before Jesse's broad back cuts off their conversation. He must have noticed what happened as well, because an hour later when Todd looks up from another conversation about bridges with Jonah—he's going to have to ask Mom to get him some books on bridges—Eric is nowhere to be seen, and Charlie is next to Daniel.

Then, there are games, board games and goddamn *Twister* that makes Todd wish that he would go to the gym more often, since his arms are trembling from holding his own weight for too long.

"Just spin the thing!" he begs. "Please."

A second later, he over-balances and falls straight onto Daniel, who lands flat on his back. Todd is just about to apologize, when he hears Daniel's laugh. He feels it too. It's vibrating through his body.

"I'm so sorry," he whispers, laughing helplessly, and signs it as he speaks. "I can't get up."

Charlie signs the last part for him.

Daniel laughs even harder as Todd tries to figure out his limbs and get to his feet. In the end, Jesse has to offer him a hand, and then Daniel is getting up next to him, and Todd meets his gaze before he can stop himself. Around them, everyone else has moved on, and the game has continued as if they were never a part of it.

"Are you having fun?" Daniel asks, and doesn't move away, though they're way into each other's personal space.

"Very." Todd needs him to stay just where he is. "Are you?"

"More so now."

Todd hopes that his face is already flushed from the game. "Thanks for helping me out at dinner."

"It's no problem." Daniel puts his hands in his pockets and then he looks over at Charlie who hovers nearby. "We're okay on our own, thanks, Charlie."

"How was your Christmas?" Todd asks when Charlie has left them to it.

Daniel shrugs. "Apart from my dad, it was fine. Like any other Christmas, really. How was yours?"

"Kinda weird. Evan's home." He chews on his bottom lip. "The dad thing, was it anything in particular, or?"

"Repeat the last part again?"

"Your dad, was it anything in particular?"

Daniel shakes his head. "No. He was himself, and I can't stand it."

Todd strokes the strip of skin on Daniel's wrist visible between the cuff of his shirt and the fabric of his pants pocket. "I'm sorry to hear that."

"It's nothing you need to be sorry for." Daniel smiles. "Hopefully I can move out soon enough."

Right. Harvard. It's two hundred-and-thirteen miles from Williamsburg. Todd might've google mapped it the other day. "Have you heard anything?"

"Not yet, no."

"Promise to tell me when you do?" Todd wants things to be the way they were a month ago, when they could share a bed, and nothing would be weird between them.

"Of course." Daniel gives him a blinding smile, then, and Todd feels almost dizzy.

Madeleine comes over to talk to them, and Daniel waves Charlie over, so Todd has to focus on something other than Daniel for a while. *It's for the best.*

They gather around the TV to watch the ball drop, and Todd moves a little to the side, when he notices that everyone else is pairing up for the kissing. Last year he kissed Mela, because they were both single and not into anyone at the party. Now she's standing close to Jesse, and he's looking at her as if she hung the moon. Todd's chest swells.

Just as the countdown begins, Daniel sidles up to him, and Todd tears his gaze away from Mela and Jesse.

Daniel looks at him and arches his eyebrows in a silent question. He should probably say no, but Daniel is offering, and it's been forever since Todd kissed him. Smiling, he counts down with the rest of them, but their voices are vague and distant, as if under water, and Daniel's focus is solely on him now.

When everyone else shouts Happy New Year, Daniel is already kissing him. Todd grasps his tie and pulls him closer before deepening the kiss. Someone once said to him that New Year's kisses shouldn't be with tongue, but Todd doesn't give a crap, and Daniel doesn't seem to mind one bit.

It's shorter than Todd would like it to be, but it still feels as if he's been holding his breath for an hour when they break apart. Daniel's eyes find his, and he smiles, a small private smile that makes Todd want to kiss him all over again.

"Happy New Year," Daniel says.

Todd signs it, just as he learned from one of the apps and practiced all day. Daniel *beams.*

∗　　∗　　∗

JANUARY THIRTY-FIRST COMES WITH COLD, but sunny, weather and Todd is vibrating beside Mrs. Floral in the gallery. The place looks *amazing.* Renatta's art is floor to ceiling, forcing spectators to look at it, to *feel* something. Emery has created his own world farther in, and when Todd went there earlier, he didn't want to come out ever again. He almost didn't find his way out, either, because it's built like a maze.

Mrs. Floral is speaking to a journalist, and Todd has smiled for more photographs than he can remember. There are people he knows here, and even more that he *doesn't* know. He thinks someone might have snapped a picture of him shaking hands with Daniel's dad, whose entire family is here too.

The place is *packed*. Dad has his arm around Mom, squeezing her tight, but his pinched look makes Todd suspect that it's more for him than for her.

All the kids are there, too, and Jamal has showed everyone who wants to see their own exhibit that they've put together this semester. He's grown at least two inches the past hour, standing tall as he answers questions from a journalist.

"I'm so proud of you," Dad tells him a little while later, when Todd is allowed to breathe since the journalists are talking to the artists. Then he sounds accusing all of a sudden. "Couldn't you have warned me about Daniel's father? I would've brought something for him to sign."

"God, Dad. That's exactly *why* I didn't tell you," Todd sighs, but then he smiles and hugs Dad so hard that his arms hurt. "And thanks. I'm glad you could come."

"Congrats," a familiar voice says, and, when Todd looks up, he finds Evan standing there.

"I thought you couldn't make it," Todd whispers and lets go of Dad. He's been disappointed about that for weeks, but it's not as though he could be angry with Evan because work got in the way.

"I wouldn't miss this for anything." Evan ruffles his hair, and Todd wonders if he got that from Dad but he doesn't mind, not today. "You've done an amazing job."

Eventually, people leave, but almost all of them have been shaking his and Mrs. Floral's hands, telling them that they're going to be back.

"Can I talk to you?" Daniel comes up to him, and Todd is surprised, because they've barely seen each other since New Year's Eve.

"Sure."

Daniel moves off to the side, behind the front desk. "I got in," is the first thing he says, and Todd doesn't get it, until he does.

"You did?" he breathes, heart hammering behind his ribs. *Daniel got in!*

"Found out this morning."

"Oh, my god," Todd whispers, wondering why he sounds all choked up. "That's amazing. Congratulations!"

Daniel smiles, then. "I promised to tell you as soon as I found out. I'm sorry it was on your big night."

"No." Todd shakes his head rapidly. "This just makes everything better."

Daniel looks away, still smiling, but it's the smile is shrinking with every second they look at each other.

"So, you're doing it? You're moving?"

"Most likely."

"That's awesome." It's not awesome at all. Well, for Daniel it is, because he doesn't have to live under the same roof as his dad anymore. He gets to see if this law thing is actually something for him. However, Boston seems billions of miles away now, though it's not *that* far. *It's not as if he's moving to California or Europe.* "I'm so happy for you. I knew you'd get in."

"It's the next adventure, right?" Daniel says, but he's pale, even for the middle of winter.

"A big one. Then you'll take on the world."

"Christ," Daniel laughs. "You've got high hopes for me."

Todd is just about to reply, when Jamal calls for him. He's standing by the door with his mom, switching from one foot to the other. Daniel must have gotten the picture from his reaction, because he smiles. "Go. We'll talk later."

"Todd," Jamal says when Todd reaches him. "I told all my friends in school about our club. So maybe some of them want to come next year. That's good, right?"

"That's great." Todd's ribcage can't fit his heart. "You told all your friends? Thank you so much, buddy."

"I only have three," Jamal confesses. "But they're funny and nice."

"That's the only thing that matters," Todd says and squeezes his shoulder. "I don't have that many friends either, but if they're good, you don't need a hundred, right?"

"Right." Jamal looks so relieved that Todd wants to hug him. "See you Thursday."

"There's always a spot for you here," Todd says, half to Jamal, half to his mom. Todd's going to make sure of that somehow.

He's helping Mrs. Floral clean up after everyone has left, when she pushes a familiar book into his hand. It's his copy of *History of Modern Art*. It's been here since his midterms.

"You should take this home with you," she says. "And we'll clean up the rest tomorrow. We both deserve some rest."

"Do you think we pulled it off?" Todd asks her and accepts the book.

She leans the broom against the front desk. "Honey, I think we just made us a name." Then she smiles. "And even if we didn't, I think we did something amazing and worth being proud of. You, above everyone else, worked so hard for this."

Todd swallows desperately. "It's all thanks to you. You hired me."

"And thank the Lord that I did," she says. "This place would have been closed months ago if it wasn't for you."

"Well, I had help from a whole bunch of people," Todd says, because working by himself didn't go all that well. He's said it a hundred times to the journalists, but he wants to make sure that she knows too. "It wouldn't have been possible without them."

"You have amazing people in your life, honey," Mrs. Floral says, and he knows. He *knows*. "I'll see you again on Monday."

"Yes." Todd hugs her tight. "See you Monday."

At home, he lies on his bed and stares at the ceiling. *History of Modern Art* is still on his chest, a friendly weight on his ribcage, and Sandwich is eyeing it with suspicion, as though it's taken her spot. He tries not to think about Daniel moving away. It's better this way, so he gets a chance to get over his crush.

"This," Todd tells her and holds the book up. "Is something I'd be happy for you to eat. It's a really terrible book."

Just as he's about to put it on the floor, thinking that accidents happen more easily if you give them a good opportunity, he notices a white piece of paper sticking up between the pages.

It's thicker than normal paper, reminding him of a postcard, but a lot smaller. It's maybe an inch tall and two inches wide, when he pulls it free. He thinks it's just a blank bookmark he found somewhere and forgot about, until he turns it over.

I'd like to give the dating thing another chance. Let me know if you want to grab that coffee sometime. /Daniel

It's simple and definitely not very out there. However, since the book has been lying around the gallery forever now, Todd has a hard time pinpointing when Daniel put it there.

Then he remembers Daniel holding this book when he came for a visit during midterms. In *October. Has he been waiting since then? For three months? Because he doesn't think he's wanted?*

"Sandwich, I'm going to be brave," he tells her as he gets out of bed, heart flat against his ribs, and gets his coat where he's left it hanging over the back of his desk chair. He grabs the painting from where it's leaning against his desk too. He never got a chance to give it to Daniel for Christmas, and now he's got a good excuse for visiting.

His pulse doesn't slow during the entire train ride; all he can think is, *what if Daniel has moved on?* It's been three months. Todd might be the only person ever to have a crush for three months and not do anything about it.

He almost slips and bashes his head against the sidewalk a few times as he hurries to Daniel's house. The paper, now deformed by his sweaty palm, is still in one hand, and the canvas in the other.

His fingers are trembling as he punches the doorbell. He tells himself that it's because he forgot gloves, but the pumping adrenaline is making him sweat.

Ava opens the door, and her eyebrows climb when she spots him and then rise even farther when she sees the painting in his hand.

"Is Daniel home?" He pulls a hand through his hair so she won't notice him trembling.

"Uh, yeah." She eyes him, not stepping aside to let him in. "Are you here to declare your undying love for him?"

"Something like that," Todd admits, helpless. "Unless you force me to freeze to death out here first."

"About time," she mutters as she steps aside. "Our parents just left for some dinner. I'll be playing really loud music on my headphones all evening."

Then she bangs the door closed and leaves him in the hallway.

"No one said anything about sex!" Todd says, exasperated.

"Dude, it's even more gross listening to you guys declare your love."

Todd rolls his eyes and swears under his breath as he fights the laces on his boots. God, he should've picked freaking flip flops or something.

He takes the stairs two at a time and reaches Daniel's bedroom door completely out of breath. It's closed, and all Todd can think is: *please don't be naked, please don't be naked* as he pushes it open.

Daniel is on his bed, reading, *fully clothed* thank god, and he startles so badly when he sees Todd that he drops the book.

"Hi," Todd says.

Daniel blinks at him, eyes wide.

The words don't come. He thinks about going with his backup plan, but then he drops the painting to the floor. Todd has no clue what to say, so he holds out the note Daniel left him.

"I found this."

Recognition dawns on Daniel's face as his gaze locks on it. "Oh," is all he says.

Doubt creeps up his spine, but Todd needs to know. Needs to ask. "Does it still stand? The offer?"

Daniel looks at him for what feels like an eternity. "You didn't find it until now?" he asks, instead of answering Todd's question.

"No. Like an hour ago. Then I came here."

Daniel still looks as though he's been struck by lightning, as if he can't quite comprehend what's happening.

Todd takes a breath. He did tell Sandwich that he'd be brave, so here goes.

"Because if it still stands, I'd very much want to have that coffee. Date. Coffee date. I mean, I hope it still stands. I've been wanting to since… well, yeah, since I met you."

"Todd, I can't make out what you're saying."

So he repeats it all, slower this time.

Daniel stands up then, and Todd shivers. "Can you say that again?" he asks, when he stops in front of Todd, and this time Todd doesn't think it's because he's been blabbering.

"I don't care that you're moving to Boston. I'd like to try the dating. If the offer still stands."

And this time, when Daniel kisses him, it's like none of the other times they've kissed. It's a little hard, and a lot desperate, and he digs his fingers into Todd's back as if he wants to make sure that he won't leave. Todd's lips are raw when they pull away, and he's out of breath for a different reason than running up the stairs.

"Is that a yes?" he asks, grinning.

"Here I've been moping all this time, thinking that you've tried to reject me nicely, and, in reality, you just don't study enough."

"Bullshit," Todd says. "I got great scores on all my finals."

Daniel's gaze roams his face, as if he's something new to discover, and his hands cup Todd's jaw. Todd doesn't think anyone has looked at him like this before.

"Is that a yes?" he asks again.

"What?"

"Is that a yes?"

A soft smile spreads on Daniel's lips. "Yes. That's a yes."

Todd is the one to kiss Daniel this time. It's so easy now, when he knows that he has all the time he wants. There's no cab, or New Year's countdown rushing them. He presses in close. Breathes in through his nose.

This is where he's supposed to be.

ONE YEAR LATER…

Todd locks his phone after checking the flight times for Mexico one last time. Travelling with Evan is nerve-racking, as he seems to think that everything will solve itself as soon as they get to the airport. Todd thinks it's pretty vital not to miss your flight. Abuela won't be happy if they do.

He welcomes a few patrons. The gallery is always less-frequented during Christmas break. In a moment, however, it will become significantly more crowded. He still has one final exam left, but most students are already finished.

A few minutes later, the door opens, and a group of kids piles through. Behind them, Daniel steps in, cheeks rosy from the cold. Todd hasn't seen him in two weeks, and the sight of him walking through the door causes his heart to malfunction.

"*Hi,*" he signs, and resists the urge to readjust his beanie when Daniel gives him one of his huge smiles. It takes a moment before he remembers that there are a group of kids here, too, staring at him with interest. "*Why don't you guys have a look around while I set things up?*" he signs.

They scatter through the next door, pulling off hats and scarves. Todd doesn't know why they bothered, since their club is in Cruella's old space next door.

Daniel steps around the counter and gives him a sweet kiss. *"How are you?"*

"Missed you," Todd signs. *"You?"*

"Tired." Daniel's hand moves to his waist briefly before he signs again. *"Just got back from Boston. When are you leaving to see your grandma?"*

"New Year's Day. Plenty of time until then." Todd grins when Daniel pinches his side. *"I have one final left, and then I'm all yours."*

"Accounting?"

"Dad is going really hardcore with the private lessons."

Daniel smiles. *"I think it's great that you decided to take the class."*

Todd doesn't like admitting it, but so is he. *"I'm not sure how great I'll be at doing this, though,"* he says, nodding in the direction where the kids went.

"You'll be great, and, if you need some assistance, I'll be there to help out."

Todd nods and takes a deep breath. *"Did you talk to your dad?"* he asks, just to stall for a little while longer.

Daniel nods. *"We're going to watch a game and have dinner on Thursday."*

Todd doesn't know what sport that would be, but the fact that Daniel and his dad have both worked really hard to reconnect after not speaking for a few months is making him proud. Todd, knowing all too well how long it takes to rebuild a broken relationship that you've put the lid on for too long, might have been the driving force behind Daniel talking to his dad about their situation.

"You're disappearing on me," Daniel says, and Todd looks up.

"Sorry."

Daniel nods and kisses his cheek. "Are you ready?"

"You're staying over after, right?"

"For sure. I'm not missing out on your dad's quesadillas." Daniel gives him a look that makes Todd's skin crawl in anticipation. "Or having you to myself for a bit. To catch up."

"To catch up," Todd snorts.

Daniel smiles against his lips before he kisses him. "Come on. Let's go teach these kids, and me, something about art."

Todd's painting was the first thing Daniel put up in his new place, and, according to Jesse, he brags about it to anyone who wants to listen. Except for Todd's own art, Daniel isn't too enthusiastic when Todd tries to drag him to a gallery or museum, but he still goes. In turn, Todd has to listen to Daniel's endless law-rants. That's more than okay with him.

The kids are in an awed cluster, gazing up at the huge, winged, clay sculptures in the next room. Daniel rounds them up, and they look at Todd with big eyes, as he flexes his fingers.

"Who is ready for a guided tour?"

THE END

Acknowledgments

Writing this book was a journey from start to finish, with its ups and downs, challenges as well as rewards. There are a number of people I need to thank for helping me come this far.

First, I need to thank my family (mamma, pappa and Lina) for supporting me and encouraging me when times were rough. You taught me perseverance and bravery, and always encouraged my creativity. Your faith in me means everything, especially when my faith in myself waivers.

I can't forget my extended family, either: farmor, faster, Ellen och Clara. I've grown up with you in my life and it's much better for it. Having incredibly strong women like you so close to me is an inspiration every day.

I want to give a special thanks to Amy, Anna, Carlos, Elias and Josh who shared their experiences, knowledge and stories with me to help make this story true. Without your feedback this wouldn't be the story it is today. I also want to thank Cinthya for generously sharing your last name with Todd.

I also want to thank the IP team, and in particular Annie, Nicki, Candy and CB who helped me bring this book to life, get the word out there, and who made this story come to life through a beautiful cover. I can't thank you enough for the understanding you've shown when things haven't been easy and the encouragement you've given me when I've needed it the most. Thank you!

I also want to thank a bunch of my close friends for all the laughs and adventures I've had with you. To have such amazing people in my life that I can trust with anything is the most incredible thing. Thank you Julia, Andrea, Emilie, Agnes, Sara, Pernilla, Anna, Ullis, Ellen, Fredrik, Lina, Maja and Carro.

Carrie, M and P: we've been friends for so long and having your support, love and encouragement has been invaluable to me during this journey. I'm grateful for your advice, knowledge and how generously you've wanted to share all of that with me.

Thank you to everyone in the TWMSG GC who's always there to share your creativity and talent.

I also want to thank my IP family who welcomed me with open arms. It's an honor to share a publisher with such amazing authors.

I want to direct a special thank you to everyone who's read my work in the past and pushed me to develop my writing style. If it wasn't for your comments and support, I wouldn't have dared to finish this book. You're too many for me to mention you all by name, but please know that I am forever grateful for the support and love you've showed me.

Last, but not least, I want to thank my high school teacher Sonja who read my work and told me to never stop writing.

About the Author

E.S. STARTED WRITING STORIES AS soon as she learned how to string letters together to create words and sentences. One of her first creations was around seven pages, eighty words, and about a tortoise living in a microwave. Since then, her stories have become a little longer, and perhaps slightly more complex. E.S. works for the Swedish government and has a master's degree in human resources. *Brush Strokes* is her first novel.

interlude**press**™

 interludepress.com
 @InterludePress
 interludepress
 store.interludepress.com

interlude  press™
you may also like…

A Tiny Piece of Something Greater by Jude Sierra

After moving to Key Largo to to make a fresh start, Reid Watsford meets Joaquim, an intern at the dive shop who is looking for adventure. As their relationship deepens, they both must learn how to navigate Reid's cyclothemia, and a past Reid can't quite escape.

ISBN (print) 978-1-945053-60-3 | (eBook) 978-1-945053-61-0

And It Came to Pass by Laura Stone

Adam Young is a devout Mormon following the pious path set forth for him by his church and family. But when his mission trajectory sends him to Barcelona, Spain, with a handsome mission companion named Brandon Christensen, Adam discovers there may be more to life and love than he ever expected.

ISBN (print) 978-1-945053-15-3 | (eBook) 978-1-945053-35-1

Into the Blue by Pene Henson
Lambda Literary Award Winner

Tai Talagi and Ollie Birkstrom have been inseparable since they met as kids surfing the North Shore. Tai's spent years setting aside his feelings for Ollie, but when Ollie's pro surfing dreams come to life, their steady world shifts. Is the relationship worth risking everything for a chance at something terrifying and beautiful and altogether new?

ISBN (print) 978-1-941530-84-9 | (eBook) 978-1-941530-85-6